TURNING THE TABLES

Caroline would have found it funny, had it not been so painfully perverse. Thomas Mannering, her rake of a husband, was actually jealous of *her*.

"I am wise to your game," he declared. "I will not be cuckolded. And you should beware. Your cicisbeo is a heartless rogue who is merely seeking another conquest. He specializes in seducing dissatisfied wives."

"You are incredibly stupid to believe such ridiculous fantasies," she charged. "Or are you attributing your own failings to me? But at least you admit I have cause for dissatisfaction."

"How dare you!" he roared, his green eyes flashing fire. Jerking her closer, he crushed his mouth across hers, as if to brand her as his own. She parried his tongue, their furious fencing suddenly transforming into a sensual duel. His hands tore wildly at her bedgown while hers frantically attacked his nightshirt, both intent only on shredding the barriers that separated them.

How could anger so light the fires of love, Caroline had to wo̶̶̶̶̶̶̶̶̶̶̶̶̶̶̶̶how could she keep those flames al̶̶̶̶̶

The Rake's Rainbow

Allison Lane

A SIGNET BOOK

SIGNET
Published by the Penguin Group
Penguin Books USA Inc., 375 Hudson Street,
New York, New York 10014, U.S.A.
Penguin Books Ltd, 27 Wrights Lane,
London W8 5TZ, England
Penguin Books Australia Ltd, Ringwood,
Victoria, Australia
Penguin Books Canada Ltd, 10 Alcorn Avenue,
Toronto, Ontario, Canada M4V 3B2
Penguin Books (N.Z.) Ltd, 182–190 Wairau Road,
Auckland 10, New Zealand

Penguin Books Ltd, Registered Offices:
Harmondsworth, Middlesex, England

First published by Signet, an imprint of Dutton Signet,
a division of Penguin Books USA Inc.

First Printing, January, 1996
10 9 8 7 6 5 4 3 2 1

Copyright © Susan Pace, 1996
All rights reserved

 REGISTERED TRADEMARK—MARCA REGISTRADA

Printed in the United States of America

Chapter 1

How can I go through with this?

The Honourable Thomas Mannering slouched beside a scarred, wooden table in the Laughing Dog's taproom. One hand supported a head that threatened to roll off his shoulders. The other upended a wine bottle, dribbling the last drops down the side of his glass. The empty bottle joined four of its mates on the floor.

Alicia.

His love's angelic face wavered insubstantially against the smoky gloom, her sparkling violet-blue eyes and golden ringlets refusing to vanish. What horrible pressures had her unfeeling parents brought to bear against her sweet innocence? Had they threatened her? Locked her away? Beat her? Had she even been informed before the notice appeared in the paper?

That was his worst fear. And had been for months. He frowned at his newly emptied glass, then imperiously demanded another bottle from the buxom barmaid. He automatically assessed her abundant charms before recalling that there was no time to dally this night. Shudders wracked him at the memory.

How could he do it?

How could he not?

Had he a choice?

The room careened dizzily in the flickering light of an ill-adjusted lantern. He squinted, focusing just enough to pour more wine.

How long had it been since his world collapsed in ruins? How many months since Alicia had pledged her undying love in Lady Debenham's rose garden? Had he dreamt their passionate embrace? His loins tightened with remembered need. Floating home, he had planned in meticulous detail the words that would request permission to pay his addresses, only to descend into hell the very next morning when the *Post* announced her betrothal to Viscount Darnley. The notice had to have been submitted before the ball. Darnley had not even attended.

Had she known?

No! She would never have played such a deceitful trick on one she loved. Nor had she willingly accepted her fate. Her distress hurt him worse than his own pain.

The new bottle emptied as he tried to forget his last interview with the love of his life. She had received him a week later in the morning room of her father's Berkeley Square town house. . . .

"Papa demanded this betrothal," she sobbed, tears glistening in her wide, ingenuous eyes as her pacing brought her close enough for him to touch. His fists clenched with the effort of not claiming one last blissful embrace. "I tried to change his mind, Thomas, but he was adamant. He refused to countenance a connection with a younger son of limited means."

He gasped at this intelligence. No one had ever questioned his background. How dare an upstart baron who was only the third to hold his own title? Thomas might be a younger son, but the Marchgate earldom dated to Richard Lionheart, and his ancestors had arrived with William.

But before he could protest, Alicia smiled in that radiant way that always sent his temperature soaring and his blood boiling.

"My love, we must look to the future. You know Lord Darnley is an old man and not in the best of health," she confided in a husky voice that started fires raging through his loins. "He cannot long survive. You must be patient, my dearest Thomas. As a wealthy widow I can marry where I choose. Papa will no longer control my life."

Resting a delicate hand trustingly against his chest, she sighed, a single tear escaping to trickle down one alabaster cheek. He shuddered at the image of his angel forced to submit to an aging libertine like Darnley. Her violet eyes begged for understanding, golden ringlets trembling in agitation. How could she endure such a plight?

Still bleary from a week-long stupor, he nearly crushed her in his arms. But embracing another man's betrothed would violate his honor. Nor could he pledge fidelity to another's wife or to a hypothetical widow—not and maintain his self-respect. Her face twisted into a momentary expression of—annoyance? Of course not, he chided himself. She was as disturbed as he over this damnable mess, and as prone to pain.

"Do not hold this frightful coil against me, my love," she continued, her hand sliding up to his shoulder, coursing desire through his body that threatened to undermine his precarious control. "I am counting on you to see me through this trial."

She did not understand the havoc she was wreaking with those caressing fingers, he reminded himself. Her natural sensuality was part of what attracted him, as were her vulnerability, her compassion, and her exquisite taste. He wanted nothing more than to protect her from life's cruelties. But fate denied him that role.

He managed to leave, honor intact, but, oh, how he wanted her! Why would a loving parent condemn a daughter to such a *mèsalliance?* Surely not merely for title and money! He could have found both in a younger, more personable suitor. Corley had been chasing her all season. With a fortune larger than Darnley's, an earl's title in hand, and a marquess's guaranteed when his uncle died, he was by far the better catch. Corley had been his principal rival since the day he had first beheld the newest beauty at Almack's.

He had never considered marrying so soon, expecting several more years of freedom before settling down. Then he caught sight of Alicia across the room and everything changed. She was a vision of heaven in a delicate blue gown, an ethereal being framed in a cloud of mist. She met his eyes and smiled. And he was lost. Her purity and innocence pierced his soul. Circe could not have enslaved him more thoroughly.

He shuddered.

In a futile effort to forget, he embarked upon a debauch that put his previous rakehelling to shame, squandering each night on wine, women, and faro. Every afternoon he pummeled opponents at Jackson's—all of whom displayed Darnley's face to his bleary eyes—before resuming his endless rounds of brothels, gaming hells, and greenrooms, all seeming alike after uncounted bottles of brandy. He succeeded in losing track of time, losing large amounts of money, and losing his legendary fastidiousness in both dress and *chère amies.* But he could not lose sight of Alicia's face. The memories refused to die.

Her wedding came and went. He drank even more, fighting to banish the image of her consorting with Darnley. The Little Season rolled by without notice. His closest friends fought to rescue him from the brink of disaster, but without success. For the first time in his life he cared nothing for what others thought of him. Reality was too barren to face sober.

But now he was caught in an even worse coil. Three days before, he had been summoned home to stand on the carpet where generations of Mannerings had meted out punishment to errant offspring. The Earl of Marchgate pinned his second son with a

withering glare and rang a peal over his head the likes of which
he had never endured in all his five-and-twenty years.

"Look at you!" the earl stormed, a condemning finger pointed
at his disheveled appearance. "Bloodshot eyes, sallow skin, bosky
at two in the afternoon! Eight months and you still wear your
heart on your sleeve. Is this the face a Mannering presents to the
world? Where is your pride? Your honor? Your debauchery is no
longer just the latest *on-dit*, nor can it be fobbed off as yet another
example of a young cub sowing wild oats. You have become the
laughingstock of the *ton*. And you are killing your mother."

He raised stricken eyes to his parent. As close to sober as he
had been in months, he was appalled at his own behavior, aware
at last of just how low he had sunk. "Dear Lord," he whispered,
"you know I would never deliberately harm her."

"This must stop, Thomas," continued the earl, his tired voice
suddenly laced with pain. "At the very least you must leave town.
Eleanor comes out this spring. Unfair though it might be, your
present behavior will seriously damage her chances." He noted
the flush spreading across his son's face and sighed in relief. Perhaps the boy was still reachable. His voice gentled. "Go down to
Crawley. Try to rebuild your life. How deeply are you dipped?"

"Nothing I cannot manage," Thomas muttered darkly.

"Nonsense," snapped the earl, anger again mastering his face.
"I've had six duns at my door this week over your debts. I will
not have a son of mine in prison. Until Robert begets an heir, you
stand second to one of the oldest titles in England. Now how
deeply are you dipped?"

"I don't know," he admitted with a groan, dropping heavily
into a chair and covering his face with his hands. Silence
stretched uncomfortably. He did not look up until a hand grasped
his shoulder.

"Are you willing to make a clean start?" asked the earl quietly.

He nodded.

"Is Crawley mortgaged?"

He nodded again.

"Gather everything you owe," commanded the earl. "I want
everything—vowels, tradesmen's bills, mortgage. I will pay the
lot. But that will be all. Your allowance will continue for one
year, then cease. Go to Crawley. You have a year to make it profitable."

"But Crawley is in ruins," he protested.

"Then I suggest you remain sober enough to restore it. It

should be a very lucrative estate. And if you run short of money, there is always your inheritance."

"You know the conditions."

"True—you would have to marry. Quite a problem. What chit would have you after the cake you've made of yourself?"

"You cannot be serious!"

"Not entirely, 'tis true. There are always antidotes desperate enough to wed anyone," the earl acknowledged brutally. "I know Lord Huntsley would welcome a suit for his youngest daughter. And she comes with ten thousand pounds."

"But at what price?" muttered Thomas to himself, suppressing a shudder at the vision of Josephine Huntsley. Though Marchgate voiced no ultimatum, the terms were clear. Thomas could hardly comprehend the sacrifice demanded for plastering over his recent follies—banishment, poverty, and a lifetime of Miss Huntsley.

He groaned.

"Think about it," urged the earl. "They are presently at home in Devon. I will expect your bills tomorrow," he added dismissively.

"Father—" He paused, then continued in a firmer voice, determined to salvage at least a modicum of self-respect. "Buy the mortgage if you like, but do not dismiss it. I find I would prefer to discharge that one myself."

He nodded firmly and left the room, his brain frantically listing all the respectable females he knew, in hopes of turning up someone better than Josephine. Anyone would be better. He could manage without a dowry as long as he had the inheritance.

But his bravura had not outlasted a round of afternoon calls. His reception finally forced an admission that not only was he a younger son of limited means, he was also considered a heartless libertine, an inveterate gamester, and a hopeless sot. Fit company for Prinny, perhaps, but matchmaking mamas barred their doors lest his very presence compromise their daughters. The polite world smiled indulgently on the sowing of wild oats, but a dedicated rakehell was acceptable only if he was a wealthy, high-ranking peer. And the highest sticklers even rejected those.

Three days later the Honourable Thomas Mannering sprawled untidily across a taproom table, his glass drooping from numbed fingers, the last portion of wine from his sixth bottle running across the uneven surface to pool under his left ear.

How could he face the fate that awaited him in Devon? Horse-faced, simperingly empty-headed, clumsily inept Miss Josephine Huntsley. Her very presence was penance, that ubiquitous girlish giggle grating on his ears until he could barely suppress screams.

Everything she did turned to disaster. Within a week of her come-out, she had tripped Oaksford (leaving him sprawled on the ball-room floor), overturned a punch bowl at the Lewiston soiree, been invited to leave Almack's after insulting Lady Jersey and criticizing the refreshments, and made a spectacle of herself on Bond Street when she stepped on her hem, causing a rip that bared her nearly to the waist. The girl needed a keeper. Living with Medusa would be preferable.

But what choice did he have? He must take a wife. Immediately. Without capital, he would lose what remained of his only possession.

Alicia, how can I live without you?

A yard of tin sounded, stirring a commotion that filtered vaguely into his brain. The mail had arrived. He staggered to his feet, the last vestiges of duty sending him to his fate.

Caroline Cummings was halfway into the mail coach when an exceedingly foxed gentleman stumbled against her back, regaining his balance by throwing an arm across her shoulders. The motion slid one hand under her cloak where it latched on to her bosom.

She gasped in speechless outrage, grabbing the door frame to keep from crashing onto the filthy floor. Her threadbare cloak, already soaked from the cold January rain, would doubtless disintegrate if ground into the mud.

"Beg pardon," he mumbled.

Glaring into a grinning face now only inches from her own, she pushed his arm and hand aside, but could think of no reply that would not be roundly criticized as unchristian by her father and unladylike by her mother. He needed a shave. And some manners.

Shivering, she took her place by the window, then glared again. Not only was he boarding the coach, the only remaining seat was next to her own. She groaned. Would the long journey into Cornwall be plagued by this amorous drunk?

Why had Papa insisted that she travel straight through instead of spending the nights at inns? After all, she was merely a governess, no longer expected to travel with a maid. And at two-and-twenty, with no looks to recommend her, she was already firmly on the shelf.

A glance at her traveling companions in no way improved her mood. Three people slept wedged into the opposite seat: a heavy-set farmer reeking of onions, whose stentorian breathing already grated on her nerves, and whose outstretched legs left little room for her own; an exceptionally stout red-faced woman who—judging from the way she leaned against his shoulder—was probably his wife; and a thin young man crushed into the corner, possibly a clerk. Even the din of the inn yard, as ostlers rushed a new team into the traces, failed to penetrate their slumbers. The third occupant of her own seat was awake, but there was little hope of company from that quarter. Well into middle age, the black-garbed spinster pursed disapprovingly thin lips and glared down a long, aristocratic nose. As the drunk dropped heavily onto the seat and slumped against Caroline's shoulder, the lady sniffed loudly and edged farther into her own corner.

Caroline twice tried to force her tormentor to sit up, but finally abandoned the effort and determinedly stared out the window. Perhaps reviewing her new position would divert her mind. The coach lurched onto the road, triggering a wave of trepidation.

Trepidation? No. Fear. There, she had admitted it. She was terrified at stepping into the unknown. Shudders raced down her spine. From fear. From cold. From the rainwater seeping through her gown where the drunk's head pressed into her shoulder. But she would survive. Pushing fear aside, she concentrated on the benefits of leaving home.

She was ideally suited to be a governess. It would be little different from what she had done for more than six years. As the third of eight daughters and four sons born to the Sheldridge Corners vicar, she was long accustomed to dealing with children. Since age sixteen she had disciplined and educated the younger half of the family.

Fortune had smiled upon her own youth when the neighboring squire invited her to join his daughters' lessons. The genial squire had also allowed her the run of his extensive library and spent hours discussing the many books she devoured. Thus she was more learned than most young men in spite of the time she had spent mastering ladies' accomplishments and overseeing her siblings. She had established regular school hours for them, opening her lessons to several village children after the first year. Some of her former pupils had since been apprenticed as clerks.

But times were bad and getting worse. The wars dragged endlessly on and tithes were down after consecutive years of poor harvests. Costs rose ever higher until the vicar could no longer support even the offspring who had not already moved out into the world. Despite lacking dowries, her two older sisters had found husbands the previous summer, for they were comely lasses, well-trained in household management. Constance married a nearby solicitor, and Prudence attracted the eye of a still-young, widowed baronet with two small daughters but no heir. After intensive coaching, Peter won an Oxford scholarship to take orders. Paul joined the navy, which did not demand he purchase his commission as did the army. Elizabeth obtained a position as companion to the Dowager Viscountess Barton, a blessing as the lady lived only four miles from Sheldridge Corners so Liza could visit the family on her days out. That left only Caroline of an age to move elsewhere. At seventeen, Anne was able to take over her teaching chores. So she accepted a governess post in distant Cornwall, where she would educate three young girls, (brats, that unquenchable internal voice reminded—spoiled, brainless hoydens) and their sensitive brother, whose delicate constitution prohibited the rigors of public school. Though not an ideal position, she was nonetheless lucky to find it.

Her father had been strangely hesitant over agreeing, despite his efforts to arrange the position. "It is so far away," he mourned, pacing the study in agitation. "And we know nothing of the family."

"I must accept," she stated calmly. "And with luck I can send you fifteen pounds a year."

"But that is more than half of your salary," he protested.

"It matters not. And Anne is more than capable of taking over my chores so Mama will not be overburdened."

"Perhaps you should wait one more year," he offered. "I had hoped you would one day marry."

She thrust her own unrealistic dreams firmly aside. "Papa, we have discussed this before, as you well know. We lack both social standing and money. Pru and Connie managed to attract beaux due to their beauty, but I can never expect to repeat their successes."

"Fustian!" exploded the vicar. "You are a fine-looking girl."

"Be reasonable, Father." She shrugged. "I am no antidote, 'tis true. But I can never claim the sort of beauty that compensates for a missing dowry. Nor can I remain content watching you and Mama struggle when I could contribute to the family well-being."

He had accepted the inevitable without further argument, though she knew he suffered over his inability to properly provide for his children. She and Mama had united in opposition when he wanted to ask his brother for help. Uncle Arthur was barely scraping sustenance out of his estate and was in no position to support others. Stifling the vision of a life of leisure she could never obtain, she continued to enumerate the benefits of this post.

Cornwall was lovely. She again ignored the voice bemoaning that the house was quite isolated. A little common sense and discipline would turn her charges into models of decorum. And where else could she impart her knowledge to a young man? She refused to entertain fears that she would have no support from that doting mother on questions of discipline, and would receive only the barest of necessities in the way of room and board. That horrid voice whispered that none but the worst nipfarthing would expect her to teach both son and daughters. Nor would she dwell on the loneliness she would undoubtedly suffer after a lifetime spent in a roisterous, loving enclave like the vicarage. And she refused to question why she would be the fourth to hold the position this year alone. An involuntary shudder raced down her spine, which she immediately imputed to the cold and damp.

A loud belch spewed brandy fumes in her face, effectively masking the farm couple's stench and directing her thoughts toward her immediate problem. Again she tried to push the drunk from her numbed shoulder. His hat rolled onto the floor, disclosing that the moisture seeping through her cloak was wine. His hair was soaked with it. What could possibly make this journey worse?

Hardly had she formulated the question when the coach lurched sharply over a series of ruts, bucking like a boat on a storm-tossed sea. He lunged across her, threw open the window, and barely shoved his head out before casting up his accounts. His stomach heaved against her hips. Swallowing her own reaction, she tried to hold the sweating, shaking body away as he continued his endless retching. Finally, one hand dug into her arm and he dragged himself back inside.

"S-sorry," he whispered shakily and collapsed onto her lap, his dark curls now dripping from the pelting rain.

"Serves you right for drinking so much," she snapped angrily but he had passed out. She exchanged an exasperated glance with the spinster, who sniffed loudly and turned to glare out her own window.

Lacking the strength to move him, she closed the window, resigned to the most uncomfortable night of her life. *Please, dear Lord, don't let this journey be a portent of my new life,* she prayed silently.

An especially bad bump jarred Caroline awake. Amazingly, she had dozed off. The drunkard still sprawled across her lap, her hand unaccountably holding him in place. Judging from the numbness in her legs, several hours must have elapsed. Even the spinster was asleep. She shivered. Water had seeped through both cloak and dress, chilling her as the temperature approached freezing. Damp gloves offered little protection for her fingers. Halfboots did nothing to warm her toes.

A glance at the window showed rain falling harder than ever. Surely even mail coaches slowed in such weather. . . . But the driver was loudly urging his horses faster. The wheels skidded sideways, sending her heart into her throat. Another lurch dug the farmer's elbow into his wife and she gasped.

"Harry!" she screamed, shaking him violently. "Wake up! Something's mighty wrong."

Snorts and wheezes were his only response.

Was some young sprig tooling the mail coach? Caroline sobbed in terror while the fat lady continued her exhortations of Harry. Though common on the stage, such irregularities were supposed to never happen on the King's mail. But their increasingly reckless pace convinced her that they were victim to just such a prank. No professional driver would handle the ribbons with this reckless abandon.

They swung wildly around a curve, the drunk's weight crushing her into the corner, his pressure making it difficult to breathe. The spinster's piercing screech woke Harry and the clerk.

"Stop, I say!" shouted Harry, pounding on the panel separating them from the driver's box.

"We'll all die!" sobbed his wife, burying her head in his shoulder.

"Imbecile! Stop, or I'll report you at the next posting inn!" he continued loudly, to no avail. He opened the window to repeat his demands, now punctuated by obscenities, but accomplished nothing beyond admitting freezing rain and wind into the coach.

The drunk groaned, his hand pawing at Caroline's bosom before he again passed out.

"Wouldn't do no good if ye did report the bloody bastard. Who'd believe ye? He must be mad," muttered the clerk, his face gray with fear, both hands exerting a death grip on the strap.

"Watch your language, young man," demanded the spinster. "There is a lady present."

Another sharp bump slammed Caroline's head into the roof, but failed to dislodge the beast in her lap.

"Harry, do something!" begged the wife, clutching his arm as the coach again skidded sideways.

"What the bloody 'ell is you doin'?" shouted the mail's guard from his perch up behind with the post. Scrabbling sounds moved along the roof and all eyes raised to follow his progress.

"Pray God the guard can slow us," Caroline gasped, meeting the terror-stricken eyes of the farmer's wife as another sickening lurch nearly landed them in the ditch. One of her hands dug into the drunk's shoulder.

"This is the most despicable journey I have ever suffered. Such low company should never be allowed to board," snapped the spinster, casting a look of such scorn at Caroline that she gasped in shock. "And now this!" Back ramrod straight, she glared at the other passengers. Only her white-knuckled grasp on the strap detracted from her haughty disdain.

Opening her mouth to protest, Caroline screamed in terror as the coach leaned sharply around another corner, poised agonizingly on two wheels, then rolled down an embankment. A horse squealed with pain. She watched in horror as her fellow passengers tumbled slowly in her direction. Then her head exploded in a cloud of sparks and the world went black.

Chapter 2

The Honourable Thomas Mannering awoke to a full cavalry brigade rampaging through his skull. His stomach churned in protest at the least movement, and his mouth had apparently been used as a nesting site by a flock of untidy birds. Altogether, a normal morning.

What was not normal was the lumpy mattress. Squeezing his eyelids tight, he burrowed into the pillow, avoiding the light he knew from vast experience would only worsen his condition. Where was he? What activities had he indulged in this time? He groaned as memory returned. Of course—the unwanted journey; the mental battle between images of Alicia and Josephine; and that moment when he could go no further. . . .

Desperately needing a drink, he had left the mail, reserving the last seat on the next coach. But the drink or two needed to restore his courage had stretched to several bottles. His last memory was of a buxom barmaid brushing suggestively against his arm.

He shifted, suddenly aware that he was not alone. One arm was draped over a deliciously soft body, his fingers cupping a generous breast. This triggered another memory—nuzzling his face against that same breast as he drifted to sleep.

Had he taken the barmaid to bed? It would hardly surprise him, nor was she an antidote like some he had lately encountered. In recent months he had cut a wide and indiscriminate swath through the muslin company, even accepting the questionable services of street prostitutes in his quest for nepenthe. It was a wonder he remained healthy. But another of his increasingly common blackouts left no memories of this particular liaison.

Shielding his eyes, he cautiously cracked one lid open, then heaved a sigh of relief. The light was too dim to hurt. He carefully turned his head to inspect the girl. Was she clean enough to risk another romp?

Pain knifed his neck.

Pain was something new, but he had no time to assess its cause.

Astonishment sent him reeling to the chamber pot without a moment to spare. Following an unpleasant interval, he grasped his swirling head, and hesitantly approached the bed.

His eyes had not lied. The woman was both a stranger and seriously injured. Her head was swathed in bandages, as was the arm that lay atop the coverlet.

"Damnation!" he muttered angrily, looking for some clue as to where he was. The sloped roof and peeling walls hinted at the top floor of an unfashionable inn. Nothing unusual about that . . . The tiny apartment was furnished as if for servants, containing a narrow bed, a single rickety chair, and an equally decrepit table. At least a fire burned in the mean grate, though doing little to suppress the January chill. Two valises rested atop a small trunk. Thankfully opening his own, he extracted a traveling flask and took a long pull to settle his stomach and clear the cobwebs from his aching head.

His eyes returned to the woman in the bed. Who was she? How had she gotten into his room? And why he was in a room? he wondered with shock. He was supposed to be on the mail, heading for Devon to pay his addresses to Miss Huntsley. A presentiment of doom was building. He could almost see the sword of Damocles poised above his head.

"Who the devil are you?" he demanded, prodding her shoulder.

No response.

His gaze sharpened. The visible hand was smooth with artistically long fingers, certainly not that of a servant. Her complexion was clear, but even in sleep he could not reconcile her features with a barmaid. Nor did she fit the mold of a prostitute. Her bag and trunk were worn but of good quality. Paradoxically, the cloak hanging on a peg beside the door was muddy, torn, and smelled strongly of brandy.

He prodded her again. What was she doing in his room? In his bed? How had she been injured and who had bandaged her? Why had he no recollection of any of this? Usually by now he at least managed a hazy outline of his evening.

"Bloody hell! What is going on here?"

His head pounded. He prodded harder, frantic when he could raise no response.

Her left hand rested atop the coverlet. She wore no rings. That precluded a widow or a wife. Terror welled in his throat as he shook her. Still no response. Acute pain knifed through his neck and for the first time, he examined himself.

"My God!"

A bandage wrapped one leg, which was surprisingly sore. Scrapes covered both hands. He peered into a cracked looking glass and gasped in shock. One eye was swollen and a long graze extended from forehead to cheek. Pain again stabbed from his neck to his right shoulder. Twisting before the glass, he discovered an ugly bruise. The agony was too great to remain in this contorted position for long, but he could not reconcile his injuries with a fight.

"An accident?" he wondered. "Bloody hell!"

But why was he sharing a bed with an unknown and apparently unmarried female? How long had they been here? That elusive snippet returned to tantalize him and he shuddered. What had occurred in the dark reaches of the night? He loosed an exhaustive and highly imaginative stream of invective, until a groan cut him off in mid-curse.

"Anne?" whispered a voice. "My head aches so. Could you bring me some water?"

He collapsed in despair as the Damoclesian sword fell. Though weak and barely conscious, she was obviously well-bred. What had he done?

"Anne? Are you here?" whispered the voice again.

Thomas rose and poured water into a cracked cup, holding it to her lips. Remembering that he was nearly naked, he slipped beneath the coverlet, taking care not to touch her. Then he waited for her to open her eyes, waited for her to tell him why they were together, and prayed that somehow his deductions were wrong.

Caroline swallowed a sip of water from the cup Anne held to her lips. No, not Anne, she acknowledged as memory returned. Her head ached abominably. She reached a shaking hand to the bandage, which had slipped down over her eyes.

There had been an accident. She remembered now. The coach had gone faster and faster until it had finally overturned. She had been on the bottom and must have been knocked senseless. Where was she?

In bed.

Someone was with her, someone who had just settled onto the edge. Was she so badly injured that a nurse had been left to attend her? But how could she hope to pay for such an extravagance? She had only a few shillings, assuming her reticule had not disappeared.

Shakily, she pushed the bandage up so that she could see. The room was dimly lit, but not with wavering candlelight. A window covered with sparse ivy admitted minimal light from an overcast day. With difficulty she turned to see who rested on the bed.

"You!" she gasped before clamping one hand over her mouth in horror. She lunged away in a reckless attempt to escape, discovered she wore only her shift, grabbed the coverlet, and retreated to the chair under the window.

Thomas jumped as though shot, remembered his own state of undress, and donned the sheet. He backed into the far corner and stared warily at the lady huddled in the coverlet. Wide, terrified eyes stared back. Her reaction was not encouraging. *What had he done?*

"What are you doing in my room?" she demanded icily. "Haven't you caused me enough trouble?"

"I have no idea," he admitted with a grimace. "I could ask the same of you. What are you doing in my room?"

"Are you still foxed?" Her nose led her eyes to the uncovered chamberpot and she sighed in resignation.

Thomas rubbed his sore shoulder. "Let us start at the beginning," he began slowly. "The last thing I remember is sitting in the taproom at the Laughing Dog. To the best of my knowledge, I have never seen you before. Who are you?"

"You must have been even more foxed than I thought," Caroline murmured in disgust.

She raked him with an objective stare. Not much older than herself, he looked as though he would clean up rather nicely. Well-cut black hair curled riotously around his face. Despite the bruises, the two-days' stubble of dark beard, and his generally dissipated appearance, he had an aristocratic face of the more handsome variety, highlighted by a wide, sensual mouth and brilliant green eyes under indecently long lashes. But his expression declared him a spoiled society buck accustomed to getting his own way and ready to ride roughshod over anyone who crossed him. Did he really have no memory of recent events? How odd. Her face snapped back into a frown.

"I am Miss Caroline Cummings, third daughter of the Sheldridge Corners vicar. I am on my way to Cornwall to take up a post as governess. We met—if you can call it that—as I was boarding the mail coach. You knocked me down, draped yourself all over me, emptied your stomach, and then passed out in my lap. Being unable to shift you, I had to endure your weight until my legs lost all sensation. Then the driver abandoned his wits and tumbled us down an embankment. As if that were not enough, you have now invaded my room. Please leave this instant!" She delivered this recital with barely suppressed indignation that raised her voice until each word pounded into his head with the force of a blacksmith's hammer.

"This situation is worse than you know, Miss Cummings," ground out Thomas, staring despairingly at the dowdy miss in front of the window. Her only redeeming virtue was height. He usually towered over women. But the few wisps of hair sticking out from under her bandage seemed dull brown, as were her eyes. The rest of her features were plain, with freckles dotting her nose. Nevertheless, he would have to make the best of things. A vicar's daughter. Devil take it, she was gentry. If this imbroglio became known, it could ruin Eleanor's Season. He took a deep breath.

"I am the Honourable Thomas Edward Alfred Mannering. I admit to being on the go last evening—at least I assume it was last evening—and have no recollection of boarding the mail. I can only apologize and hope that my illness did not disturb you too greatly."

"Well," she conceded, "you did make it to the window—over my poor body."

He groaned at the picture her words painted.

"Again," she returned to her original complaint, "what are you doing in my room?"

"I could ask you the same question. I fear that someone has carefully placed us here together," he explained. "I awakened to find myself sharing a bed with you."

She reddened, then her face paled. "What—"

He shrugged helplessly. "I have no idea," he admitted, "but I was three sheets to the wind rather than senseless, so anything could have happened."

She was visibly shaking.

"We will have to marry, you know," he added resignedly. "Neither your reputation nor my honor as a gentleman would survive otherwise." Which was the worse sin? Ignoring honor's demand? Or disgracing his family by wedding beneath him? Unfortunately, honor delivered the more impassioned plea. But how could he survive being shackled to vicarage prudity? *Oh, God, Alicia! How could fate have turned so badly against us?*

Caroline stared as if he had gone mad. *Surely this is a dream. Soon I will awaken, safe in the room I share with Anne. We will laugh at such a fanciful nightmare and finish packing my trunk for Cornwall.* But Mr. Mannering was still there, partially wrapped in a dingy and slipping sheet, and try as she might, she could not wake up. Must she really spend her life with this perpetually foxed stranger who blithely admitted that when in his cups he would of course expect to ravish any female foolish enough to cross his path? He belonged in Bedlam.

"But who would ever know?" she protested desperately.

"These things have a way of getting out," he said. "There is no telling how many people are aware we spent the night together. Think it over. I will try to discover where we are and what has happened. Mayhap I can learn how we find ourselves in this fix. Not that it will improve our situation any."

She merely nodded and turned to stare out the ivy-covered window.

Once he departed, she numbly proceeded with her own *toilette*. There must be some way to escape this coil! But she could remember nothing beyond the accident. Not the faintest glimmering. Someone had carried her to an inn, removed her clothing (her cheeks reddened), dressed her wounds, put her to bed. That same someone must have done the same things to Mr. Mannering. Her blush spread clear to her toes. But who would have assumed that they were wed? She slumped dizzily onto the bed. At least nothing had been stolen. Her few coins still lay in the reticule she found tucked among her clothes. Except her virtue, mocked that inner voice she hated.

Mr. Mannering returned with a breakfast tray, keeping his expression carefully neutral. Dowdy didn't begin to describe her dress. Never fashionable, it was at least ten years old, having originally belonged to someone both shorter and stouter than Miss Cummings. Innumerable washings had softened the fabric until it hung like a muddy, brown tent. The bandage bleached her face even paler. And her right hand was nearly as scraped as his own.

"The innkeeper's wife fixed this for us. It is dusk, by the way. We are at the Blue Boar, some forty miles west of Sheldridge Corners." He placed the tray on the table, drew it nearer the bed, then seated himself on the chair.

"What did you learn?" She poured coffee. He was already quaffing ale. This parody of normal dining set her teeth on edge.

"I spoke to a thin young man who was another passenger."

She nodded in confirmation to the question in his eyes.

"He claims that the driver was well into his cups, at least according to the guard. The fellow's betrothed had just jilted him for a soldier and he has repeatedly been criticized for failing to average the nine miles per hour mandated for mail coaches. Slowness is one thing the company will never tolerate. But all tales are hearsay. The guard departed, along with the King's mail, some hours ago. No one really knows why the coachman forced that sudden burst of speed. The accident broke his neck."

Caroline shuddered.

"I owe you a vast number of apologies, it seems," he continued ruefully. "According to report, my attentions were far worse than you implied. So familiar did I act that Miss Spencer was convinced that we are married. She so informed our rescuers and as neither of us was able to contradict her, they placed us in a room together."

"Is she the spinsterish lady?"

"Right."

"That would explain why she glowered at me while delivering her diatribe against the low company allowed onto the mail these days."

He cringed. "Again, my heartfelt apologies. But we must settle our future. Your father is a vicar. Have you other relatives?"

"Papa was the fourth son of the late Lord Cummings, so there are numerous aunts and uncles on that side. But no money. He had to make his own way and preferred the church to the army or the government. He met my mother while assigned as a curate in Lincolnshire. She was the old Earl of Waite's second daughter, but was disinherited for marrying so far beneath her, so I know little of that family. You might learn from her example. I have no dowry at all."

So her breeding was actually quite good, he reflected in surprise. Which made his own behavior even worse. But such a connection would not reflect badly on his family.

"That matters not. I see no possibility of explaining away the past eighteen hours, Miss Cummings. I have hopelessly compromised you. There can be no solution but marriage."

"Who will ever find out? No one knows my name. I spoke to none on the coach. I can simply continue my journey."

"Word will get out," he insisted. Honor aside, the more he considered Miss Cummings, the better he liked the idea. While no beauty, she was an improvement on the horse-faced Miss Huntsley. A governess surely had more sense than that brainless widgeon. And she would probably not complain over conditions at Crawley, never having known luxuries. Clearly she had few sensibilities. Most ladies of his acquaintance would produce weeklong hysterics after what she had been through. It seemed that fate was offering at least a partial reprieve. All he had to do was convince her of the inevitability of their union.

He flashed the most understanding of his stock of charming smiles.

"The accident has delayed your arrival and your injuries will be impossible to hide. Once it is known you were on the coach whose driver died, someone is bound to connect you with Mr. Mannering's mysterious wife. They know me, you see, having checked my card case. Who would overlook such a scandal involving their governess, Miss Cummings?"

She cringed. "But you cannot wish to marry me, Mr. Mannering. You know nothing about me. Nor I of you, for that matter."

"True, though that can be easily remedied. I will not deceive you, Miss Cummings. I am no bargain," he began. "To give you the words with no bark on them, I have spent the bulk of the past year in continuous dissipation, surfacing only recently to find myself deep in the River Tick. That is the worst of it, however. I am the second son of the Earl of Marchgate and have a small estate of my own, though it is in considerable disrepair. My father has decreed that in exchange for bailing me out, I must stay on said estate and see to its restoration. The only capital I can obtain is an inheritance from my grandfather that comes to me upon my marriage. But my recent misbehavior has not helped my reputation any. Father claims that Lord Huntsley would welcome my addresses to his youngest daughter. I had not yet given him my answer, deciding in my cups two evenings ago to first travel to Devon and see whether she is really as disgustingly inept as I remember. Frankly, your advent is a blessing. Already I know and like you better than Miss Huntsley."

Hardly a complimentary declaration, but acceptable under the circumstances, she reflected. He obviously had no desire for a wife but must accept one for financial reasons. So their compromising situation would not become a bone of contention in the future. He seemed to consider her an improvement in his fortunes.

"I will be equally frank, sir," she countered, pacing the room restlessly. "I am the third of twelve children. Times are bad and Father can no longer afford to feed such a brood. I accepted a position as governess, planning to send a portion of my salary to my family. That remains important, so in addition to bringing no dowry, I would constitute a modest drain on your admittedly straitened circumstances. To my credit, I am excellent with children and well-versed at running a household. I even know a bit about estate management. However, my education will seem shockingly broad to the polite world for I am the worst sort of bluestocking. And while I have acquired all the manners expected of one in my position, I have no idea of how to go on in higher circles and cannot produce the inane chatter acceptable to drawing rooms. I still cannot accept that marriage is the only solution to our predicament. And I have no desire for a husband who is both an admitted gamester and a drunkard."

He reddened. "Plain speaking indeed, though I had not previously shown a penchant for gaming and believe that I have now come to my senses regarding my recent behavior. As for drinking, after last night I have a profound antipathy to over-indulging ever again. But speaking of last night, I do not know exactly what happened. Nor do you, seemingly. However, we must proceed on the assumption that the worst occurred, with the worst likely consequences."

She blanched.

"Precisely, my dear Miss Cummings," he confirmed. "And if there are to be no long-standing repercussions, then we must marry immediately."

"All right. But how am I ever going to explain this to Papa?"

She burst into tears.

Chapter 3

Closing her eyes, Caroline rested her head against the squabs and reflected on the last four days, grateful that Thomas had chosen to ride. She needed this respite. Fate had forced another night together at the Blue Boar, for they could not engage a second room without precipitating the very scandal they sought to quash. At least he volunteered to sleep on the floor. They had returned to Sheldridge Corners the next morning.

Rumors of the accident abounded and the Cummings were appalled to discover that Caroline was involved. In deference to her pounding head, Thomas sent her to bed and himself informed the vicar of their situation. They had agreed on a suitable tale: being somewhat disguised, he had fallen asleep slumped against her shoulder. This had led an elderly spinster to assume that they were man and wife. When the accident rendered them both unconscious, the good lady had so informed the innkeeper, who then assigned them a single room. Naturally, he was prepared to take Caroline to wife and would ride immediately to London to obtain a special license. The vicar was agreeable, so Thomas departed forthwith. She had not seen him again until their wedding in the vicarage parlor that very morning.

Not that she had been allowed time to either regret or celebrate her fate. The intervening days had flown by in a flurry of congratulations and preparations. Her mother and married sisters overwhelmed her with conflicting advice and all worked feverishly to improve her limited wardrobe now that she was no longer restricted to governess drab.

Thomas spent most of their abbreviated wedding breakfast with his friend, Lord Rufton, so they exchanged few words. Nor had they spoken beyond the commonplace at lunch. She thus had no idea how anyone had reacted to their forced nuptials. Even her parents never mentioned it. Nor had she voiced her own misgivings to her family, restricting her comments to the challenge of restoring Mr. Mannering's estate and the unexpected advent of such a personable young man. For despite his scrapes and bruises, he did clean up very well indeed. And sober, he possessed such charm that her entire family had fallen instantly under his spell. She shook her head. They had certainly seen a different side of his character.

"Such a handsome man!" fourteen-year-old Esther sighed when Caroline appeared at breakfast the morning after her return. "That curly black hair is so like Evelyn's description of Lord Byron. And those eyes! Who would have believed you could meet such a beau at our own Laughing Dog Inn?" Esther spent the wedding breakfast gazing in mooncalf adoration at her new brother-in-law.

"I'll bet he's a warm one," murmured Constance as she helped her dress for the wedding. "Mark my words, you will bless the day you met." Connie had been visiting the vicarage when they returned. As the prettiest of the Cummings daughters, she always attracted the attention of every male in the vicinity and had undoubtedly set those green eyes gleaming. Caroline had always wished she shared Connie's looks.

"What a great gun!" enthused eleven-year-old John. "He told me the funniest story about a curricle race!" And he launched into a confusing tale of barking dogs and frenzied poultry that left her laughing even though she had no real idea just what had occurred.

"He says his youngest sister is just my age," reported Anne longingly in the darkness of their shared bedroom. "Oh, I hope I can meet her. Do you suppose we could both visit you this spring? Imagine growing up on an earl's estate. If only Grandfather had not disowned Mama, we might have managed a come-out!"

Caroline listened, and wondered at their enthusiasm. Clearly he had charm to spare when he chose to exert it. He was probably one of London's leading rakes with half the *ton* at his feet. She must guard her heart against his wiles if she was to avoid a lifetime of misery. For she harbored no illusions. He would never love her. She was but the means to acquire a small fortune. And though he might treat her as a savior now, she must never forget that she was merely the lesser of two evils.

The coach hit a bump, drawing her eyes to the window. Thomas rode alongside, offering a partial view of his profile. He certainly cut a fine figure, sitting his glossy black stallion as though they were one, his own black curls a perfect match. Tonight they would discover whether he had ravished her. Not that it mattered. His mere presence was condemnation enough. She had seen it in her mother's eyes, though the good lady believed that both were unconscious and blameless. But others would never consider mitigating circumstances. And he had not been unconscious.

She shifted her thoughts to the estate that was now her home. The house was fairly new, dating from the reign of Queen Anne, so should be free of most drafts. That alone made it attractive after the vicarage. Though Thomas called it a small manor, his description made it seem a veritable palace, at least double the size of the squire's grange. But she would manage, even if he had not exaggerated its deterioration.

She was less sanguine about meeting his family. None of them had returned with him from London. She didn't even know if they had been informed of his hasty wedding. What would the earl think of this coil? His title was one of the oldest in England. And what about the countess? Would she look down on this vicarage upstart? Her breeding was hardly up to Marchgate standards, even if Thomas considered her an improvement over his father's choice. Then there was Viscount Hartford, Thomas's older brother, and his two sisters, the youngest poised to make her bows to society. Who knew how they would take the news.

She shuddered.

How would she cope? She hoped her lack of social graces wouldn't embarrass him. Would his consequence diminish because she was too far beneath his touch? She would know in three months, for he intended to spend the Season in London.

In the meantime she must mold herself into a dutiful spouse. She enumerated her roles. The house would require hard work, but she was used to that. Caring for the tenants was little different than the vicar's duty to his parishoners. Her biggest challenge was Thomas himself. The ultimate goal was friendship, but that lay far in the future. She must first learn to respect him, despite their disastrously vulgar introduction. They must achieve a workable partnership if they were to restore Crawley. She would remain matter-of-fact over their personal relationship, for he did not deserve a missish spouse. But above all, she must accept his behavior outside their home without comment or complaint, for he owed her nothing but his name. *Please, Lord, let me never lose sight of that fact.*

Thomas was also using this time to assimilate his drastic change of fortune. The previous days had flown past in a whirlwind of arrangements, giving him no time to reflect. And he still felt out of control. The biggest decisions had been made when he

was too cupshot to think clearly. But little could be altered at this
late date. For better or worse, his future was settled.

The interview with Vicar Cummings—Thomas's first truly
sober act—had gone well. There had been a momentary flash of
anger at their compromising situation, but the vicar immediately
agreed that no fault could attach to either of them and blessed
their forthcoming union. And his new father-in-law was undeni-
ably relieved that Caroline's lack of dowry posed no problem.

The interview with his own father had been far more painful.
Having just been raked over the coals for excessive drinking, he
dreaded disclosing how disguised he had been.

"You what!?" the earl barked when he admitted the entire,
sorry tale—except just how thoroughly he had compromised her.

He patiently reviewed every detail until his father agreed that
no other honorable course existed. At least he was suitably impressed by Caroline's breeding and even volunteered to arrange
the release of his inheritance. Nothing was said about his recent
behavior.

Nor did either of them mention Alicia.

Just back from Doctor's Commons, he was strolling down St.
James Street, deep in thought, when he bumped into another
oblivious pedestrian. His eyes widened as he recognized George
Mason, Viscount Rufton, who happened to be his closest friend.

"George, what are you doing in town?" he exclaimed with
pleasure. "I thought you were buried in the wilds of Northumber-
land until spring."

"Mother invited the Coffertons and Delaneys for the holidays
in an unsubtle attempt to see me leg-shackled." George grinned.
"I escaped just after Twelfth Night. After all, I am only six-and-
twenty." He cast a comprehensive eye over his friend. "Good
Lord, that must have been quite a mill. Is your opponent still
breathing?"

Blinking his purpled eyes, Thomas ruefully shook his head.
"No mill, George. Just a coaching accident."

"You?" The incredulous voice carried, causing several heads to
turn in their direction.

"I wasn't driving," he disclaimed immediately. "Come up to
my rooms and I'll tell you about it."

"Gladly. But injuries aside, you look better than I've seen you
in months. Have you decided to rejoin the living?" The tone was
bantering, but Thomas was embarrassingly aware of the serious
concern that underlay George's words. They turned out of St.
James and headed for Albany, where both kept rooms.

"I fear so," he conceded with a shake of his head. "I have sworn off serious drinking—a little late, I must admit. You are looking at a man about to take personal charge of his estate in exchange for financial assistance from the pater. I will be at Crawley in two days, as soon as I finish acquiring a wife. Would you care to stand up with me?"

If he had not still been dazed at the speedy upheaval of his own fortunes, he might have laughed at the way George's eyes suddenly protruded from their sockets. Unlocking his door, he poured brandy and embarked upon the saga of how fate had tricked him.

George was a brick. The tale had spread no further. And he had indeed stood up. Thomas appreciated the gesture. It was especially fitting, since George had participated in every milestone of his life since they met at Eton.

But now he and Caroline were headed for Crawley. Alone.

The stone wall flanking the road gave way to wrought-iron gates marking the entrance to one of Picton's estates and offering a view of well-kept grounds bordering an elegantly curved drive. Even in mid-winter, the sight drew his eyes, shooting envy through his breast.

He tried to picture Crawley as he had last seen it. Though he had inherited the estate some five years earlier, he had actually visited it only three or four times, leaving its supervision in the combined hands of his bailiff and man of business. The house would need a thorough cleaning, though the finished effect should be quite charming. Likewise, the grounds required attention. But there was less urgency about that chore now that Alicia's beauty would never grace them. He had often pictured her presiding over al fresco entertainments along the lakeshore, her blue eyes mirroring the clear water, her golden ringlets casting the sun into shadow.

His teeth clenched against the pain in his tightening loins and he deliberately pushed memories of his love into the background. Somehow he must forget her. She was lost to him for all time. Even Darnley's demise couldn't help them now. He would lock her memory into a private mental compartment and not allow her to intrude on his daily life. Visions of her beauty could warm his heart when he hit one of life's rough spots, but she would otherwise remain hidden.

Thank God, Caroline was plain. Though not as dowdy as she had first appeared, she would never be mistaken for a diamond. Her freckled face and neatly coiled hair were acceptable, but there was no comparison between her and his love. And that was good.

It eliminated the temptation to do so. Nor did she seem prone to chattering, giggles, vapors, or other missish behavior. And she was sensible. Once she had accepted his hand, there had been no more protests over their union, merely practical discussion of how best to accomplish the deed. It boded well for the future. He would not be subjected to pouting or second thoughts. Now if he could just coax a little passion from her. . . . That was the one thing he could not live without. *Oh, Alicia, how deeply you touched my soul. . . .*

He determinedly returned his thoughts to Caroline. It was quite possible that passion lurked beneath her unpromising exterior. Her grandfather, the late Earl of Waite, had been a lusty devil who reputedly passed his appetites on to most of his numerous offspring. He grinned at remembered tales of old Waite's eldest daughter, now a dowager viscountess. And she was Caroline's aunt. The future looked brighter. He wished he could remember their last encounter, not that it would provide any guidance. That an encounter had taken place he knew quite well. The signs were all present when he had cleaned up, which would make tonight easier. . . .

They arrived at Crawley just before sunset. Thomas had not exaggerated its condition, conceded Caroline as the coach bounced along a heavily rutted drive toward the house. If anything, he had understated the case. When had he last visited his estate?

Neglect was everywhere, overshadowing the usual January barrenness. Weeds choked the drive, fences sagged in forlorn disrepair, deadwood threatened anyone foolish enough to walk beneath the trees, and several fields that should have been under cultivation appeared not to have supported a crop in years. A handful of sheep grazed over a sparse pasture, confined only because someone had jammed brush into the breaks in the estate wall. Water pooled in a meadow whose natural drainage had been blocked by feral shrubs, threatening to back up onto the drive.

The house appeared little better. The sun's last rays illuminated windows that had not been cleaned in years. Several roof slates were broken, wood showed little trace of paint, and the stonework needed pointing. However, the charming facade would offer a warm welcome once they tamed the surrounding shrubbery and pruned back encroaching ivy.

Thomas handed her down from the carriage. "This looks worse than I remember," he admitted in chagrin.

"You certainly did not exaggerate conditions, sir," she agreed. "When were you last here?"

"I suppose it has been all of two years, but Tibbins should have kept better order."

"Tibbins being your bailiff?"

He nodded.

Caroline sighed. "That is for tomorrow. First things first. Are there servants? And are we expected?"

The door was not yet open and he was fishing in a pocket for his key. "Yes and no. I forgot to send ahead, and it would seem my valet has not yet arrived from town with my luggage."

"Then the servants are probably at dinner."

But this speculation proved false as footsteps finally sounded in the hall. A stately butler opened the door.

"Mr. Mannering, sir!" he exclaimed, his staid mien slipping for a moment, revealing more than a trace of chagrin.

"Peters, this is my wife, Caroline," injected Thomas with a charming smile. "I take it Cramer has not put in an appearance?"

"No, sir, ma'am." Peters's eyes twitched to the adjacent drawing room which was under dusty Holland covers.

"I understand my husband neglected to send notice of our imminent arrival," she said easily. "I'm sure that can be put right on the morrow."

"For now, if you will see that the master bedroom is readied and our luggage carried up, we will stretch our legs in the garden. And some food would not be amiss. Trays upstairs will do for tonight."

"At once, sir," agreed Peters, hurrying toward the servants' hall.

Thomas turned to Caroline, a rueful smile on his face. "I fear I am not making much of an impression, am I?" He looked like a little boy trying to escape some well-deserved punishment. He undoubtedly had years of practice at charming himself out of scrapes. She firmly suppressed the smile his hangdog look elicited.

"That depends on what else you have forgotten, sir. What others did you neglect to inform of our nuptials?" But the twinkle in her eye belied the stern tone.

"I hope nobody. The notice should appear in the papers this week. Father is looking after my business in town and has expressed a desire to meet you soon as possible. The exact date is undecided as Mother is laid low with a chill and is unable either to travel or to receive visitors."

They had reached a terrace along the west side of the house. Caroline caught her breath, for despite the lack of care, the view was delightful, lit to its enchanting best by the setting sun's rosy rays. The manor occupied a low hill from which paths wound south through terraced formal gardens to a lake nestled in the valley. Beyond its shores rose a line of larger hills, most of them forested. A stream drained the lake, winding across parkland and meadows before turning out of sight.

"It's beautiful!" she exclaimed. "How sad that it has been let go for so long." Then she gasped at the implied criticism.

But he was not perturbed. "Yes, it is sad, though not entirely my doing. I have never lived here, you know, and have not owned the property very long. There has been no one in residence for over a decade."

"Then the house should be in poor shape, indeed. I wonder if we will need more help. There cannot be much staff. Is there a housekeeper?"

"Yes, Mrs. Peters. But you will need to hire additional servants."

They reached the western edge of the formal gardens, so they retraced their path back to the house, where he led her on an abbreviated tour. Covered as it was, she could not evaluate the furniture, but every room told the same story of decayed neglect—dingy carpets, faded draperies, wall coverings varying from loose to tattered, cobwebs and dust everywhere. The only room that elicited a second glance was the library. It was nicely proportioned and appeared considerably less neglected than the rest of the house. The shelves seemed well-stocked.

"Don't get your hopes up," warned Thomas, noting the enthusiasm in her eyes. "Collections of sermons dominate this undistinguished assortment if I remember correctly from my last visit. However, my own books will arrive by the end of the week, which you are welcome to peruse. And feel free to order anything else. There is an excellent circulating library in Banbury, and when we go up to town, I have subscriptions at all the booksellers."

"Thank you, Thomas," she said, smiling as she filed away the surprising information that he appeared to be bookish, a tendency she would never have suspected from his previous behavior. If so, it could provide a foundation for a tentative friendship.

He next led her upstairs to the master suite. "You will have to share my room until yours is renovated. It is quite untenable at the

moment, or at least it was when I was last here. Order whatever
you need and make that your first project."

Shivering, she gazed at the enormous bedroom. If this was the
best Crawley offered, she did not yet have the fortitude to peek
into her own rooms.

The carpet's color was impossible to discern, as dirt had turned
its pattern to mud. The previous tenant had kept cats. Snags and
tears decorated the bottom half of both draperies and bedhangings, and the wallcoverings were destroyed. But the bed was
freshly made up, the fireplace burned merrily—already reducing
the chill of an unused room—and the furniture appeared solid,
though in need of a good polishing. A table was laid for supper.
She suddenly realized that Thomas was speaking.

" . . . will bring bathwater. I must check the stables before the
light is gone, for I dare not have my cattle sent down without adequate facilities. One of the maids will be up to help you shortly."

"Thank you, Thomas. Take your time. I am weary after traveling all day and will rest. We can eat later."

He lightly kissed her hand and strode away.

She immediately set out to explore the suite. Thomas's valise
was in the dressing room so she unpacked it, then did the same
with her own. Her trunk had not yet made an appearance, but
sounds from next door heralded the arrival of bathwater.

"I am Sarah, ma'am," greeted a rosy-cheeked maid when Caroline returned to the bedroom. She did not look a day over fifteen.
"Mrs. Peters sent me to do for you."

"Thank you, Sarah, but I am not accustomed to much assistance. Do you know what has become of my trunk?" She was already slipping out of her traveling dress, the sight of hot water
reminding her of how dusty she was from the road.

"It will be up directly," promised Sarah. "There is not much
staff, so the groom will have to be summoned to carry it. Have
you nothing in your valise that you can wear this evening?"

"Oh, yes." Positioning a screen around the hip bath, she removed her shift. The screen caught the heat from the adjacent
fireplace, creating a cozy nook. "I have already unpacked it. The
blue muslin will do. How large is the staff? Mr. Mannering suspects that we will need additional workers."

"Not very big," admitted Sarah. "The house has been empty
ever so long. Besides Mr. and Mrs. Peters, there's myself and
Polly for maids, and Mrs. James in the kitchen. Polly just started
and is still in training."

"Is she replacing someone who recently left?" asked Caroline curiously, wondering how even an abbreviated staff had allowed the house to get so filthy.

"N-not exactly," stammered Sarah, suddenly sounding embarrassed.

"What is wrong?" Caroline put as much sympathy in her voice as possible. "Everyone has to start somewhere."

"Oh, please, ma'am. I warn't meant to say that about the training as Mr. Tibbins don't know about it and we're not supposed to give it away."

Vastly surprised, Caroline nonetheless managed to hide that fact. "I take it the official staff consists of Peters, Mrs. Peters, and Mrs. James. So how do you and Polly come to be here? I want the truth now. Frankly, I am glad to find you."

"Well"—Sarah hesitated before continuing in a rush—"after the old owner left, Mrs. Peters had no help and no company, for Mr. Tibbins would spend nothing on the house. But there are often girls from the farms and the village who want to go into service. Boys, too, sometimes. So Mr. and Mrs. Peters have got into the habit of accepting us for training and then helping us get positions in respectable houses. Mostly we work in the servants' hall and the housekeeper's apartment, but before we can be placed, we have to do one of the big rooms. I did the library just last month. Please don't hold it against Mrs. Peters. She is ever so good to us."

"I think it an excellent program," agreed Caroline. "We will undoubtedly continue it. I will speak to Mrs. Peters myself. Now perhaps you can find my blue dress and lay it out."

Sarah bobbed a curtsy and took herself into the dressing room to collect the required gown. Caroline luxuriated for several minutes in the warm bath, thinking over the girl's fearful confession. She was not at all impressed with the bailiff, either with his refusal to countenance staff for the house or for his apparent ignorance of a long-standing apprenticeship program that flourished under his very nose. Thanking Sarah for her assistance, she sent the girl back downstairs, then dressed and resumed her explorations.

Beyond a second dressing room lay what would undoubtedly be her own room. Thomas was right about its condition. Deplorable was her own impression. Too bad none of the training had been perpetrated up here. Silk hung in tatters from the walls, matching the draperies. It was impossible to discern either color or pattern from the remains. Besides the cat damage, years of sun had shattered the fabric, leaving long tears along each fold. The bedhangings were not much better. The carpet contained scattered holes too large to mend. What little furniture remained was damaged—a chair with a broken leg, sagging drawers in the chest, a mattress that appeared less comfortable than sleeping on the floor. . . .

Clearly whoever had previously owned this estate had spent nothing on it for a very long time. Tibbins was not solely to blame. Was the rest of the house this bad?

One of her first priorities must be determining how much money she would have in her household budget, and what Thomas's plans were for indoors. Obviously, the bulk of his inheritance would have to go to improve the estate's productivity if they were to manage in the future. But an earl's son would not tolerate living in squalor. Footsteps sounded and she turned just as Thomas stepped through from the dressing room. He had already bathed and changed. Had she fallen into a trance?

"Contemplating sleeping in here tonight?" he teased, then smiled at her shudder.

"You are right. It is uninhabitable," she agreed. "Did you deliberately minimize the deterioration for fear of driving me off?"

"No, but my memory certainly played tricks on me. Now that I am here, I realize that little has changed, but I did not recall the details. It makes me shudder to think what tomorrow may disclose."

She shivered. "Is the rest of the house this bad?"

"I've no idea. I never looked beyond the mess downstairs. And I've a confession. The rooms I showed you earlier are all I've ever seen. But come, Peters has brought up dinner."

Over the meal, which was plain but surprisingly good considering the lack of advance notice, Thomas set out to charm his wife and set her at ease. He refrained from any further reference to sleeping accommodations or what activities the night would hold, instead conversing on the estate and what must be done to rescue it from its shameful condition.

"The stables are in unexpectedly good shape," he reported over the soup. "I have long toyed with the idea of raising hunters and plan to give it serious consideration. This is excellent hunt country and my groom is an outstanding trainer. What think you of the idea?"

"I will have to defer to your judgment, Thomas. Though I ride modestly well, I have had little opportunity to exercise the skill and know next to nothing about horses themselves."

He welcomed the intelligence that she rode. "We must find you a mount. Do you drive, as well?"

"Alas, no. I used to ride with the squire's daughters, but Papa's resources never extended even to a gig. I would love to learn. It would seem necessary if I am to deal with the tenants."

"Then I shall have to teach you," he offered, greatly pleased by her enthusiasm. "I will spend tomorrow morning with Tibbins and should have a better understanding after that of just where I stand. Perhaps you could spend the time with Mrs. Peters. Then we can compare notes and decide what is to be done first."

"Ask him about the roof. Several tiles appear damaged."

He nodded.

"And may I bring in helpers from the village to clean for the next few days? We can discuss permanent staffing later, but this dirt has got to go."

"Amen to that, wife." Thomas grinned. "Do whatever is necessary, though I begin to think it will require a miracle and far more cash than I have to set Crawley to rights."

She refused comment, instead asking about hunters. This topic lasted for the remainder of a leisurely meal and convinced her that he not only knew horses, but had seriously studied the problems of setting up a breeding and training facility. He was not a dedicated wastrel, she concluded in relief. So what had triggered his admittedly lengthy debauch?

Following dessert, he left to track down her missing trunk while she prepared for bed. She could not avoid a measure of terror at the thought. Five days ago she had not even met this man, yet now she was expected to not only allow, but to encourage the ultimate intimacy. Never mind that he had probably already indulged himself in that regard. Having no memory of the occasion, it did nothing to alleviate her anxiety.

She pondered what she knew of the marriage bed. Both of her sisters had reported that the procedure was nothing to fear and could even be enjoyable. Of course, Constance was in love with her husband, and Prudence shared a comfortable friendship with hers that predated their wedding. But at least their words were encouraging. And she instinctively knew that the success of her own marriage would be greatly enhanced if she found that she could enjoy intimacy. For her husband gave every impression of doing so. If this became something they could share in amity, it would provide yet another link between them. If not, she foresaw a lonely future, with her at Crawley and Thomas in town.

She finished brushing her long hair and deftly braided it for the night. Now what? Should she climb into bed? She had no idea when he would return. What if she fell asleep? That would hardly endear herself to him. Nor could she lie for any appreciable time without succumbing to fear. She decided instead to settle into a chair near the fire with the volume of *Marmion* that had been in her valise.

Ten minutes later Thomas opened the door. Her heart immediately began to pound and she could feel her muscles tense.

"Your trunk will be up in the morning," he reported casually. "Sarah will help you unpack. At the moment, she and Polly are cleaning the breakfast room so we will have somewhere to eat."

"Thank you. There is nothing in it I need right now." Her voice came out in a squeaking croak that brought a blush to her cheeks. Did she have to sound like the veriest ninnyhammer? They had already spent two nights together, after all.

He flashed his most seductive smile and disappeared into the dressing room. She determinedly returned her eyes to her book, though no words registered on her brain. The more she tried to relax, the tenser she became.

She nearly jumped out of her skin when soft hands suddenly caressed her shoulders. "Relax, my dear," he murmured, gently massaging away some of the stiffness. Chills and prickles tumbled down her spine. His lips brushed lightly against the back of her neck, his warm breath and sensual voice wrapping her in the silkiest velvet.

"May I undo this braid? I love long hair," he said, hands already untying the ribbon. As his fingers combed through her waist-length tresses, she shivered, her book sliding unnoticed to the floor.

Noting the effect he was having on his wife, Thomas smiled. His instinct was confirmed. This was a woman who could be wildly passionate if she would allow herself that freedom. Hopefully she was not one of those raised to believe that enjoyment of her marriage bed was unladylike. He must take great care to make her first time pleasurable for her. Pulling her gently into his arms, he smoothed his hands over her back, then lowered his lips to hers.

Caroline froze for an instant before relaxing into his embrace. He was now her husband. Undue missishness could doom their marriage. His warm lips moved lightly over her own, sending a new regiment of chills marching down her spine. She experimentally moved her own lips in response and felt his arms tighten, pulling her closer. The pressure of his mouth increased and his tongue gently requested entrance. She stopped thinking and allowed instinct to take over. Her lips parted and he slipped his tongue inside, teasing and cajoling, inviting her to participate in an erotic dance that was already swirling her emotions into the misty realms of ecstasy. The kiss deepened, with her arms now tightly wound around his head, her hands combing through his hair, drawing him closer. His hands traced the lines of her back, her sides, her hips, and the tightness of his embrace made breathing difficult.

Her height was perfect, he decided, allowing her body to fit comfortably against his own. He lifted her into his arms and set her gently on the bed, his mouth tracing her cheeks, her neck, nipping at her ears. She moaned.

"One moment, dear wife," he whispered hoarsely, the velvety voice now reduced to something elemental and even more stimulating. He pulled away long enough to extinguish the lamp and divest himself of his dressing gown. He had not bothered with a nightshirt. *Easy*, he admonished himself. *Don't frighten her.* Grasping the frayed edges of his control, he forced his breathing slower. The last thing he wanted was to instill an aversion to intimacy.

She flushed at a fleeting glimpse of his nakedness, but forgot embarrassment as he once more wedded his lips to her own. She resumed her exploration of his shoulders, reveling in their muscularity despite his admitted history of dissipation. He must have spent time on something more than debauchery in recent months.

His lips again drifted down her cheek and onto her neck, this time continuing along her shoulder. At some point during this mindless embrace he had unbuttoned her nightrail. One hand caressed her breast, thumb rubbing enticingly across the stiffened tip. She moaned again, arching against that wicked hand, in search of she knew not what.

He groaned in his own right, pushing her gown from her shoulder and shifting his lips to that rigid peak. He was moving far faster than he had planned, but he could no longer contain himself. She was incredibly responsive, more than he had hoped in his wildest dreams. He could not recall when he had last been so urgently aroused. Her fingers dug into his back, fiery against his bare skin. He shifted his attentions to her other breast and fought for control. He must calm down, draw things out, not chance scaring her. But oh, how he needed this. Her breasts were even more enticing than he remembered from that hazy awakening four days ago—firm, generous, and delightfully erotic. One hand slid down her thigh, inching up the hem of her gown until he could reach underneath, sending her into writhing delight, her breath gasping as raggedly as his own.

He could no longer wait. There was no doubt she was ready for him. By sheer will, he forced himself to go slowly, but she showed no signs of discomfort or distress. In fact, she instinctively drew him deeper, propelling him over the edge until he could not think at all. His mouth crushed onto hers as he drove them into ever higher spirals of dizziness until together they burst into a thousand pieces and crashed back to earth, practically unconscious.

"Dear Lord," he gasped, shifting so she could breathe.

"Mmm . . ."

With his last ounce of energy, he drew the sheet over their still-entwined bodies and was instantly asleep.

Chapter 4

Caroline retrieved some stationery from the library for making notes and tried not to dwell on her first night as a wife. It would take time to fit the evening into proper perspective, but her impressions were encouraging, confirming several of her previous suspicions.

That Thomas was an established rake seemed probable. He was so obviously adept at the art of seduction. And the strength of his passion was equally clear. Despite their devastating initial encounter, he had awakened her twice during the night. Thankfully, she had enjoyed herself as much as he so obviously did, and she blessed her sisters for their encouragement. Society held that ladies were expected to barely tolerate the duty of the marriage bed, and her mother had seemed not to know how to broach the subject given the suddenness of her marriage and the lack of any pretense of affection.

But how did such mutual satisfaction fit with separate bedrooms? More than ever she resolved to guard her heart. Any rapport was purely physical. It was dangerous to read more into the night than actually existed. A rake rarely cared who the partner of the moment was. All he required was a woman who willingly accepted his advances.

"Good morning, ma'am," said Mrs. Peters as Caroline reached the hall.

"Mrs. Peters." She nodded. "Shall we begin? I want to see every room today so Mr. Mannering can decide where to start."

"I must apologize for the state of—" the housekeeper began.

"No apologies are necessary," interrupted Caroline, loath to endure a day of such sentiments. "I am aware of the estate's history, but the past is over. We are now concerned with the future, starting with a top to bottom cleaning. How many temporary workers can be located by tomorrow?"

"Quite a few, I am sure. There is little to do in the fields this time of year, though farm laborers are not trained for indoor duties."

"We will manage quite well. I spoke at length with Sarah last night. She described the domestic servant apprenticeships you have offered." She was surprised to see a flush spread across the housekeeper's face at this change of subject and noted a flash of trepidation in her eyes. "I approve of your efforts and have every intention of continuing such a worthwhile policy," she assured her. "Why would anyone expect otherwise?"

"Well"—Mrs. Peters hesitated, then succumbed to temptation—"the previous owner was a regular nipfarthing, never willing to spend a groat on the estate, even if that meant poor service and decaying surroundings. Mr. Tibbins had been ordered to extract all possible profits, especially after the old gent moved on to stay with a sister in London. He would not have countenanced even the room and board I supply to the girls."

"But Mr. Mannering has never expressed such sentiments," she riposted before catching the housekeeper's unbelieving eye and forcing herself to think. "Of course, he has not previously spent much time or thought on Crawley," she conceded.

"There you have it," agreed Mrs. Peters. "And he left Mr. Tibbins in charge with no change in his instructions."

"There will be changes now," she promised, "for he cannot have known what those instructions were."

No more was said about the past for the rest of a long morning. Sarah, Polly, and Peters had already removed the Holland covers in the drawing room, dining room, and library, and were busy making the rooms usable. She skipped them, resolving to examine them closely after lunch. Now she wanted a broad overview of the manor, and she especially wanted to make note of any furnishings that might prove useful. It seemed unlikely that anything in the main rooms would be in very good shape.

The house was even larger than it had appeared the evening before. Thomas had pointed out the rooms now under assault by the limited staff. Most were located in the west wing, and the terrace flanking that wing led to the delightful overlook of lake and valley. What she had not detected in the fading sunset was that this wing represented but a portion of Crawley Manor. Beyond a large central block was a more extensive wing, the whole cupping a south-facing courtyard that caught and held the sun's rays even on this chilly January day. It promised a delightful retreat in the years ahead. But the immediate future was daunting. To eyes accustomed to the Sheldridge Corners vicarage, the manor was enormous. Swallowing a wave of terror at the magnitude of her task, she began making notes.

Neglect was visible everywhere, though some areas did show less wear than others. She sketched quick plans of each floor, using a simple code of numbers to indicate her superficial impression of each room's condition before jotting down specific problems and noting the presence of anything useful. She discovered several carpets that should clean up well, although she could only guess at their color; bedroom furniture that needed but minimal repair; and even draperies on northern windows which had escaped the sun's damaging rays. And the attics proved a virtual treasure trove of discarded but usable items. Much of the furniture dated from earlier eras, but the house would look better old-fashioned than run-down.

On the negative side, dirt lay thick in every room, and January was not the ideal month for a massive turnout. Washing only the Holland covers that would be immediately redeployed would be a Herculean undertaking. To say nothing of cleaning the draperies, bedhangings, and carpets. The Augean stables seemed trivial in comparison. The carpets alone could require an army of field hands. *Please, Lord*, she prayed silently, *we desperately need a week of unseasonably warm, sunny weather*.

And the roof definitely leaked.

By lunch Thomas was almost as overwhelmed as Caroline.

He had awakened in a burst of enthusiasm. The physical side of his unexpected marriage was proving to be everything he could have wanted. How had Caroline managed to extricate herself without disturbing his slumbers? He grinned. Her face might be plain, but her body was as voluptuously enticing as any he had encountered. And her response to his overtures was certainly not what he had feared once the words *vicar's daughter* fell from her disapproving lips. So his forced rustication offered certain attractions.

The estate would not be among them, he conceded by noon. He spent a quick hour skimming the ledgers, and the rest of the morning in the saddle. His impression of Tibbins slipped steadily until by midmorning he could no longer deny that the man was both lazy and incompetent. Why had he not noticed these problems on his previous visits?

And why had he asked that particular question? he cursed moments later. His mind refused to let it go unanswered. And the ensuing reflections were far from comfortable. To his chagrin, he discovered that the Honourable Thomas Mannering was a useless fribble.

Had he accomplished anything in five-and-twenty years?

Unfortunately not. A third of his lifetime gone for nought. He had put in the expected time at Eton and Oxford, enjoying his studies enormously but reluctant to admit to such an unfashionable pleasure, producing adequate but unexceptional work lest he be singled out by the tutors. Why was he hesitant to appear different? Such cowardice did not uphold the honor his ancestry demanded.

From school he had embarked upon life in the *ton*, sowing his oats with wild abandon, rapidly acquiring a reputation as one of London's more charming rakehells, but as he never seduced innocent maidens, society smiled indulgently on his rumored prowess and welcomed him with open arms. Espousing both the dandy and Corinthian sets, he sparred, fenced, and tested his marksmanship at Manton's. He lounged at his clubs, gamed, and attended innumerable sporting events. He wasted uncounted hours on dressing, driving through the park, exchanging endless *on-dits*, and doing the pretty to society's denizens. And none of it was worth a damn. He deliberately ignored the months of Alicia, and shuddered at the abysmal aftermath of her rejection. But how had he allowed himself to drift so aimlessly? Unlike most of his friends, he was not heir to a title and fortune so he had nothing to wait for. Why was he wasting his life?

What was he to do with his future? It was true that he had often considered raising horses, but he had never taken the idea beyond the dreaming stage. Nor, in spite of inheriting Crawley five years since, had he spent even a minute assessing its condition, discussing its problems, or planning its future. He had left all decisions in the hands of a bailiff he did not know, and a man of business he did not supervise. He shuddered at his own negligence. If the two were robbing him blind, it was no more than he deserved. And he knew next to nothing about agriculture. Yet in twelve months' time, Crawley would represent his entire fortune.

He tried to honestly evaluate what he saw, rapidly discovering that there was no point in making mental notes of urgent problems. Everything constituted an urgent problem. He would require a week to obtain even the broadest overview. Instead, he sought any sign of good news. That the stables were marginally acceptable was due to the estate's sole groom. Two of the tenants seemed knowledgeable and willing to try modern innovations. And several cottage industries flourished in the village.

But bad news predominated. The farms were in deplorable condition, with families housed in hovels, fences and outbuildings derelict, and little noticeable attempt to improve crop yields or livestock. His own acres were in worse shape. And the sight of the grounds in full daylight was enough to make the sturdiest heart quake. Without a gamekeeper, vermin abounded. The drive was all but washed out. The gardens formed impenetrable thickets capable of hiding follies. Even the lake was choked with deadwood and weeds. In low spirits, he returned to the house for luncheon. Would Caroline be speaking to him after viewing the devastation that was now their only home?

But lunch proved a milestone in their developing relationship. Both weary after a long morning, they exchanged formal greetings and concentrated on food. But once Peters retired, Thomas turned his attention to his wife.

"What think you of the house?"

"It will be quite delightful," she responded diplomatically.

"But not for a long while"—he grinned—"be honest."

"If we are being frank, it is deplorable," she agreed. "You must join me in praying for sunshine—lots of sunshine."

"And why is that?"

"January is hardly suited for large-scale cleaning, sir. What did Tibbins say about the roof?"

"The damage occurred in last week's storm." He frowned as he recalled the bailiff's hesitation at the question.

"Is he generally reliable?" she probed. Tibbins was clearly not carrying out his duties, yet Thomas had employed him for five years.

But she needn't have worried. He laughed. "Do not ever fear the truth, wife," he admonished. "I have never really talked with Tibbins, but after half a day in his company viewing the estate he has supervised, I judge him lazy and inept. I will keep him on only until I learn enough to take charge myself. How bad is the roof?"

"Critical," she rejoined, with relief. His words indicated a trust in her judgment that established the beginnings of a partnership. "Judging from the water damage on all floors in the east wing, the leak is large and has been growing for at least a year. Perhaps longer. I did not examine anything in detail so cannot begin to guess how extensive the rot is."

He groaned. "And at least three tenant cottages must be replaced, with significant repairs necessary to the rest. I cannot in good conscience allow those people to spend even one more year in such squalor."

"I suppose Tibbins has not gotten around to planning the spring planting," she commented dryly.

"He would undoubtedly follow the same plan as he has for each of the last ten years. I wonder that he still coaxes forth any yields. As near as I can tell, the man never heard of crop rotation. Even the tenants complain of his inflexibility."

"There was an interesting book published last spring, titled *Improved Field Cultivation Techniques*. Have you perchance read it?"

Guilty at the reminder of his not-so-youthful follies, he grimaced. "I have not been myself this past year, remember? Who wrote it?"

"Unfortunately, I do not recall, though the squire has a copy and could certainly tell us. I merely skimmed it, so cannot trust my memory for details. But it might make a good starting point for planning."

"I must ride in to Banbury tomorrow and will check the booksellers. If they don't know, then you can write the squire. I would take you along, but my carriage and horses will not arrive until the end of the week. Have you any commissions?"

"Several. I will put together a list." She paused. "I have made other discoveries since we arrived. It seems the maids Sarah and Polly are not officially employed here. Tibbins refused to authorize indoor staff beyond Peters, Mrs. Peters, and Mrs. James."

He glanced up in surprise. "Then why are they here? Without notice, they could hardly have been brought in for our benefit."

"True. But the Peters long ago took upon themselves—I suspect to relieve boredom—the task of training area girls and boys to be domestic servants and helping them find suitable positions. Tibbins is unaware of the practice. But I like the idea and wish to continue it."

"Certainly. This is yet one more negative to lay at the man's door. Tibbins will not remain much longer."

Encouraged by this reaction, she voiced yet another idea she had formulated that morning. "I could not help noticing the deplorable condition of the grounds. With planting due to start so soon, the tenants will be busy in the fields. What think you of hiring former soldiers to make a start on clearing? We had many of these poor men near Sheldridge Corners. They cannot find jobs, nor can most return to combat because of their injuries. But many are able to do moderately heavy work, especially where there are no time constraints as would exist in planting or harvesting."

He bit off an equivocation and turned her suggestion over in his mind. Many veterans littered the streets of London, men in the tattered remains of uniforms, who lacked an arm or leg or worse, and were reduced to begging to stay alive. Like most of his peers, he had pointedly ignored them, but her appeal prompted him to consider their plight. How would he survive similar deformities? And he could so easily have acquired them. Second sons frequently turned to the army for their livelihood. Without Crawley, he might well be on the Peninsula.

"An excellent idea," he agreed. "I will inquire about area men while in town tomorrow and see what labor may be found."

"Thank you, Thomas. May I turn out the library while you are gone? Or would you prefer the drawing room? Both need much more than today's cursory cleaning."

"The library will be fine. Best to finish in there before I find myself neck-deep in paperwork." He grinned.

"So I thought. And I will put together a preliminary list of essentials that we can discuss tonight."

Thomas rose and helped her from her seat. "Until dinner then, Caroline. I must spend the afternoon trying to make sense of the estate records." He raised her hand to his lips, sending shivers up her arm.

That day set the pattern for the following week. They ate all meals together. The evenings passed in amity in the library. Thomas alternately perused estate records and devoured the agriculture and horse-breeding books he purchased in town. He discovered a hitherto unsuspected interest in estate management. But the more he learned, the angrier he became with his great-uncle for dissipating a prosperous property and at Tibbins for abusing what was left.

Caroline spent these evenings sitting quietly before the fire, mending linens and draperies. She was always willing to discuss estate problems, but rarely initiated a conversation, knowing that he was wrestling with a host of new concepts. Though she had spoken to the squire several times about estate management, she had not studied the subject herself, so refrained from offering her own views. Ladies were not expected to be knowledgeable and she did not want to endanger their developing friendship by setting herself up as an expert. Instead she limited her input to common-sense statements and an occasional pertinent question that pointed his thinking in interesting new directions. She discovered that he possessed a lively mind and a keen sense of humor. These attributes and a week of hard work and no drinking went a long way toward earning her respect.

Days found Thomas riding over the estate and Caroline supervising a truly gargantuan cleaning effort. She had been forced to scale back her plans. There was simply too much to do. Roofers arrived to repair the leaks, but Thomas agreed to postpone other work on the east wing. She closed it off and concentrated on the rest, praying daily for continued dry weather. A dozen powerful men beat carpets from dawn to dusk, raising enormous dust clouds. An even larger army toiled indoors. Men stripped or reattached wallcoverings and shifted furniture. Women scoured, waxed, and polished. Lamps doubled their output of light with the advent of clean chimneys. Silkwood paneling in the hall and library glowed. Windows sparkled and furniture gleamed.

By week's end the drawing room, dining room, and main sitting room were places of welcome, despite fraying draperies, worn carpets, and appallingly bare walls. Most of the west wing and the central block was clean and aired, though she had made no attempt to decorate or even make habitable the bulk of the rooms. But in an attic she discovered a set of French furniture that had graced the drawing room some fifty years earlier, its condition better than the heavy, worn pieces preferred by Uncle Bertram. In like manner she moved a better carpet into the breakfast room, undamaged draperies to the dining room, and found several almost-matching pieces suitable for her own rooms.

Her most surprising discovery was a lovely pianoforte in the drawing room. With the manor's history of neglect, she had expected nothing beyond a derelict harpsichord. But though it was badly out of tune, it seemed in excellent condition. In her only personal extravagance since her marriage, she immediately sent for a tuner. Music was both her greatest love and her most striking accomplishment.

After a week of nonstop labor, she celebrated with an afternoon of playing. She had her own music, of course, but had discovered a cabinet holding other pieces, many of them new to her. Lost in a Haydn concerto, she did not notice Thomas's amazement as he halted in the doorway. Nor did she see the pain that marred his face before he fled the room. Thus she did not worry when his evening's study lengthened so that she fell asleep long before he stumbled up to bed.

On his part, Thomas suffered a shock when he had returned

early to the manor. The last thing he had expected was finding that his wife was an accomplished musician. Not that he disliked music. To the contrary. Alicia was an exquisite pianist and he had spent several memorable evenings listening to her entertain guests. This was yet another thing he had banished to a mental attic when he lost her. He could never enjoy music again.

His first thought upon hearing the concerto was that an angel had dropped in to pay its respects, immediately followed by the painful memory of Alicia's golden head bent over a keyboard. Worse was the realization that the musician was his wife, his ears proclaiming her more accomplished than anyone he had ever heard.

He fled.

How could he entertain such an idea? Alicia was the most exquisite musician in the world, better than the most talented professional. She could charm the birds from the trees or induce the stars to dance in the heavens. Caroline could not be that talented. It was merely shock that she played at all. Anger burst through him. She should have mentioned this. Her secrecy was hardly in keeping with her agreement to be honest. Instead, she had sprung her skills as a surprise, forcing him to make the comparison he had sworn to avoid.

Confusion reigned.

He was still young, and though he had enjoyed countless women in his five-and-twenty years, he understood little of the fair sex beyond the purely physical and still considered life in absolute terms. From the beginning he had known Alicia was perfect, an angel surpassing all others—her beauty unmatched, her wit enchanting, her talents divine. His acceptance of a leg-shackle was possible only when he decided to admire her from afar while he gouged out life with an imperfect wife. But perfection was impossible for a mere mortal. To find others with abilities that even approached hers reduced Alicia to human terms and revealed his own foolishness. Thus came his anger at Caroline for shaking Alicia's pedestal. He had reconciled his loss and accepted his fate, but his wife was unwilling to live a life of relative contentment. She chose to challenge his love head-on.

The illogic of this idea never occurred to him. How could she challenge someone whose existence remained unknown to her? For he had also been less than honest, neglecting to mention the love of his life. But he could no longer keep them separate. Neither could he allow his wife to surpass his love. That would call into question the legitimacy of his continued adoration and turn his agonizing debauch into a childish tantrum, affronting his honor.

He remained in the library, morosely drinking and pondering his life. Again, he relived the agony of the past year, now worsened by a new awareness of just how permanent marriage was. And how far from utopian. Unwilling to question his own actions, unable to accept an imperfect Alicia, he could only blame Caroline.

His initially favorable impression had now swung far in the other direction. She was too secretive. And far too retiring. Her refusal to introduce herself to their fellow passengers had resulted in their forced marriage. Her reticence concerning her accomplishments was causing untold agony. Though he had established a policy of open honesty, she clung to her secrets. What devil had forced him to wed someone bent on making him miserable?

And why had he been so anxious to accept her partnership? He had rushed his fences unpardonably in trying to befriend her before she had proved herself worthy. He knew little about her. How could he assume that she deserved his friendship? Now he was faced with the unpleasant chore of pushing her to a suitable distance. Too bad he was tied to Crawley. . . . Of course, he could always manage some business trips. Setting up a breeding stable would require travel to buy stock. Needing time to sort out his ideas, he might as well start immediately.

By the time he determined the proper course, it was well past midnight and the brandy decanter was empty. He briefly considered sleeping somewhere else, but there literally was not another comfortable bed in the house. Sighing, he resigned himself to one more night with the wife he now resented and slipped quietly beneath the sheets.

"Alicia!"

Caroline awoke with a start, not sure what had disturbed her slumbers.

"Alicia, my love!" he called again.

Tremors shook her from head to toe. Thomas was dreaming, agitation and passion vibrating through his voice.

"Alicia! How can I live without you?" A sob wracked the plaintive cry.

She slipped from bed, unable to breathe through the sudden pain. Her first reaction was to dismiss the episode as a meaningless dream, but his aching desire was hard to ignore. Who was

Alicia? She padded softly to the window and noted that it was just past dawn.

"Alicia-a-a—"

She drew in a shaky breath. Tears trickled down his cheeks. She had felt increasingly comfortable, her hope of developing a solid partnership seeming a reality. She had not anticipated anything beyond mild affection, knowing that a man of his ilk was unlikely to care deeply for someone lacking both beauty and background. Not a day passed without her stern self-reminder that she was merely the lesser of two evils. She had never expected love, but neither had she expected to find he already loved another. He had certainly been less than forthright when urging marriage, claiming his dissolute behavior was the worst she would discover about him. An attached heart was far worse.

She paced across to the fireplace, but no coals remained to warm her. Why had he not married Alicia when he needed a wife? Had she died? *Dear Lord, I hope so.* Grief would eventually pass and they could continue to build their partnership. In the meantime, she could not remain here listening to this continued mourning for his love. Nor could she awaken him. Admitting that she had overheard his impassioned cries was impossible.

She slipped into the dressing room, quickly donned a warm gown and cloak, then headed for the garden. Perhaps an invigorating walk would clear her brain and lift the gloom that had enveloped her at the first sound of his voice.

Half an hour later she had achieved a measure of peace, and common sense again ruled. She had not expected love. Nor was there anything of which she could complain in their relationship. If his heart still grieved, he was not allowing it to interfere with their marriage. Did he know he talked in his sleep? Was that why he had insisted that she complete her own suite as soon as possible?

She dropped onto a bench to consider this idea as the rising sun cleared the eastern hills, bathing the garden with golden light. Her rooms were nearly ready. With a little extra effort she could move in by nightfall. Then he could cease worrying about accidentally exposing his heart.

"Yer wits are addled!" a male voice exclaimed from the other side of a hedge.

"You ain't been here long enough to see the way the master and mistress work together," rejoined a second man. Alicia recognized him as Willy, the estate's groom.

"Bah!" responded the first in disgust. "I been driving the guv since 'e first come up from Oxford. 'E's allus known 'ow to cozen the ladies. But the only one 'e ever cared for was Miss Alicia. Lived in 'er pocket for months, 'e did. I'll never forget the night she pledged 'er love to 'im for all eternity. Floatin', 'e were. In a reg'lar trance. Coulda carried the coach 'ome on 'is back an' not noticed."

"And how would a coachman know the master's thoughts?" scoffed Willy.

"Oh, 'e's a dab 'and for the 'orses," the second man bragged proudly. "Ain't never put on airs, neither. Allus 'elpin' in the stables. Talks to me like a friend, 'e does."

She had by now recognized him as Jacobs, Thomas's coachman and trainer who had arrived with the remainder of his stable the previous afternoon.

Jacobs seemed anxious to parade his superior knowledge before the country groom. "Rode up top that night," he related. "I reckon 'e needed someone to talk to. Excitement fair bubbled out. Described 'er as the most beautiful angel in the world. An' the wittiest. An' the most talented. 'E 'spected to pay 'is addresses the next day. 'Ardly surprisin'. All Mayfair'd been lookin' for an announcement for weeks."

"So how did he wind up with Mrs. Mannering? Not that she ain't a fine woman. Did the lady turn him down after all?"

"Worse. Turned out she was already pledged to Viscount Darnley—old goat must be past sixty, though still randy as the devil by all accounts. The guv took it 'ard. Fell into a black melancholy from that day to this."

Caroline was shaking so hard she could scarcely stand, but she had to flee before she was discovered.

The pieces fit all too well, she acknowledged, almost running toward the lake. Thomas had admitted wasting the past year in debauchery. Now she knew why. He had been trying to forget Alicia. And obviously failing. But whatever had or had not happened, her own future was perceptibly bleaker. Though she daily reminded herself that he would never love her, a stubborn hope had lingered that time would prove differently. That hope was now shattered. Nor did the future seem at all comfortable, for the aging Darnley would undoubtedly die before many more years had passed. What would happen when the beautiful and most cherished Alicia was free? *Dear Lord, help me cope with this! Can I really ignore his actions if he turns to her? And how am I to react?*

Two more hours of vigorous exercise failed to restore any trace of peace, but shock and fatigue finally numbed her thoughts. She returned to the house in a trance.

Thomas was already at breakfast, dressed, as always, for riding. Neither offered their usual morning greetings. Neither noticed the omission.

"I am going to Graystone Manor to purchase some horses," he announced baldly some minutes later, pushing his barely touched plate away in disgust.

She kept her expression neutral. "I wish you a pleasant journey, then. And luck in your endeavor."

"Thank you." He strode quickly from the room.

She remained at the table for some minutes, shredding a piece of toast and repeatedly rearranging ham bits on her plate. This sudden departure was perfectly logical, given his morning dream. And most welcome. He needed time to get his emotions back under control. So did she. A period of calm would allow her to adjust her ideas and come to grips with this new scenario before having to face him either in a discussion or, worse, in bed.

Thank you, Lord.

Chapter 5

Thomas left immediately, driving the carriage himself. Handling the ribbons kept thought at bay. Jacobs accompanied him, for he would perform much of the actual training, making his input important to the success of the breeding enterprise.

Thomas deliberately avoided thinking of his marriage as he drove along the lanes and highroads. With morning had come the realization that he was too close to the problem. Events had swept him along without pause, but whatever imbroglios he had fallen into, the undisputable permanence of his union remained. And honor demanded that he accept and adapt. He must set aside his love of Alicia and carry out his duty to Caroline. The best course was to concentrate on horses for a time. Perhaps a different perspective would emerge in a week or two that would suggest a workable solution.

Turning his mind to business, he determinedly talked horses, concentrating on his plans for Crawley's future. He drank sparingly at the inn and fell instantly asleep. The previous night had been far from restful. Anger, pain, and resentment over lacking control of his life had kept him awake for most of the few hours he spent in bed, and Alicia had invaded his dreams when he slept. But this night afforded sound refreshment, and he awoke in better spirits.

It was late afternoon when he turned through the gates of Graystone Manor, unwillingly comparing the immaculate grounds with the desolation that was Crawley, overwhelmed yet again by the magnitude of his dilemma. Atlas shouldered a lighter burden. How many years of uphill battles did he face? Was success possible with his limited resources? He shook the question away. He *must* succeed. No other outcome was tenable.

The Earl of Graylock was renowned both for the excellence of his own horses and for the quality of those he offered for sale. It was his remarkable success that had first piqued Thomas's interest in raising hunters himself. Besides purchasing stock, he hoped for advice about his own fledgling business, for Graylock was not only a top breeder. Ethical in a field that attracted the greedy and sleazy in droves, rich enough that he continued his endeavors out of love—though his stables returned a handsome profit—Graylock welcomed newcomers and unhesitatingly assisted their efforts. He had already been instrumental in directing Thomas's interest to hunters rather than racers.

"You are honorable, Mannering," he had expounded over a bottle of wine at White's two years before. "Stay away from racehorses. Too many copers in that line. You cannot make a living and remain honest."

"Why?" He had long suspected that truth, but wondered what reasons Graylock would give. And the track did exert a glamorous fascination.

"Your honor could not survive," stated the older man baldly, a note of regret tinging his voice. "Cheating and sabotage are firmly embedded. It is all too common to find promising horses maimed and even killed by rival trainers. And plenty of lesser crimes occur—inflicting minor injuries that affect performance, shocking horses with nervous dispositions, even bribing riders. That is why I seldom wager on races. Regardless of bloodlines, training, and track conditions, cheating and sabotage make the outcome too chancy. Just last year fire destroyed Lord Dunhollow's stable before Newmarket. Injured the odds-on favorite, and the rest of his horses couldn't compete for months. Jockey up on the second favorite blew the horse out at the start and limped home in eighth. Not the careful handling one expects from an experienced rider."

"Who did it? The ultimate winner's trainer?"

"Possibly. Or his owner. Or any of the half dozen gentlemen who bet heavily on him at long odds. Or someone connected with one of the other top finishers. Or perhaps another individual whose scheme failed. There is no way to know and the imprudent jockey disappeared."

"But surely an honest breeder can survive."

"Possibly. Many are trying to clean out the scoundrels. But there are other factors. Consider the horses. Racers have been bred for short bursts of speed over a flat course. It is true a top runner can pull down big purses and stud fees. But what happens to those who cannot win races? They lack the stamina to cover longer distances. They tend to be nervous, which makes them unsuitable for riding or carriage work. Many are prone to leg injuries, rendering them useless for jumping. And a slow horse is hardly likely to breed speedier offspring."

Thomas slowly nodded as the truth of the earl's comments sank in.

"Now consider the hunter," Graylock continued. "The best can be sold in the shires for top dollar. The terrain requires speed, stamina, strength, heart, and great jumping. The fastest even make good steeplechasers if you are set on competing. But a horse lacking any of those attributes is still useful. One with less stamina can become an excellent hunter over more benign terrain. And even the least talented jumpers make outstanding riding hacks."

Thomas reviewed that and other conversations he had held with Graylock over the years. Without question, the man knew hunters. His estate lay but a few miles from Melton. Four of his horses had sold for more than a thousand pounds each to top Quorn huntsmen.

He sighed in envy when the house came into view. Sprawled over an area several times larger than Crawley, Graystone Manor was the product of many generations and almost as many styles. From a great hall barely postdating the Conquest, it had mushroomed into a maze of wings and towers. Gothic arches graced a chapel. One tower boasted narrow archer's slits, a second displayed leaded Elizabethan windows. Greek columns graced a Palladian addition, and Georgian austerity characterized another. But surprisingly, the gray stone from which the estate took its name unified these disparate parts into an attractive and welcoming whole.

Excitement over at last embarking on his dream left Thomas a trifle shaky as he turned the ribbons over to Jacobs and mounted the steps. Graylock was in the hall when the footman opened the door.

"Mannering!" he exclaimed in apparent pleasure, clasping Thomas's hand in a firm grip and drawing him inside. Afternoon sun glowed on centuries-old paneling. "What brings you out this direction?"

"I was hoping to look over your operation with an eye to buying a horse or two." He smiled.

The Earl of Graylock appeared more relaxed in his casual country clothes than he ever had in London, his shock of silver hair complementing light gray eyes. A widower in his early fifties, he had never remarried after losing both wife and heir in childbirth, content that his title would ultimately pass to a favored nephew.

"Wonderful," he enthused. "Are you finally setting up your own stables?"

Thomas swallowed a surge of embarrassment at the words, for he had last discussed horses with Graylock before he met Alicia.

"Yes, and I would appreciate your advice."

"Can you stay a few days? Sharpton, Heatherford, young Blakeley, and several other breeders are arriving tomorrow for a fortnight's stay. We get together once a year. You are welcome to join us."

"I would be honored, my lord." Thomas's eyes brightened and he blessed fate for dropping this opportunity in his lap. What better way to slip back into the society he had ignored for the past year? And a modest break might provide the distance he needed to decide what kind of relationship he wanted with Caroline.

"Are you still in town?" asked Graylock.

"No, I moved down to Crawley a fortnight ago." Thomas shuddered. "Uncle Bertram cared nothing for the estate, and it shows. You would not believe the shape it is in."

"What are the stables like?"

"Tolerable. That was my one surprise. The lone groom takes pride in his work and maintained the place on his own, even in the teeth of opposition from an inept—and soon to be out of a job—bailiff."

"Sounds like a jewel," commented Graylock. "How is he with horses?"

"Jacobs is impressed. I've not had time to watch him myself. Crawley is in appalling condition otherwise. I left my wife turning out the manor."

Amazement lighted the earl's face. "You are married? I hadn't heard."

"Ten days ago. To one of Waite's granddaughters—old George, I mean. It should have been in the *Post* by now."

"Congratulations. I will understand if you choose not to remain the full fortnight. But I have several mares you might be interested in. If you still have that black stallion . . ."

"Greatheart?"

"That's the one."

Thomas nodded.

"What a hunter!" Graylock enthused. "He would make an outstanding stud. Crossing him with my mares could create a line of truly superior horses. But why am I keeping you in the hall after such a long drive? Once you are refreshed, we can visit the stables." He signaled a footman. "I will be in the library when you are ready."

Caroline spent the days of Thomas's absence on cleaning and

restoration. By working as hard as possible from dawn until long past dusk and devoting her evenings to music, she was able to hold thought at bay until enough time had passed to clearly evaluate her problems.

She moved into her own rooms the day he left, then initiated a turnout of the master bedroom. The carpet was really quite beautiful, she discovered, with a glorious pattern in blues and reds that had been invisible beneath twenty years of accumulated dirt and grime.

One of the rooms in the closed-off wing held draperies and bedhangings in a matching red that showed but slight fading. She located a chair in an attic that was not only in superior condition to the one drawn up in front of the fireplace, but whose color blended well with the restored room.

Another project she pursued was Thomas's suggestion that she learn to drive. He had been too busy to teach her himself, but a still-usable dogcart was stored in the stables, and she prevailed upon Willy to hitch up a placid old gelding—the only horse on the estate when they arrived—and instruct her. Her aptitude for this skill proved adequate and within three days she was sufficiently confident to pay a round of calls on the tenants. By week's end she dared drive as far as the village where she made the acquaintance of the vicar, and Mrs. Perkins, the squire's wife.

Mrs. Perkins called the next day.

"I do hope I have not arrived at a bad time," she apologized when Caroline bustled into the drawing room.

"Not at all," she disclaimed. Peters followed just behind with a tea tray. She had taken a moment to straighten her hair, but despite streaks of dust near the hem, she still wore the gray round gown she had donned to supervise the day's cleaning. "Besides, I expect you are curious to discover how derelict the manor has become. I would have been." Brown eyes twinkled into Mrs. Perkins's rueful face.

Only a few years older than Caroline, Edna Perkins boasted strawberry-blond hair and handsome features, though several childbeds had noticeably thickened her figure. Hazel eyes reflected whatever color she wore. Today it was green.

"You must understand that no one has been inside Crawley for fifteen or twenty years, my dear. And rumors have been rife since your arrival."

"Started by those helping us clean, I suppose." Caroline laughed. "Well, as you can see, conditions could be better. However, Mrs. Peters is a wonder and we are slowly gaining control."

The drawing room was half presentable to a discriminating eye. The carpet and French furniture complemented the room's ornate ceiling, drawing attention to the four oval frescoes radiating from its center. The marble fireplace surround had been well cleaned and the piano's satinwood case glowed with polish. But the draperies were worn and faded and the walls unacceptably bare.

"Was it really as bad as rumored?" Mrs. Perkins dared ask.

"Worse, I've no doubt. We could easily have grown crops in places. Mr. Bertram Mannering was horridly eccentric."

"How?" Mrs. Perkins asked in breathless anticipation.

"Thank heavens he was unique in the family," began Caroline. "My husband is nothing like him. The man was a nipfarthing of the worst kind, refusing even to maintain sufficient staff to clean more than the few rooms he used. There are rooms in the east wing that I suspect had not been entered for more than thirty years."

"Heavens! Had he a wife?"

"She died young, in childbirth. He remained secluded even after mourning, becoming increasingly reclusive as the years passed."

Thomas claimed his uncle was obsessed with his wife, continuing to talk to her daily until his own death forty years later, but Caroline refrained from offering that tidbit to the local rumor mill.

Her guest was again examining the drawing room.

"Have you planned the rest?"

"Not yet," she admitted cheerfully. "There has been no time and I have not received the latest edition of *Ackermann's*. I need to go to Banbury, but am not familiar with the shops. Could you advise me? My husband is away on estate business and will not return for another week. Besides, he knows this area no better than I."

"Delighted, Mrs. Mannering. In fact, I am going to town tomorrow. Perhaps you would care to accompany me."

This met with Caroline's approval, and she happily spent the next day arranging for new wallcoverings in the drawing room, dining room, and Thomas's bedroom, hiring a painter for her own suite, and ordering new chair covers for the dining room and library. And she managed everything at a very reasonable cost, with the promise that the work would be complete within a fortnight. Mrs. Perkins was amazed.

"I don't know how you do it," she exclaimed over a plate of cakes at the confectioner's. "I have no head for color and dither forever over samples before finally choosing something abominable. And invariably expensive. Jonathan despairs of me."

"I am sure he does not," soothed Caroline. "Nor do I believe such fustian. You are doing it much too brown. But save the praise until the work is complete. As you pointed out, I took home no samples. It may be a dreadful mess."

They visited more shops after their tea, finishing at the booksellers. Caroline was everywhere welcomed, the shopkeepers delighted that Crawley had a tenant at last. By the end of the day she and Edna were fast friends.

She had managed to ignore the problem of Thomas for several days and finally felt able to consider it. Did knowing of his attachment change anything? It did not. Why should he treat her any differently? He had known the situation from the beginning. If she allowed Alicia's existence to alter her behavior, she could only drive him away. Was that what she wanted? Of course not. The only change must be in her own expectations. She must not push her way into his confidence lest he turn on her in disgust. It would take far longer to create a true partnership. And she must redouble her vigilance over her own heart. Any *tendre* was out of the question. But with care, she could hope that eventually they might become friends.

Jacobs returned the next day leading a string of four broodmares, two yearlings, and a two-year-old stallion. He also carried a note from Thomas, inquiring about her activities and explaining that Graylock was hosting a gathering of breeders and trainers. He had been invited to stay and hoped to acquire valuable information. He would, he said, return in a fortnight and added that he missed her. *I would invite you to join me, but none of the gentlemen brought their wives.* It was signed, *Fondly, Thomas.*

She had overreacted, she concluded in relief. She would forget that Alicia existed and concentrate on the future.

Thomas was enjoying his visit with Graylock. Two of the houseguests had started breeding operations in recent years and were able to offer invaluable advice about potential pitfalls. He spent many hours putting horses through their paces, finally settling on a reasonable assortment.

His most surprising discovery was how much he missed Caroline, especially at night. He did not love her, of course, but her passionate sensuality made her the most desirable bed partner he had ever encountered, and her instant availability added a previously unknown dimension to his life. He had never had the means to set up a regular mistress. Even his lengthy affair with Swynford's widow had not been a dedicated relationship on either side, so marriage offered uniqueness. For the first time in his life, he commanded someone's entire attention.

Time had worked to ease his emotions. And his mind had been busy modifying its impressions. Caroline was not as accomplished as he first thought. He had exaggerated her abilities in his surprise that she played at all. She and Alicia were equally accomplished musicians, heaven having blessed his otherwise undistinguished wife with one exquisite talent. Musical prowess aside, she could not compare with Alicia in any other way. Nor did equity in one arena detract from his love's other angelic qualities. He could once again enjoy music. Truly, fate had offered him a reprieve from a lifetime of despair. He had a wife who could satisfy his passion and entertain him in the drawing room. He had Alicia, whose exquisite beauty could be called to mind whenever life grew dull. He had only to maintain his relationship with Caroline in a businesslike and friendly manner and life would be sweet. He thus firmly remounted Alicia on her pedestal. Caroline would care for his house and eventually provide him with heirs. They were separate once more. Peace reigned.

Having reached this comfortable compromise, he penned her a friendly note, to be dispatched along with Jacobs and his new cattle, then joining Blakeley and Sharpton for a game of billiards and a discussion of effective training methods for recalcitrant horses.

But he received the shock of his life the next day.

He had just seen Jacobs off to Crawley when he noticed a crested coach drawn up to the front door. Curious at the quantity of luggage—for none of the breeders had brought wives to this annual meeting—he paused to decipher the crest.

"Well, Thomas," cooed a well-loved, seductive voice just behind him, "I certainly never expected to find you gracing this mausoleum."

"Ali—Lady Darnley, what a surprise," he choked, spinning around as he scrabbled to recover his poise, knowing his mouth gaped at her unexpected appearance. "I did not know that Darnley was interested in horse breeding."

Alicia laughed gaily. Caught unawares, Thomas fought to bring his raging emotions under control. *Honor, honor*, he repeated in a silent litany until the word no longer conveyed meaning. All he wanted was to crush her in his arms.

"Horses hold no interest for the viscount," she murmured, "but he is Graylock's cousin and needs must confer on some trifling matter, so here we are. I suppose I will be reduced to rusticating with horsemen's wives." Her eyelashes drooped demurely, her mouth drawn into a charming pout.

"Hardly. You will be the sole lady in residence. We left our wives at home for this meeting." Pain ravaged him at the flicker of surprise in Alicia's eyes.

"You are married?" she gasped.

"Just after Christmas. Caroline is one of the Earl of Waite's brood," he exaggerated in a flash of male need to flaunt what she had thrown away. But even as the words formed, he castigated himself. It was not her fault. Her parents had forced this situation on them both. The hurt in her eyes knifed his soul. Not only were they apart, he had now injured her with his own conceited tone. And she was all he had ever wanted.

Her beauty still captivated him. Today she wore a blue traveling gown and matching pelisse that emphasized her incredible eyes and made her golden curls appear even brighter. And her smile could instantly enslave him. Yet he could not apologize without making things worse.

Again repeating his unspoken litany of *honor, honor,* he excused himself lest he forget his pride and admit how much he loved her, and lose all control over his need to possess her.

Caroline was experiencing some of the happiest times of her life. Each day increased her sense of accomplishment, her efforts making immediate improvements in the house and estate. Given Tibbins's ineptitude, she quietly assumed his duties, ordering the changes that would address the most pressing problems. Thomas had left in such a hurry, that he had made no other arrangements.

He had hired three army veterans, and four more appeared in search of work the first week he was gone. She assigned them to the most urgent tasks on the grounds, including repairs of the estate wall, cleaning up the drive, and pruning around the entrance to the house. By the second week she moved one crew to the meadow to improve the drainage lest the spring rains again flood the road. Once Jacobs had returned, half the veterans labored under his direction to repair fences and expand pasturage for the horses.

The note from Thomas also contributed to her contentment. Not until two days later was she brought up short.

Jaimie Griggs, one of the tenant children, was laid up with a chill so she assembled a basket of remedies and foodstuffs to take to the family. Not having been raised to the aristocracy, she was not in the habit of leaving small tasks to the servants. She walked to the stables instead of requesting that the dogcart be brought to the door. Thus she inadvertently overheard another exchange between Willy and Jacobs.

"The master's due back next week?" asked Willy, freezing her progress at the stable door.

"That's wot 'e said," confirmed Jacobs, "though 'e may stay on a spell. Lady Darnley arrived jus' afore I left."

"That one you claim he's barmy on?"

"Right-o, my lad. Ye shoulda seen 'is face when 'e caught sight of 'er. Cor blimey! Mouth 'angin' open, eyes poppin' out, and 'is fists clenched like 'e could 'ardly keep 'is 'ands off'n the wench. But I told you what a beauty she is."

Caroline slipped unseen back to the house, threw herself across her bed, and cried till there was no emotion left in her heart.

Why? She did not love him and had known that sooner or later Alicia and he were bound to meet again. And Alicia's feelings were unknown. Her impression—admittedly based on one overheard conversation between two servants—was that the girl was a heartless flirt. Caroline had never expected love. Nor had she expected fidelity, so even the worst should neither surprise nor wound her.

Thomas owed her nothing. Marrying her was an expedience that had been his least undesirable choice at the time. So why was she behaving in this odiously missish way, as if her dearest love had deliberately broken a vow of eternal faithfulness? She finally explained the unexpected pain as sadness that a basically decent gentleman could throw himself away on an undeserving baggage.

On her own account, she must remain a helpful, uncomplaining, and undemanding wife, continuing her efforts to restore Crawley and assist him whenever asked. But she would not allow even the slightest *tendre* for this admittedly handsome rake. And that included permitting emotion to intrude on their bedroom activities. Physically, she could hardly help enjoying the things he did, for he was an accomplished lover and made sure that she was involved and satisfied. But she must remain detached. The alternative was a lifetime of unhappiness.

Having soothed her feelings, she picked up the basket and asked Peters to summon the dogcart.

Nor did her thinking change over the next several days. Her organizing skills soon had the estate functioning smoothly, leaving her with excess time on her hands. Evenings could be spent playing the pianoforte or mending linens and draperies. She began to devote a portion of her afternoons to drawing and watercolors. Not that she would ever match her sister's work, but sketching served to fill the time and some of her pictures were passable. In fact, she framed two and hung them in the morning room to dress the otherwise bare walls until she found something better.

Her gratitude for Thomas's absence evolved into anxiety over his return. Better to face their next encounter than to remain in suspense. What had Alicia's intrusion done to their relationship? Could they remain partners, if not friends? Or had they already moved down that road of estrangement she had envisioned once before that could only lead to separation?

Chapter 6

Alicia's arrival increased Thomas's strain. He had last set eyes on her at that single morning call following her betrothal and had looked forward to their next encounter. But he had expected some advance warning and time to prepare. Certainly it should have taken place in the context of London's superficial social whirl, which would provide both a framework and a buffer. To meet in the country at an informal house party was worse. Her being the only lady in residence was worse. How could he seek her company without betraying his honor? Yet ignoring her was an exercise in futility. He was but a moth to the flame of her beauty.

Each day he walked a precarious tightrope between honor and adoration, pain and passion, duty and desire. The sight and sound of her inflamed his senses while intellect and honor fought to control his actions. It did not help that she was even more alluring than he remembered, nor that she exuded a thinly disguised sensuality aimed pointedly in his direction. Too young to understand their changed relationship, she persisted in treating him as a much adored suitor, ignoring both his newly married status and her own very-much-alive husband.

"It is so warm in here," she murmured one night, too softly to be overheard. "Would you show me the conservatory, my love? It must be cooler there."

"That would be improper, as you well know," Thomas reminded her, wanting nothing more than to comply. His own temperature needed a dose of cooler air, though until she had voiced her request, he had considered the room chilly. He gave her no chance to coax a change of mind, beckoning a passing footman.

"Lady Darnley has expressed a desire to see the conservatory. Would you conduct her there?" Ignoring her sad eyes, he joined Sharpton and immersed his thoughts in horses. Or tried to.

Every day she loomed larger in his mind. Her natural grace lent a seductive sensuality to every movement. Her husky voice caressed his ears, even when uttering commonplace sentiments.

How could he find the words "horses bore me" provocative? She lit up every room she entered, a mobile ray of sunshine whose presence left him burning.

Fortunately, he had a great deal of will power. His code of honor had always reigned supreme. Even during his periods of deepest debauchery, he had never bedded another man's wife. And though he had occasionally pursued widows of quality, he experienced twinges of guilt over the subsequent liaisons, preferring to conduct his affairs with courtesans, who freely bestowed their favors with no expectations beyond payment for services rendered.

But neither could he tear himself away from Graystone while Alicia remained in residence. God knew he had tried. It seemed that fate was allowing him one last chance to enjoy her company. Yet memories of his uncontrolled debauch forced him to limit his attentions, both for the sake of his family's sensibilities and to uphold his own dignity. *Honor, honor*, became his waking litany. He stayed away from her as much as possible, spending his days riding, working, and discussing horses with the other men. Only in the evenings did he allow himself to watch her.

News of his marriage led to congratulations by all and sundry. Lord Darnley had initially looked askance at his presence, fully aware of his very public obsession. But the viscount relaxed when he discovered Thomas had since wed, and observed that his attentions to Alicia were no more marked than the other gentlemen's. With his noticeably failing health, he rarely appeared during the day, saving his waning energy to join the company in the evening for cards.

Alicia made Thomas's honor more difficult to uphold with each passing day. Her innocence worked on him like a drug, her sympathy with his pain enslaving him as much as her beauty, but capitulation would betray all he held dear. He drank in every sight of her, his eyes absorbing the tiniest nuance of her being, for he would have nought but memories to provide comfort in the future. Yet he refused to do more than look.

"You must understand how wretched my life is," she pleaded one night, tears trembling in her violet-blue eyes. With great difficulty he turned aside her determination to confess her troubles.

"I feel so sorry for you," she commiserated another day, "being tied to a country nobody in place of your love. We both face the same intolerable situation." Again he deflected the conversation. Discussing his marriage would breach the rampart he had erected around his core, but that risked breaching his self-control.

Every day she turned to him with her joys, fears, and curiosity. Yet he could not administer a set-down, understanding all too well her unhappiness. An innocent forced into marriage with an aged and ailing reprobate could find nought but fear and loathing in her marriage bed. And no sympathy out of it. Was it any wonder that she would turn for support to the man she loved? Needing warmth to counter Darnley's cold possessiveness, could he blame her for occasionally forgetting her vows and turning to him for comfort? She did not understand the burden her love placed on him. Even if he found the means to repudiate his love—something honor knew he should do—he could not simply leave her dangling. Having courted her affections so assiduously, his victory made him responsible for her heart. His responses tried to achieve the impossible—forging their mutual passion into friendship, not merely as a cloak, but in reality. Her naiveté made his efforts doubly difficult. *Dear Lord, give me strength enough for both of us.*

Would will power be enough? He should leave. But he could not tear himself away. Only honor kept his instincts in check. Honor demanded fidelity—for both husband and wife—and explained his gratitude for Caroline's passion. She could keep him fulfilled. The resentment that had driven him from Crawley had long since dissipated. He missed her, though he would not try to push for a close relationship when he returned home. Partnership would come in time if she proved herself worthy. But Alicia was right, as usual. Caroline was a country nobody. He must remain emotionally aloof until he discovered how maladept she proved in London, restricting their encounters to business and to bed. Meanwhile, he would feast his eyes on Alicia. Looking was no sin. Nor was dreaming. He had only to remain honor-bound.

Or so he thought. He awoke one dawn knowing he must remove from Graystone immediately. He missed his nightly encounters with Caroline. Not since his first forays into the muslin company while still at Eton had he gone more than a few days without at least one woman. This was a terrible time to push his limits. A fortnight of celibacy was rapidly undermining his resolution. He had come within an hair's breadth of joining Alicia the night before.

She had appeared at dinner in a low-cut gown of the sheerest gold silk that clung to her figure, revealing every enticing curve. Daring for London, it was scandalous for a masculine house party. It was all he could do to keep from sweeping her out of sight of other eyes. Nor was his mental state improved when she accidentally brushed against his arm in the drawing room, her taut nipples sending waves of desire clear to his toes. Dear God, how he wanted her!

Only a frenzied midnight hike under icy February skies had conquered the urge. He shivered. If he had been unable to leave the house, he would have succumbed to his lust, invading her room, even raping her. The idea appalled him. Nor could he guarantee that such measures would work in the future. His obsession—and he freely admitted the word—was growing stronger with each passing day. Dignity, respect, honor . . . all were rapidly eroding under the force of unbridled passion, and he could not allow that to happen.

He would inform Graylock at breakfast of his imminent departure. And he had excellent reasons to leave—Crawley, his new cattle, and a young bride. No one need know that his own weakness drove him away.

Unfortunately, he never made it to breakfast.

As he passed Darnley's room, Alicia stumbled into the hall, cannonading into him before she was even aware of his presence.

"Oh, Thomas, I am so thankful you are here," she sobbed, anguish highlighting her face as she clutched the lapels of his coat.

"Lady Darnley," he chided her, forcibly removing her to a more discreet distance. "What is amiss?"

"Darnley suffered a seizure and I fear he is dying," she cried, clutching his hand as a drowning sailor would a lifeline.

His heart turned over. "Has the doctor been summoned?"

"Of course. He just arrived." She lifted her tear-stained face, sending a wave of longing through his breast. "Stay with me, my love," she pleaded. "I cannot face the day alone."

He could not deny her plaintive request, though he retained enough sanity to escort her to the drawing room, seat her in a chair by the fire, and choose a second chair some distance away for himself. He immediately rang for chocolate. Servants made an excellent leash for runaway passions.

Alicia regaled him with anguished details. Darnley's valet had awakened her in the night and summoned her to her husband's bedside. He was unconscious, one side of his face dragged down as though a clay sculpture had been carelessly handled. Nothing they tried would rouse him to any activity beyond breathing in irregular gasps, wheezes, and snorts that threatened to cease at any moment. Nor could any in the room put aside their terror as they agonized through lengthy periods of silence, waiting to see if he would breathe again.

"I do hope he goes quickly," she blurted. Then answering his shocked expression she continued, "You of all people know how little I wanted this marriage, but he has been good to me in his fashion and I would not wish him to suffer."

"Perhaps he will recover," he offered, concentrating on finding words that would offer comfort while ignoring all thought of whom he addressed. Neither task proved easy. His body strained to move closer. He had little experience with illness and death, so could offer no insight. Nor did her description disclose what Darnley's future would hold if he survived. That was Alicia's greatest fear. Eyes glued to the fire, he mouthed banalities. When he could no longer stay aloof, he found the strength to excuse himself.

But he could not leave for home.

A bruising ride restored his equilibrium and gave him the courage to face another day. *Please let this be resolved soon.*

Darnley did not die. His coma continued for the rest of the day and the night, but he awakened with the dawn. Thomas learned of the improvement at breakfast.

"Word is Darnley will never completely recover," commented Sharpton between mouthfuls of kidneys and eggs.

"Tough on Lady Darnley," was all Thomas could manage. He made a great show of spreading marmalade on his toast.

"Heard she went into strong hysterics over his infirmities," said Lord Crompton.

Thomas's stomach tightened. He continued to eat, despite a sudden loss of appetite.

"I don't know why," snorted Sharpton. "Marrying a man old enough to be her grandfather! What did she expect?"

Thomas closed his ears to the ensuing discussion of other May-December matches and the health problems the couples inevitably encountered. When he judged that he had consumed an unremarkable amount of food, he thankfully excused himself and escaped the breakfast room.

Think! You must escape before it is too late, urged his conscience. His feet turned to the book room that opened off the library. It was usually empty this time of day, so he could relax and pull himself together.

Not until he crossed to the fireplace did he realize that someone had preceded him. He stifled a groan.

"Thomas." Alicia's husky voice floated from the window. "Have you heard about Darnley?"

"He has recovered." Voice carefully expressionless, he wondered how he could escape. Already treacherous desire threatened to take control. *Honor, honor, honor* . . .

"Recovered?" Her voice turned hysterical as she restlessly paced the floor. "You cannot understand one word in ten that he utters! He cannot move his right hand or arm. How is that recovered?"

"Give him time, Lady Darnley," he suggested calmly. "You know the effects of apoplexy frequently prove temporary."

"The doctor says he could remain in this state for years," she sobbed. "How can I possibly live with that?"

"You will find the strength," he assured her.

"I cannot believe it to be possible," she countered. "If I cared for him, perhaps it would be so. But you know my heart belongs to you." She eyed the door, then deliberately shut it. "We are both married. I must talk to someone and cannot risk the servants overhearing."

"All right," he agreed helplessly, nervous about spending so much time alone with her. His cravat was intolerably tight.

"You must understand how things are. Father was so insistent about this match," she choked. "After he refused to allow me to marry you, it made no difference who I wed, so Darnley seemed acceptable. I did not expect him to live long and hoped the resulting freedom would allow me to fashion life on my own terms."

She sent him a smoldering look that declared more clearly than words that he had figured prominently in those future plans. His loins tightened despite his efforts to remain detached. He retreated to the far side of the fireplace as Alicia's pacing edged closer. Why was she bringing up old history? Such a future was no longer possible. He tried to focus his thoughts on Caroline, but her dowdy image produced only cold shudders.

"But I cannot tolerate being tied to an invalid. Can you see me severed from London society?" Her eyes glittered as she turned her full stare on him.

"No," he choked, rapidly lowering his gaze before he became lost in those violet depths. *HONOR, HONOR, HONOR* . . .

"What am I to do?" she pleaded, her hands sliding up his chest. "He will not allow me to live in London without him, but I despise his estate. It is so utterly isolated. I need society . . . and gaiety . . . and you . . ." Sobs punctuated her words. Her unhappiness pierced his armor. Tears trembled on her curved lashes. He tried to push her away but the movement dragged one hand down his chest where it came to rest on his groin. . . .

Passion exploded through him, obliterating all else. His control

shattered. Arms crushing her in a fierce embrace, he lowered his
lips to hers. And once he tasted her, he could not stop. Nothing
mattered but the woman in his arms. Endless dreams of making
love to Alicia had tormented his nights for nearly a year. He entertained no thought beyond plundering her mouth and attacking
the fastenings of her flimsy gown. Alicia. The culmination of his
every desire.

Nor did she offer any resistance to his overtures, her fingers
frenziedly tearing at his buttons in return.

"Alicia, my love, my angel. Dear God, how I need you," he
moaned, stripping her dress off even as he lowered her to the
floor.

"Thomas!" she gasped, reveling in the fierceness of his embrace. "My only love! Oh, yes . . . please . . ."

His mouth crushed hers, his last coherent thought a desire to
muffle her impassioned cries lest someone overhear.

Much later he slipped from the room, hardly noticing that he
unlocked the door, his concentration focused on regaining his
bedroom without encountering someone who might remark his
disheveled appearance. Already awash in guilt, he dared not name
his other reaction—disappointment. Not due to Alicia, he hastily
assured himself when the feeling first surfaced. It was the inevitable result of his own disgrace.

Anger at his weakness surged through him, as powerful as the
recent storm of passion. Not only had he committed the unpardonable sin of bedding another man's wife, thus demeaning his
honor, but he had broken a sacred vow. Never mind that much of
the *ton* ignored that portion of the wedding service that pledged to
forsake all others. From early childhood he had considered his
word to be absolutely inviolable. He could still recall his father's
scold when he had been caught, at the tender age of six, teasing a
stableboy to allow him to groom the horses after promising his
sire that he would remain in the Abbey as punishment for some
forgotten misdeed.

"A gentleman's word can never be broken, Thomas," Marchgate declared, his features twisting into an expression of disappointment the memory of which caused pain for years to come.
"It is one difference between us and the lower classes. When you
ignore a promise, you also give up the right to be considered a
gentleman. I will not condone such dishonor in my son. You belong to one of the proudest families in England, directly descended from one of the Conqueror's chief knights. You stand
second to one of the oldest earldoms, bestowed by Richard Lion-

heart himself. You will never again demean your honor by breaking your oath, is that clear?"

The lesson was reinforced many times during his minority as the lies and half-truths of others came to light. As he grew older, the nuances grew clearer. The hallmark of a gentleman was honor, and the heart of honor was honesty. A gentleman never went back on his word. Nor did he encourage others to break their sworn word or to act without fully understanding the consequences. Thus he never bedded married women of any class, never seduced maidens, never tempted green youths to game beyond their means.

But now he had reneged in an unforgivably spectacular way. Not only had he coerced Alicia into breaking her own wedding vows—he had blatantly ignored his own. It didn't matter that he did not love Caroline. He had pledged himself to her and she deserved his respect. She had more than upheld her end of their bargain. But infidelity was hardly a form of respect. Nor could he guarantee that he would not again fall from grace if he remained in Alicia's company. He was weak. His obsession bordered on madness. His brain ceased to function when she was near.

He took the only course left, packing his bags and bidding Graylock farewell. Within the hour he was at the ribbons of his coach, driving toward Crawley as if all the demons of hell were in pursuit. How would he ever live down this disgrace?

If only he had left yesterday!

Chapter 7

Thomas turned his weary horses through Crawley's gates and headed for the house. Exhaustion numbed his emotions. There had been little sleep and no rest the night before, his self-flagellation continuing even into the dream world.

He was weak . . . weak and dishonorable . . . dishonorable, disrespectful, odiously undeserving of either sympathy or forgiveness . . . and he had dragged the world's most perfect lady into hell. How could he have sullied both Alicia and his own self-respect? The questions wound round and round in his head. As did the recriminations. With each repetition, his own actions seemed more reprehensible and Alicia's purity more rarefied until he would have expressed no surprise if accused of brutally raping her. What price would be exacted from him for his shame? So grievous a lapse in honor would demand a harsh punishment. He shivered.

He was nearly to the house before his brain registered the improvements wrought during his three-week absence. The estate wall and drive were in markedly better repair. A rebuilt fence enclosed the meadow where his new horses grazed. Grounds and pastures appeared less derelict. And the house offered a distinctly warmer welcome.

Another wave of guilt deepened the self-loathing he had nurtured since the debacle with Alicia. He should have been supervising Crawley instead of sporting at Graystone. It was unconscionable to stay away so long, leaving only the incompetent Tibbins in charge. Again he had proved himself a useless fribble who left it to others to carry out his responsibilities. His father had rescued him the last time. Who was bailing him out now? The sight of three soldiers working on the stable provided a possible answer. Jacobs must have shouldered more burdens than training horses.

"Mr. Mannering, sir." Peters bowed as he opened the door. The hall glowed with polish, an unfamiliar deal table and several chairs now gracing its expanse. "Welcome home."

Thomas glanced through the open door of the drawing room and gasped at the difference. Gold-patterned silk and pale green paint ornamented the walls, uniting furniture, carpet, and ceiling into an elegant whole. Even the worn green velvet draperies look better. And other accents had appeared—a pair of marble figures, several paintings, Sevrés bowls and vases, wall sconces, lamps, an ornate ormolu clock on the mantle—reminding him of his mother's London sitting room in his youth. Clearly, Caroline had been hard at work. Guilt intensified. She was more than upholding their bargain. Given the same budget constraints, not even his mother could have produced a more elegant result.

"Thank you, Peters," he responded. "Cramer will need help with my luggage. Where will I find my wife?"

"Mrs. Mannering took the dogcart out some time ago, sir, visiting tenants. The Griggs boy is still poorly and Mrs. Hendricks was delivered of a daughter yesterday."

"Who is driving her?" It could not be Willy, as the groom was even then unharnessing his coach horses. Was Jacobs wasting valuable time squiring Caroline about the estate?

"She drives herself, sir," explained Peters woodenly. "And quite well, I believe."

He forbore comment, his guilt now tinged with disappointment and a touch of anger. He had promised to teach her to drive, had even looked forward to it. But she had not waited. A lady relied on her husband for direction. *A country nobody*, Alicia's voice echoed. He stifled the sound, but the thought remained.

"Is Tibbins about?" With Caroline gone, he might as well move to the next order of business—releasing the bailiff. Graylock had recommended a competent replacement who would arrive in a few days.

Peters flushed. "Ah—Mr. Tibbins is not on the estate at present, sir."

"Why?" Surprised by the butler's hesitation, his own unstable emotions lent sharpness to his voice. "Come, come, man, what is going on? Did he run off with the silver?"

Peters coughed discreetly and resumed his wooden mask. "Mrs. Mannering sent him on an unimportant errand to Squire Hatchett of Sheldridge Corners. He was becoming a nuisance, sir, raising unreasonable objections whenever she needed cooperation, particularly over the hiring of additional grounds staff and the repair work she ordered to the drive and water meadow."

His anger increased. At himself for his absence. At Tibbins for short-sighted incompetence. At Caroline for interfering in estate business. He thrust it down. Gossiping with the butler added yet another crime to his growing list of transgressions.

But by the time he reached the library his temper had abated. Whatever her faults, Caroline had not shirked her duties. Evidence of care abounded—clean, inviting rooms in which worn furnishings were overshadowed by judiciously chosen new wall-coverings, upholstery, or draperies. The attics must have been a treasure trove, for everywhere he discovered objects he had never seen before.

The morning room contained a pair of watercolors depicting Crawley in better days. One showed the manor, its front magnificently set off by manicured shrubbery, riotous plots of colorful flowers, and a well-maintained sweep of drive. The other depicted the panorama of lake and hills seen from the west terrace, the view framed by the graceful arch of an elm tree. Again, the gardens and grounds displayed a perfection that would require years to restore. He studied the paintings for several minutes before choking out a gasp of surprise. The signature on each was "Caroline Mannering." Shaking his head, he turned his steps toward the library. Her talents had again exceeded his expectations. While not up to Alicia's standards, the pictures were quite passable, far better than he would have expected from a vicar's bluestocking daughter. Few dedicated students had the time to pursue female accomplishments.

The library, too, was transformed, its shelves rearranged so that his own books occupied prominent, easily accessible positions. A portrait of one of his Tudor ancestors hung above the fireplace. The estate records lay open on his desk. A glance showed that Jacobs was following his instructions, that the worst estate problems were being addressed, and that several new employees had been added to both the house and the grounds staffs. He nodded approval. Not until he turned to leave did his eyes suddenly fly back to the ledger. Every entry since his departure was in Caroline's hand.

Anger blazed in a red fire. She had taken control of Crawley. Not only that, she had the temerity to effect more progress in three weeks than he would have expected in three months. His own efforts seemed paltry in comparison. Her dedication to the success of their partnership contrasted badly with his behavior with Alicia.

Damnation!

How dare she overstep her place? he fumed as he stomped upstairs to be greeted by a bedroom glowing with rich reds and blues (his favorite colors), a better shaving stand ensconced in the corner, and an invitingly comfortable chair drawn up to a welcoming fire. New wallcoverings set off a pair of unfamiliar paintings. He threw himself across the bed, its unexpectedly soft mattress igniting another wave of fury. Curses flowed freely, lurid enough to burn the ears of the soldiers working outside. All his anger and guilt focused on this new target. Insufferably managing female! Ladies did not trespass on gentlemen's preserves. How many times had his mother uttered that very statement?

"A lady does not interfere in a gentleman's business, Emily," she would declare. "You may be intelligent and better educated than most, but you can never understand a gentleman's affairs. Nor should you try, unless you desire the social censure and ostracism handed out to those who choose bluestocking pursuits over proper ladylike decorum. So never question a gentleman's judgment."

Crawley's transformation was amazing, but she had no business meddling in the estate operation. And certainly no business doing it well. He would be the laughingstock of London if this got out. Thomas Mannering and his paragon of a wife! He'd never be able to set foot in his club again.

But guilt returned and he buried his face in his hands. Who else was in a position to run Crawley? demanded his conscience. The incompetent Tibbins? Jacobs, who was performing the work of two or three men already? The Honourable Thomas Mannering who forgot all responsibility once his eyes encountered Alicia, who preferred dishonorable dalliance to duty, who had undoubtedly called the wrath of God down upon his head, who had made such a miserable mess of his life he could scarce hold his head up in public? Where had he gone wrong? How could his love for someone so noble recoil into something so base? Anger, guilt, frustration, longing . . . all fought round his head until he dropped into exhausted slumber.

He awakened late in the afternoon to numbed unreality. Cramer brought bathwater in answer to his summons.

"Has my wife returned?" he asked, tossing his crushed cravat and shirt onto the chair.

"Mrs. Mannering is in the drawing room entertaining guests," the valet responded stiffly. "Will you be joining them, sir?"

"Perhaps. Who is here?"

"Neighbors, I understand."

"Ah." He slid into the warm bath. "That will be all, Cramer. Lay out the blue jacket and embroidered waistcoat for dinner. I will wear the brown now."

"Yes, sir."

Thomas tried to calm his mind as he relaxed in his bath. But try as he might, he could neither identify his problems nor decide how to approach Caroline. His brain was in a state of chaos. Wearily, he toweled off and donned clean clothes. Not until he finished tying his cravat did he notice that Caroline's toiletries were gone. Lunging through their respective dressing rooms, he halted in amazement in the connecting doorway.

Her room was awash in golds and greens. A patterned carpet in those colors set the tone, with gold velvet draperies, green walls, and vibrantly lustrous oak furniture reflecting the warm afternoon sunlight. Not until he had continued into her sitting room did he realize that none of the furniture matched and she had settled for painted walls. Clearly she had expended no money on herself. Fury again flared, but he could not have explained why. He stared for several minutes, unable to discern the cause for either anger or frustration.

The root of his problem, of course, was his love for Alicia. It had precipitated the crisis resulting in his unwanted marriage and had led to his own dishonorable behavior and subsequent guilt. He had abandoned his responsibilities to sit in her pocket, for her presence kept him at Graystone at least a sennight longer than he would otherwise have stayed. She was the epitome of his ideal wife—beautiful, talented, passionate, yet needing the protection and care of a strong male—a prize to engender envy in the breast of every acquaintance. Caroline approached that ideal only in passion. An admitted bluestocking, in his absence she revealed herself to be managing and competent to an unladylike degree. And alarmingly independent.

In his present mood, he declined to join the company in the drawing room, instead stalking off to the stables. He did observe as he passed, that she was entertaining two gentlemen and three ladies. Anger again flared. The men were young, good looking, and hanging on her every word. She had lost no time in ingratiating herself with the local gentry.

Two strange carriages were drawn up in the stableyard.

"Whose are those?" he asked as Jacobs appeared in the door.

"That one belongs to Squire Perkins, guv. 'E an' 'is wife an' Miz Barlow is visitin' with the missus. T'other belongs to Vicar Stokes an' 'is sister."

Negligible callers. She should not get too chummy with them for they were beneath the dignity of her new position. Dismissing them, he turned his attention to business.

"The stables and paddocks are impressive," he complimented. "You've done well."

"Thank ye kindly, though 'tweren't all my doin'. The missus sent Bob an' Ted down to Willy with orders to start on the fences afore ever I returned. Later she added Jim an' Mac to the crew. For all their problems, they work 'ard."

"Problems?" He beat down another surge of ire at his wife's meddling. The results were odiously impressive.

"Cor, guv, I forgets ye don't know 'em. Bob's got a bum leg, Mac's 'ip was shot up, Jem took a bullet in the chest that left 'im short-winded, an' Ted lost an arm. I didn't much like hirin' cripples, guv, but the missus talked me into givin' 'em a chance, an' damned if I weren't impressed. Ye got yerself a jewel, beggin' yer pardon. She's got an 'eart as big as the earth an' the sense to match."

Thomas let this remark go unanswered, instead making a detailed examination of the stable and each of his horses. He paused when he came to the one sorry beast who had come with the estate.

"Now that my cattle are all here, we might as well get rid of Dobbin."

"I wouldn't just yet, guv," ventured Jacobs. "The missus uses 'im with the dogcart. 'E's steady an' too slow to bolt with 'er. She's got a sweet touch on the ribbons, but ain't 'ad 'nough practice to let out alone even with Ajax," he concluded, naming the gentlest of the carriage horses.

Thomas shuddered. He must find something better for Caroline to drive. Having her plodding around the neighborhood with Dobbin and a dogcart would do nothing to enhance his consequence. Nor would it aid the reputation of his stables.

But planning was difficult for he could not think clearly. His head swirled—anger at the disruption of his life, irritation at Caroline's independence, chagrin that her accomplishments exceeded his own, guilt over his indiscretions, horror at his treatment of Alicia, longing to hold her again. By the time he entered the drawing room before dinner, his internal war manifested itself as chilly formality.

"Good evening, Caroline." No trace of charm warmed the aloof voice.

"Good evening, Thomas. I trust you had a pleasant trip." She

chose to be cordial, unsure whether his demeanor stemmed from
weariness or anger that she was not Alicia. She had hoped that he
would join them while her callers remained. It was time he became acquainted with the neighbors. But she had not missed his
black look as he stomped past the drawing room.

"Quite productive." The suspicion that her felicitations harbored both sarcasm and full knowledge of his activities added
chilliness to his tone. "You have been busy, I see. The house is
improved."

"Thank you."

"When does Tibbins return?"

"Tomorrow." Should she enumerate her problems with the infuriating bailiff? But he hardly seemed receptive so she remained
silent.

"Good. I have a replacement. Talbert arrives next week."

Peters announced dinner, which they consumed in near silence.

Thomas joined her in bed that evening. Resolved to protect her
heart, she welcomed him with appropriate enthusiasm but divorced her mind from the proceedings. He hardly noticed her limited response. Each touch sent images of Alicia blasting through
his mind, leaving guilt and self-loathing in their wake. Caught in
his own hell of recrimination, he brought the encounter to a rapid
conclusion and thankfully returned to his own bed. Both lay
awake long into the night, dissatisfaction clouding their respective
analyses of the future.

That day set the tone for the weeks that followed. Talbert
proved to be a hardworking, talented steward, able to effect as
many miracles on the estate as Caroline. Within days, the two
men finalized plans for the spring planting and agreed on priorities. Thereafter, Thomas left operations in Talbert's hands, meeting briefly with him each morning to discuss problems but
otherwise directing his attentions elsewhere.

He threw himself heart and soul into the stables. Burned by his
lapse with Alicia, disenchanted and resentful of his forced marriage, he turned his obsessive energy to horses. Willy Larkin had
proved to be an adept manager and now occupied the position of
head groom, with two boys working under him in addition to the
contingent of soldiers effecting repairs. Jacobs and Thomas spent
long hours together training the young horses from Graystone and
several others acquired on additional buying trips. He discovered
an ability to concentrate on the painstaking task of schooling a
raw horse to the exclusion of all else, finally reaching—for those

hours, at least—the nepenthe he had so long sought from pain and disillusionment.

His relations with Caroline remained coolly formal. They seldom met at breakfast and he never returned for lunch, so contact was limited to dinner. Conversation centered on Crawley, but without the exchange of ideas that had characterized their first week. She occasionally mentioned neighbors, but he rarely responded. Afterward, he retired to the library to continue his course of study, losing himself in books on estate management and horses as another way of holding the world at bay.

A week elapsed before he again joined her in bed. Fearful of a repetition of their last encounter, he carefully focused his mind elsewhere until he obtained the necessary release and returned to his room. He would have been horrified to learn that he had treated his wife worse than the lowest of his casual liaisons, for even deeply in his cups he had worked to involve his partners, but such a thought never entered his mind. However the experience offered so little satisfaction that he repeated it only when absolutely necessary.

Caroline's welcome for his return quickly faded as she accepted that cool formality would be the norm in the future. It did not require much thought to conclude that his love for Alicia still flourished and that a fortnight in her company had left him resentful of his forced marriage. Despite Alicia's own marriage, his wife must be the symbol of his loss. Any immediate hope of friendship was gone. It would be months or even years before such a chance might reappear. In the meantime, she must build a life that did not depend on his assistance, or even his presence.

She threw herself into caring for the house and the tenants. Rapidly discovering that Thomas no longer accepted her suggestions, she learned to take problems to Talbert. When two more soldiers came to her for jobs, it was Talbert who officially hired them. When she discovered that the Griggs's roof had been damaged in a heavy storm, Talbert juggled the priorities to effect an immediate repair. He instinctively understood that all was not well between the Mannerings and never mentioned her involvement to Thomas even while offering her suggestions for his approval.

As conditions at Crawley improved, she found extra time on her hands. Finances precluded extensive decorating. Thomas welcomed no interest in Crawley outside the manor itself. Nor did he spend even a minute more than necessary in her company. She filled the hours by furthering her friendships with neighboring gentry, and by spending long periods in the still room concocting remedies. The thanks she received from grateful tenants made her efforts seem worthwhile and almost compensated for the dearth of compliments from Thomas, who rarely acknowledged her efforts. Evenings she devoted to music, able to lose herself and banish the world while at the keyboard.

Thomas's increasingly rare excursions to her bed offered no comfort. Even more aloof than at dinner, he took no interest in her needs, instead accomplishing his purpose quickly and in silence. Unable to tolerate comparisons between this cold stranger and the seductive charmer of before, she learned to divorce her mind from the proceedings, lying quietly until he had left and then concentrating fiercely on other things lest she cry herself to sleep.

This last tendency was profoundly disturbing. Unwilling to admit even in the deepest recesses of her mind that she might have formed a *tendre* for her husband, she daily concentrated on his faults. His heart was committed to Alicia. He resented their marriage and was bent on blaming her. This possibility had worried her briefly at their first meeting, but she had thought his father's edict and the conditions of his inheritance would prevent it. However, he seemed to have forgotten his escape from the undesirable Miss Huntsley. Far worse were the comparisons with his beloved Alicia which she could never hope to overcome. With little hope that he would undergo a change of heart, she was forced to accept the bleakest of futures. *Dear God, why did you allow him to fall in love with someone he could not wed?*

As Thomas's activities fell into a predictable routine, he also found it harder to keep thought at bay. He firmly stifled memories of those early evenings when Caroline had joined him in the library, her calm presence and intelligent conversation enlivening his studies. Or of the pleasure to be found when a passionate, willing woman shared his bed. Still determined to vent his frustrations on her, he would entertain no approval. She represented the antithesis of what his wife should be.

He also stifled a growing loneliness. He was unaccustomed to solitude, having spent his entire life in company with others. Thoughts of Alicia tormented him, reminding him at frequent intervals of the dreams he had entertained of what marriage would be like. It wasn't fair that he should be locked forever into so imperfect a union. What had he done to deserve so miserable a fate? The punishment surpassed even the worst of his crimes.

"We leave for London on Friday," Thomas announced at dinner one night.

"All right, sir," Caroline agreed, stifling irritation at his high-handed manner. When had this plan been made? "Where will we stay and for how long?"

"Marchgate House on Berkeley Square and I do not know. Father demands our presence. Mother has recovered from her illness." He paused to drain his wineglass. "We will not remain long as I cannot neglect the stables. You must purchase some clothes when we arrive. I cannot have you shaming me in town." The cold voice conveyed nothing but boredom.

"Yes, sir," she managed, hiding her pain and anger. She knew her limited wardrobe was far from fashionable, and would be the first to admit she had nothing suitable for London, but his icy condemnation hurt. Perilously close to tears, she dared not voice any of her myriad questions. Would the Marchgates disapprove of her as strongly as he so obviously did? What about the rest of the *ton*? How was she to fill her days with no household to oversee and no friends or even acquaintances available? The thought filled her with terror. It required two hours of vigorous walking before she slept that night.

Nor did she learn any further details. Thomas gave no thought to her predicament, instead concentrating on arranging his absence. When he thought of London, it was with a surge of excitement. Alicia was in town while Darnley consulted his physicians.

He joined Caroline at breakfast early Friday morning, an intimidating frown darkening his eyes until they appeared nearly black.

"Jacobs fell and broke his leg last night," he announced baldly.

"How is he?"

"He will recover, but cannot work in the meantime. I will have to find a replacement before leaving for town."

"We can send a message to your parents. They will understand the delay."

"No." His eyes glared as he instantly rejected her suggestion. "You must go as planned. I will join you as soon as possible."

"Very well." Anger suffused her at his words. And trepidation. She was now condemned to meeting a house full of strangers without even an introduction from her husband. *Dear Lord, please don't let me make a cake of myself.*

Her spirits tumbled further as Larkin turned the carriage down the drive. Thomas loosed a stream of blasphemy just before they moved out of earshot and she knew his temper had little to do with Jacobs. He was angry because Alicia was in town.

Chapter 8

Caroline arrived in London at dusk. Never having seen a town larger than Banbury, her eyes widened at each new sight—the skyline, dotted with a forest of church spires, including the impressive bulk of Westminster Abbey and the dome of St. Paul's; carriages, curricles, carts, and wagons of every description jostling together through jammed city thoroughfares; enormous buildings, most five and six stories high, crowding the streets and dwarfing the throngs of pedestrians; streetsweepers, peddlers hawking their wares, liveried footmen racing to deliver messages, and linkboys, their torches held high, lighting the way for elegant town coaches; lamplighters igniting the new gas lamps recently installed along several Mayfair streets; and top-of-the-trees dandies escorting fashionable ladies into magnificent town mansions aglow with myriad candles and lamps.

Restraining the urge to stare, she resolutely firmed her backbone. Really, there was nothing to fear. She belonged to Mayfair as surely as did Thomas. It was her destiny. She was granddaughter to one earl and daughter-in-law to another, to say nothing of her uncle, Baron Cummings. She repeated the litany endlessly, but without conviction. Nor could it dissipate her nervousness.

Terror mushroomed when the coach pulled up before an imposing four-story house in Berkeley Square. Larkin let down the steps. Torches flared on either side of a door held open by a formidable footman in blue and gold livery and powdered wig. A very proper butler showed her into an elegant Chinese drawing room redolent with lacquer, jade, and priceless ceramics. Dragons writhed on dark red walls, separated by panels depicting bamboo forests populated by peacocks and other exotic animals. Table legs had been carved to resemble bamboo. Silk brocade hung at the windows.

Please, God, she prayed silently, *help me survive this meeting without shaming Thomas or giving his family a disgust of me.* She pasted a smile to her chilled lips, determined to appear calm despite shaky knees, fluttering stomach, and an enervating trepidation that swirled fog between her eyes and the rest of the world. Never would Thomas have cause to rue her conduct. She would die first.

"Welcome, Caroline. I am Lady Marchgate."

The cool greeting did nothing to assuage her nerves, but she glided forward to curtsy demurely before the lady seated near the fire. As though she were the Queen, Caroline thought suddenly and had to stifle a giggle at this inopportune surfacing of her irreverent wit. She would have known the lady anywhere. Thomas's green eyes glowed below still-black hair in a feminine version of his face.

"My lady."

"But is Thomas not with you?" Disappointment warmed her hauteur. Was he a favorite son?

"I fear not, my lady," she explained, accepting a seat opposite her mother-in-law. She carefully kept her back firm and her posture erect. "Jacobs broke a leg last night. Thomas must locate a qualified assistant before he can leave Crawley."

"I trust Jacobs will recover without incident. Thomas's groom, is he not?" Her voice was again coolly detached.

"He was, though Thomas recently promoted him to head trainer. He should recover but cannot ride for some time."

The butler entered with a teatray, which he set at Caroline's elbow on signal from the countess.

"You will pour," she commanded.

Caroline nodded and automatically set about the task, fully aware that it was a test of her training or lack thereof.

"You are related to Lord Waite?" It sounded more like an accusation than a question.

"Yes, my lady. The old earl was my grandfather though he disowned my mother." She kept strict control over her voice, achieving—though she was unaware of it—the same cool tone as the countess.

"And why was that?"

"He did not approve of my father."

"A vicar is beneath the touch of an earl's daughter."

The sideways jibe at her own background angered her. "That was not his objection. Father is a baron's son, but he had no fortune and Waite had his eye on a wealthy suitor."

"So they eloped." Contempt permeated the words.

"Not at all. Mother was of age. They wed in her own church

with several relatives in attendance. Most of the family approved the match."

"So how does she like life as a penniless vicar's wife?"

"She has no complaints. We have always been a happy family."

"And how many are you?" Her voice remained cool but was no longer icy.

Caroline again described her home and family, politely answering questions about her education and training. Resentful of the examination, yet she conceded Lady Marchgate's concerns. It was not usual for one of society's sons to wed a complete unknown. If their positions were reversed, she would wish forewarning of potential pitfalls. Many of the countess's queries undoubtedly parroted those posed by her friends.

Rapid footsteps approached and an excited young lady burst into the drawing room with unladylike abandon.

"Eleanor, dear," Lady Marchgate reproved her daughter, "decorum at all times. May I present Thomas's wife, Caroline? My youngest daughter, Eleanor, who makes her bows this Season."

"I am thrilled to meet you at last," enthused Eleanor, patently ignoring her mother's critical stare. "Imagine Thomas whisking you off to Crawley without even letting us see you first!" She was quite unlike her mother in appearance, her brown hair arranged in ringlets around a narrow face glowing with impish mischief. Gray-green eyes sparkled above a retroussé nose and pouting mouth.

"Eleanor, you know I was ill all winter," admonished the countess.

"We needed the time at Crawley in any case," added Caroline lightly. "Conditions were positively gothic when we arrived. At least the house is livable now."

"You must be tired after your journey," noted Lady Marchgate, her voice clearly indicating dismissal. Had she interpreted Caroline's remarks as criticism of Thomas's stewardship? Her tone conveyed neither warmth nor acceptance.

Caroline quelled a spurt of anger at her husband. The least he should have done was introduce her to his family. Or should he?

No.

Her back straightened. She was building her own life, was she not? For the first time his absence seemed a godsend. *This is a battle I will win on my own,* she vowed silently.

"Eleanor, please show Caroline to her room. Her luggage will be there by now."

"Thank you, my lady." Caroline curtsied properly to her hostess and departed.

"You need not be so formal," protested the irrepressible Eleanor as she led the way upstairs. "Mama can appear starchy, but you are family after all."

"That is for Lady Marchgate to decide," reminded Caroline. "I can hardly be described as either a suitable or a welcome match. She will wish to become better acquainted before adopting a more relaxed form of address."

"What precipitated such a hasty wedding?" wondered Eleanor. "I have been immured at the Abbey for over a year. No one ever explained." Her eyes glowed with speculation, undoubtedly the result of an overindulgence in gothic novels.

"Thomas needed his inheritance to restore Crawley," declared Caroline, anxious to erase any hint of romantic attachment when she noted that starry-eyed expression. "An accident designated me as the bride," and she repeated the tale they had told her parents.

"Good heavens!" exclaimed Eleanor in a burst of artless candor. "No wonder Mama sounded so formal. She can be odiously high in the instep."

"So I understand. I could hardly expect otherwise." She cast a rueful glance over her gown. "Particularly as I am far from fashionable. What can you tell me of London modistes? My wardrobe needs immediate attention."

"I am sure Madame Suzette can help. Mama is most impressed with her. Why not accompany me for my fitting tomorrow? Mama will not have to rise so early if you chaperone me."

"We will ask what she thinks of the idea." She refused to promise, unsure whether such an action might contravene London convention. Nor did she believe the countess would entrust either her daughter's care or reputation to an unknown stranger.

"This room is yours. You are lucky. It has always been one of my favorites," babbled Eleanor, pushing open a door. Without waiting for a response, she continued. "I hope you ride. There is no one to accompany me but a groom. Don't you just hate grooms? They never allow one to gallop or jump challenging fences or anything. Of course, neither did Emily before she got married. She was as much an old stick as Mama and Papa." She giggled. "Oh, I do hope to attract some handsome beaus this Season—exciting, romantic suitors who will shower me with poetry and flowers, waltz with me at Almack's, and steal kisses in the garden."

A servant interrupted this chatter, arriving with a can of warm water.

"I would love to get better acquainted"—Caroline smiled at Eleanor—"but I must change for dinner. Will you excuse me?"

"Of course. How thoughtless of me." She whirled out of the room as rapidly as she had entered. Caroline shook her head. Eleanor reminded her very much of Eppie, the squire's youngest daughter and an empty-headed hoyden. But her silliness was never annoying because it was always accompanied by loving charm.

Her room was beautifully decorated in blue and silver with heavy velvet draperies, silk wallcoverings, and a thick Aubusson carpet. A welcoming vase of violets rested on the dressing table and a fire, obviously lit long before, burned merrily on the hearth. A connecting door stood open to a green and silver room. She could see Cramer busily unpacking Thomas's luggage.

Refusing to dwell on Lady Marchgate's catechism, she set about the daunting task of composing her nerves for her upcoming introduction to the earl. Which gown would prove least inappropriate? She scanned her meager wardrobe in despair. There really was little choice. It would have to be the primrose, despite knowing that the color made her face appear sallow. But her only other evening gown showed distinct signs of wear. Shrugging off what could not be changed, she washed and recoiled her hair.

Excepting Marchgate, the family was already gathered in the drawing room when she descended. Thomas's older brother and married sister had joined them for the evening. Eleanor introduced her brother, then drifted over to converse with Emily and the countess, leaving the two alone.

Viscount Hartford was quite outside Caroline's previous experience. Slender and of medium height, he had light brown hair, pale blue eyes, and a long face, but none of this drew an observer, for he was undoubtedly the pinkest of the pinks. Pushing the bounds of even foppish attire, he appeared in a silver-blue tailcoat with lapels extending well beyond his excessively padded shoulders, and with buttons as large as his palm. Nor could she visualize how he had squeezed into it, so tight was the fit. Rose satin breeches clung to padded thighs. His waistcoat was heavily embroidered with pink, blue, and yellow flowers and butterflies. A matching posy of hothouse flowers covered one lapel below shirt points so high and a foot-tall cravat so stiff he could turn his head not at all. A plethora of fobs and seals in assorted shapes dangled from his slender waist. His face rippled in a faint shudder as he quizzed her with his glass.

"I agree," Caroline said with a smile. "My first stop in the morning will be at a modiste's."

"But naturally, you have jutht arrived. How horrid of me to expect perfection tho thoon," he lisped, mincing closer and finishing with an affected giggle. He made an exceedingly elegant leg and smiled.

She hurriedly composed her face lest she laugh at his antics, unable to tell if he was serious or clowning. She rather suspected the former.

"Such rudeness!" she declared, a broad smile softening her words. "Do you quiz everyone you meet, my lord?"

"Merely depressing pretensions. Does it really bother you?"

"No, for I have no pretensions to depress."

"I was shocked to learn of my dear brother's marriage," continued the viscount, applying a delicate pinch of scented snuff to each nostril before returning his elaborate gold and crystal snuffbox to a pocket.

"Not unpleasantly, I hope," she rejoined.

"No, no, my dearest Caroline—I may call you Caroline, may I not?"

She nodded.

"And I am Robert. But I cannot think what bedevils me tonight. My manners are sadly lacking. I meant no insult." He daintily dusted his fingertips with a lacy handkerchief.

"I took none, Robert," assured Caroline. "Thomas decided it was time to claim his inheritance."

"Ah." A languid hand fluttered with understanding, his lisp growing more pronounced. "But here ith my thithter Emily, Viscounteth Wembley. Emily? Caroline. Thomath'th wife."

Emily's coloring matched Robert's, as did her features. Caroline knew her to be her own age, married three years before and mother to a young daughter. Her husband devoted his time to politics. She exuded an elegant sophistication that Caroline could only admire even as she was swept with embarrassment at her own countrified appearance and lack of address. But Emily showed no signs of censure. She greeted her warmly while Robert minced across the room to speak to his mother.

Caroline discovered an instant rapport with her sister-in-law and soon broached the subject of clothes.

"I must acquire some decent gowns," she declared. "But I am

at a loss. Eleanor has invited me to accompany her in the morning, but I do not know what to buy. We will not be in town for long, nor can I spend a great deal. Thomas needs all he can find for the estate."

"Madame Suzette, Eleanor's modiste, can help you decide. Her prices are reasonable and her styles becoming." She paused a moment to evaluate Caroline's appearance. "I expect you would look best in soft greens, roses, and perhaps muted blues, but there may be other colors that would flatter you. And what about your hair? A looser style would help, I believe."

"I had not thought about it." Caroline frowned, trying to picture her face surrounded by either Eleanor's ringlets or Emily's upswept knot. She failed. But she had to admit that her tightly coiled braid was more suited to the governess she had expected to be than to a young matron of the *ton*.

"Why don't I join you tomorrow? We can spend the morning shopping, then return to Wembley House for luncheon. My dresser is an *artiste* with hair. Perhaps she can contrive something."

Caroline's thanks were cut off by the arrival of the earl. Emily tactfully slipped away.

"I am enchanted to meet you at last, my dear." He smiled warmly, raising her hand to his lips.

"As am I, my lord," she responded. One look placed the origin of several family characteristics. His height had passed on to Thomas, his coloring and long face to his other children. Thomas had also inherited his address and his unconsciously seductive voice.

"I understand some emergency kept Thomas at Crawley?" None of his wife's disappointment tinged his voice. Instead, she detected a hint of . . . What was that elusive note? Pride? Yes, pride. And why not? Given Thomas's history, a demonstration of responsibility would certainly raise pride in his sire's breast.

"Only briefly." She explained yet again about Jacobs's accident.

The earl nodded approval. "And how is Crawley?"

"Improving. Have you been there yourself?"

"Not for twenty years or so. It was run down even them. I assume it is worse now."

"As near as I can tell, not a shilling has been put into the place from that day to this. Nor has any attempt been made to maintain buildings, improve productivity, or apply even the slightest form of modern agricultural practice."

The earl almost suppressed a shudder. "That bad, is it?"

"You would not believe its appalling state when we arrived. Indicative of conditions was the manor's roof which contained a large, long-standing hole noticeable to anyone approaching along the main drive, but of which the bailiff was unaware. But things are improving. Thomas's new bailiff has worked wonders, as has a crew of ex-soldiers he hired. And he has completely renovated the stables."

"I am glad to hear it, and not as surprised as you might think. Thomas has always pursued his interests with obsessive single-mindedness. I only hope this one lasts longer than the others." He excused himself, leaving Caroline with much to consider as she chatted with Eleanor.

Was the earl implying that Thomas's pursuit of Alicia was now history? Very doubtful. Besides, no one knew she was aware of the attachment. Was his purpose to warn her that Thomas was prone to obsessions? What other activities had he embraced to excess? Raking, for certain. He had denied drinking and gaming before Alicia and she had no reason to doubt his word. Was he a prankster? Or perhaps the earl's last comment was merely an aside to himself.

She moved on to greet the countess. It was interesting that Thomas received his coloring from his mother but his height and physique from the earl. His siblings were the opposite. Emily and Marchgate seemed to share Thomas's intelligence. It was too early to tell if it lurked beneath Eleanor's giddiness, the countess's cool reserve, or Robert's silly affectations. But one thing was clear: Lady Marchgate obviously doted on her eldest son. At best, she would treat Thomas equally.

Dinner proved to be another unobtrusive test. Despite holding continuous conversation with Eleanor and Robert, who flanked her at the table, the countess surreptitiously watched everything Caroline did, from her manners to the way she treated her dinner partners. Fortunately, Mrs. Cummings had taught her well and she had attended enough meals with the squire and other local gentry that formal dining posed no terrors. The only new experience this evening was the food, for Marchgate employed an exceptional cook. As the ladies adjourned to the drawing room, Caroline hoped she detected a slight thawing.

The addition of Emily to Eleanor's proposed expedition proved acceptable and the three arrived at Madame Suzette's early the next morning. Not that Caroline considered it early. Unaccustomed to town hours, she had awakened at her usual time, surprised to discover only the earl not still abed. He was taken aback when she entered the breakfast room, but they spent an amiable hour discussing Crawley and her family, parting in mutual approval that allowed her to relax for the first time since Thomas had announced this trip.

Eleanor was immediately whisked off to complete her fittings, but Suzette was busy with another customer. Unsurprised, Emily and Caroline perused fashion plates until Suzette could attend them.

"This would look stunning on you," said Emily, holding up an evening gown with a neckline so low Caroline gasped.

"Surely that is scandalous," she murmured.

"Not for London," insisted Emily. "I will show you my wardrobe this afternoon if you do not believe me. But your reaction is quite common among first-time visitors."

"Well, perhaps," she conceded. "But I will not believe stunning. Some improvement I would expect, but my face is too plain."

"You exaggerate. I grant you are not a diamond, but then neither am I, and glad of it. I have yet to meet an incomparable who is not spoiled and self-centered. But you have a nice-looking face. The severe hairstyle just exaggerates your cheekbones. And we must do something about that country tan. Dawson, my dresser, has a cucumber concoction that she swears will fade it in a few days."

"We shall see. What about this?" She held up an unusual afternoon gown with sweeping lines.

"Lovely. You have the height to carry it off. I never could. And here is another one perfect for you." She proferred a riding habit cunningly embellished with braiding.

"Yes. Interesting. With a shako hat, I believe."

"Excellent eye. For you a shako would be far more effective than this," and she tapped the plate.

A noisy altercation suddenly erupted in one of the fitting rooms. "Incompetent fool! How dare you imply that I ordered this rag!" an imperious voice demanded. "I never wear periwinkle, and the sleeve doesn't begin to fit!"

Emily glanced up only long enough to ascertain that Eleanor was not misbehaving, but Caroline's mouth gaped at such rudeness.

"*Oui,* my lady," soothed a heavily accented voice. "*Impossible* that we cannot fix today. You prefer the blue of the morning sky, *non?* With just a hint of *violette*. *Trés bien*. All will be well by luncheon."

"Impossible," snapped the first. "I never deal with bacon-brained idiots. Cancel the order. I shan't be back."

"Good heavens," murmured Caroline in shock. "Who is that?"

"Lady Darnley," responded Emily automatically, her mind on fashion plates. Her eyes lit up over an evening gown that would perfectly enhance her own figure. "She has the most waspish temper in the *ton.*"

"Why would anyone receive such a harridan?" Surely this could not be Alicia, reflected an amazed Caroline. Thomas had more sense than that.

Emily laughed lightly and turned her full attention on her sister-in-law. "You have much to learn about society, Caroline. An unpleasant personality does not doom any titled person to anonymity. Nor does a wretched reputation if that title is high enough. Do you believe she shows this face to either gentlemen or the patronesses of Almack's? Her bad behavior is reserved for tradesmen and social inferiors. She is a diamond of the first water, drawing men to her side like flies to honey. And there is little we can do. No lady can criticize another to a gentleman without diminishing her own consequence. Not even to expose a Tartar like Lady Darnley. She regularly mistreats her servants, but they are helpless to stop it. Without a reference, none can leave her service and expect to find another position. Lady Stafford saw her take a carriage whip to a street urchin last year when a crowd jostled the boy into her path, forcing her to swerve. We had hoped that time would steady her temperament. But marriage has certainly not improved her. She has been far worse since she returned to town last month. Darnley reportedly suffered an apoplectic fit several weeks ago that left him partially paralyzed."

"The poor woman," Caroline murmured.

"Save your sympathy for someone deserving, Caroline. She certainly spares none for him. Rumor has it that she is furious at him for tying her to a sickbed. She certainly expected him to die quickly. After all, he is well past sixty and she barely nineteen."

Caroline stifled a gasp. It was, indeed, Alicia. How could Thomas idolize such a bad-tempered shrew?

Emily continued. "Everyone was shocked when she accepted his hand for half the *ton* was pursuing her. Darnley didn't even figure in the betting books. The wagering heavily favored—" She suddenly stopped in confusion as she recalled whom she addressed.

"You needn't worry," retorted Caroline dryly. "I am well aware that Thomas was the leading contender for the fair Alicia's hand. He made quite a cake of himself over her."

"True. He has always thrown his heart into everything he does. But I am glad you know. It makes conversation less delicate. And I was ecstatic at her betrothal. Imagine having that for a sister-in-law! Did he really tell you about it?"

"No, and I doubt he is aware that I know, not that he would deny it if asked. Ours is not a love match, as you well know. But he is throwing his heart into Crawley at present and we muddle along quite well together."

"Is he finally over her, then?" dared Emily.

"Oh, no. Nothing has changed. It should be an interesting sojourn in town," she added bleakly.

Emily's response was forestalled by Alicia herself, who chose that moment to exit in high dudgeon. Caroline refrained from staring, but could not help a comprehensive glance at her husband's idol.

Even with her features twisted in fury, Alicia remained beautiful. Golden hair cascaded from a high knot to drift in tantalizing ringlets about her face. Sensually gowned, her figure both invited protection and demanded caresses. But no visual charms could erase the image her own temper had created. Caroline would not have liked her even if Alicia exerted no hold over her husband.

She wondered about Darnley's seizure. When had it occurred? What had triggered it? Was Thomas somehow responsible? But she dared not voice these questions lest she start further rumors connecting them. She refused to be responsible for any revival of old gossip.

Madame Suzette appeared and an enjoyable two hours ensued. Caroline bought more than she would normally have considered prudent, urged on by Emily's assurances that every gown was necessary for town, by Thomas's sneer about not shaming him, and by her lingering irritation at Alicia. The modiste had several dresses already made up that were easily altered to fit. Others would be finished within the week. Caroline wondered at this, and at the peculiar look she received from Suzette when Emily introduced her.

"But, of course," explained Emily as they examined gloves and fans in a nearby shop, having dispatched Eleanor and her maid back to Berkeley Square, "she will wreak revenge on Lady Darnley by turning you out as elegantly as possible. She is well aware of the connection and equally aware that every compliment paid you will poke a dart in Lady Darnley's pride."

"You exaggerate!" protested Caroline, laughing.

"Not at all. But you must understand the rules if you are to succeed in town. The *ton* is a remarkably petty and shallow institution revolving around appearance and consequence. Rumor is king. Common sense is an alien concept. Ridiculous, I agree, yet we all play the game. Even those who are eminently sensible and intelligent become frivolous in town. It takes years to learn the difference between those who don the garb only in London and those who embody it always. Robert is one of the latter. The lisp and clothes are affectations, of course, but the empty-headedness is real. Papa frequently despairs of ever turning him into an earl. Wembley and Thomas are genuinely intelligent and usually quite sensible—though I grant my brother seems a candidate for Bedlam lately. Father is sensible as well. Mother falls somewhere in between, unfortunately making most decisions based on what society would think rather than what is right."

"I could never live like that," said Caroline, shuddering in distaste.

"Of course not. You weren't raised to it. But don't condemn the fribbles out of hand. Many literally have nothing else to do. That is true of most of Thomas's friends, by the way. They are heirs to titles but they own no property and control no fortunes. They are discouraged from military or government pursuits, ineligible to sit in the Lords even if their parent has no interest in doing so, and barred by convention from pursuing trade. And so they fritter away their lives gaming and drinking and strutting about town. Once they finally accede to their titles and become absolute despots over their properties they cling to their newly won importance by denying their own heirs any responsibility."

There really was no response to Emily's analysis, reflected Caroline. Nor was there a solution. A few fortunate heirs with understanding parents were encouraged to learn about their estate or even given small properties to manage. But too many men would die rather than relinquish even a portion of their authority.

The coach returned them to Wembley House for a delightful luncheon and a lengthy session with Dawson. Emily had not exaggerated her dresser's abilities. Caroline was amazed at her transformation. Several lemon rinsings lightened her hair and added a range of blond and bronze highlights. Dawson then cut it and arranged soft waves around her face that modified its shape, devising several styles that complemented her regal stature. And that was another surprise, for her new gowns, with their lower bodices and simple lines, bared a long, arched neck that added elegance to her height. And delight in the results put a sparkle in her eyes.

"But how will I ever manage this myself?" she wondered aloud. "The maid assisting me has no talent for hair."

"I believe I can help," assured Emily. "Dawson's sister is free just now. Her employer moved to Scotland but she refused to leave town. Would you give her a try, knowing she would never move to Crawley?"

"Certainly," agreed Caroline, and her new dresser appeared at Marchgate House that evening.

Chapter 9

"If I cannot find a better way to occupy my time, I shall go mad!" Caroline addressed the novel she had just slammed shut. The words refused to engage her mind, merely dancing on the page like so many ants. After four days in town, time hung heavy.

Not that the Marchgates ignored her, she admitted as she pulled out a sketch pad and idly began a picture that rapidly evolved into Crawley Manor against a stormy sky. She had accompanied the countess and Eleanor on morning calls, acquitting herself well in the drawing rooms of some of Mayfair's most powerful hostesses. But the quiet reserve that cloaked her lack of insipid chatter and ignorance of *ton* gossip would never promote friendships.

Turning the page, she penciled an exaggerated sketch of Lady Debenham's oppressively Egyptian drawing room with its clawed furniture, lotus-blossom tables, caryatid-supported mantel, and a lion-headed chair that had to be the most uncomfortable she had ever endured. A giggle erupted as her pencil made the torturous chair devour Lady Debenham.

Rain precluded outings to the park. Her only exercise since arriving had been a turn around the square with Eleanor and the footman, Sam, who despite his terrifyingly formal appearance turned out to be a lad of sixteen. The square itself was elegantly lovely, surrounded by brown-brick town houses and boasting a central garden set amidst sheltering plane trees, its focal point an equestrian statue of the King. But rain again confined her to the house, falling so heavily she could barely make out Gunter's on the far corner. And there was nothing to do.

Her fingers idly moved on to produce a rapid study of the Laughing Dog Inn. Now why would she draw that? True, it represented the point at which her life had swerved to a new course, but was that good or bad? Was her present situation an improvement? Even if this visit to London proved congenial, she had no assurance that life as Mrs. Mannering would do so. Thomas grew colder each day until they barely spoke to each other. It would be easier to bear if they had not shared so comfortable a first week together. But these days, being the lesser of two evils did not make her acceptable. Even commonplace messages passed via the servants. And she had no assurance that the polite world would receive her differently.

Invitations did not yet include her, a situation neither she nor the countess bothered to correct. She needed time to adjust. Nor was she anxious to throw herself into the giddy marriage mart rounds, though she expected to attend many of its entertainments. She already partook of Eleanor's sessions with the dancing master, both to polish her skills and to learn the waltz.

She had made one interesting acquaintance at Hatchard's that morning. Arms full of books, she rounded the end of a shelf and collided with another lady equally laden.

"I am so very sorry, ma'am," Caroline apologized, gazing ruefully at the volumes now scattered on the floor.

"Entirely my fault," insisted the other, a pretty blonde about her age and only a couple inches shorter. She wore a gold pelisse with bronze trim. "I am Helena, Lady Potherby."

"Mrs. Mannering, my lady." She was already sorting books. "I hope you enjoy this as much as I did," she added, stacking three volumes of *Sense and Sensibility* onto Lady Potherby's pile.

"I'm sure I will. Jane Austen is always entertaining. Is this treatise on education yours?"

"Yes." Caroline blushed. "I started a day school in our village and hope for ideas on improving it."

"Wonderful! I want to do the same but my husband is adamant about maintaining our consequence. He fears anything that caters to the lower classes." Her face twisted into exaggerated disdain.

"How shortsighted. Perhaps your vicar could suggest someone willing to run it with your backing. Before my own marriage I invited village children to attend the lessons I taught my younger siblings."

"It is possible. If I was not actively involved, perhaps James would reconsider."

"Consider it part of your duty to your tenants. In this era of enclosures and agricultural reform, their future may depend on an ability to read and write."

As they discussed the problem, she discovered that Lady Potherby was also a vicar's daughter. She had married Lord Potherby seven years before and now had three children. Unlike Thomas, her husband disapproved of bluestockings so she had to pursue her studies unobtrusively. Caroline's spirits lifted. Despite their problems, Thomas had much to recommend him as a husband. He was tolerant and had become an able estate manager, willingly authorizing programs to better the lives of his tenants.

"I would love to hear more of your school," explained Helena. "But I am already late for a fitting at my modiste's."

"Perhaps you could call tomorrow," suggested Caroline. "Morning hours?"

Helena laughed. "I would love to." She gathered her books and they bade each other farewell.

But for now, Caroline was bored. Not even the sketching helped. Her fingers moved on their own, leaving too much time for thought. What was Thomas doing? Still looking for an assistant for Jacobs, she supposed. When could she expect him in town? As soon as possible, for he knew Alicia was here. Would he ever discover her true nature? If so, what would he do? But speculation was worthless. Jacobs's words teased her mind, describing Thomas's reaction when Alicia arrived at Graystone. Such lack of control could only create scandal in town. How would she maintain her own poise in that event?

Her mind circled dizzily, thankfully interrupted by a summons to the drawing room.

"Ah, Caroline," said Marchgate as she paused in the doorway.

Lady Marchgate was enthroned near the fire, with Eleanor diligently attacking a piece of needlework nearby. The fourth occupant of the room was a stranger, but he seemed oddly familiar. On the shady side of fifty, his salt-and-pepper hair was fashionably cut, as were his clothes. Clad in a blue tailcoat, fawn breeches, and highly polished Hessians, he exuded an air of elegant importance. Brown eyes twinkled as he turned to appraise her.

Thankful that she was wearing one of her new gowns (a walking dress of sprigged muslin with a fashionable flounce) and grateful that Dawson was just as talented as her sister, she smiled.

"Yes, my lord?"

"Caroline, I would like to introduce my good friend William Morris, the ninth Earl of Waite and your uncle. William, my daughter-in-law, Caroline Mannering."

She turned surprised eyes to the earl, unsure how to greet the head of the family that had disowned her mother. That explained his familiarity. The shape of cheek and chin resembled his sister's, as did his eyes.

"I cannot describe how delighted I am to meet you, my dear," said Waite, his charming smile lighting the room. "I never approved of Father's behavior, you must understand, but he forbade any mention of Fanny and his effects did not disclose her direction."

Relieved at the words, her smile spread to her eyes. Marchgate now noted their similarity, for Caroline strongly resembled her mother.

"Thank you, my lord. We live in Sheldridge Corners on the Bath road west of Hungerford."

"No 'my lording,' Caroline," he admonished her. "I am your Uncle William. Have you brothers and sisters?"

"You told him nothing?" She turned to Marchgate in surprise.

"That is for you." He motioned to a nearby couch and tactfully joined his wife and daughter by the fire.

"I am the third of twelve, Uncle William," she confided, eyes sparkling with mischief as she gracefully seated herself and motioned him to join her.

"Good Lord!" he burst out. "Poor Fanny!"

She laughed. "I doubt she would willingly part with any of us. She is a devoted and loving mother. We range from Constance, now six-and-twenty, to Angela, who just turned two."

"So," murmured Waite, his mind doing rapid sums, "Father lied when he claimed she eloped because she was increasing."

"Heavens! Mother would never condone such behavior," she exclaimed in shock. "Nor would Father. And one could hardly term it an elopement as they wed in your own parish church, following the usual banns. I always understood that the old earl disapproved of the match and disowned her when she insisted. The only hint of why was one comment I overheard some years ago when she mentioned that he was so high in the instep he could never countenance a connection with a younger son of a mere baron. The remark struck me as odd, for she never allows herself to disparage anyone, however well deserved."

"It sounds true, however," confirmed her uncle. "Father was odiously puffed with conceit. We all suffered from it. I am only sorry that I was making my grand tour at the time and was unable to assist her. But tell me something of your family."

She spent the better part of an hour with her uncle, describing her brothers and sisters and life in the vicarage. The most telling points for the earl were the Cummings' closeness and the love that prevailed despite economic hardships and the loss of Fanny's entree to society. A weight he had not previously noticed lifted from his heart with this intelligence. At the end of her recital Caroline felt comfortable enough to ask about the rest of her mother's family.

"Fanny and I had a brother and three sisters," he told her. "The oldest, Beatrice, lives in town. She is now the Dowager Viscountess Shelby and you should avoid her for she has become notorious. Every family has its black sheep, but you are young and unknown as yet. Your reputation would suffer if linked with hers. Of the rest, Timothy stays almost exclusively on his estate in Devon, Margaret married a Scottish earl and never comes to town, and Sylvia succumbed to consumption some five years ago. My own wife died in childbirth after presenting me with two sons and two daughters."

"Goodness," gasped Caroline, her head swirling with new people. "And I suppose there are other cousins as well."

"Some five-and-twenty, if memory serves. But that does not include the more remote connections. The family is rather extensive."

"I wonder if Mother has followed your lives."

"I must ask her. Does she still take surprises well? I would dearly like to see her again and long to surprise her, but would hardly risk shocking her by suddenly appearing after eight-and-twenty years."

"I doubt she would suffer from so pleasant a shock, Uncle William. But you must not expect lavish treatment. Times are bad and the vicarage none too opulent."

"I understand. Perhaps I can offer some belated support from the family. At the very least, she should have the dowry Father refused to provide. But enough of the past. Will you attend the theater with me this evening? It is more than time you were introduced to society."

"Thank you, Uncle. That sounds delightful."

The theater proved to be both better and worse than she had anticipated. The building was opulent beyond belief, with a domed Corinthian rotunda and twin staircases curving up from the lobby. Everywhere she looked, stunningly dressed ladies and fashionably garbed gentlemen abounded. Nor did she feel out of place, for the first time confident that her own *toilette* did not shame her. Dawson had outdone herself, sweeping her hair upward into a high knot with soft waves framing a face whose tan was already beginning to fade. The smooth lines of Madame Suzette's green silk gown further accentuated her height and displayed her fine figure. Pearls borrowed from Lady Marchgate drew attention to her swanlike neck, as did the long pearl earrings that had been a wedding gift from her mother, one of that lady's few remaining pieces of jewelry. The total effect implied a sophistication and elegance she hoped would not be spoiled by any lack of address.

"Caroline!" exclaimed a nearby voice while she was still dazedly taking in her surroundings.

Her eyes focused on a black-haired lady of medium height whose gray eyes were wide with surprise.

"Cissy, how wonderful to see you again." She smiled at Squire Hatchett's older daughter with whom she had daily ridden and studied in their youth.

"Papa wrote that you had married, but I had not heard of your arrival in town."

"I only just got here. Your papa was very disappointed that you were unable to be home for Christmas."

"I know it was wretched for him, but we were promised to Nigel's family. His sister had just presented her husband with an heir, so the season included a christening. But did Matt Crawford really make a fool of himself Christmas Eve?"

"Worse, but this is no place to talk. May I present Thomas's father and sister, Lord Marchgate and Lady Wembley? And my uncle, Lord Waite. This is Lady Carstairs, wife of Sir Nigel Carstairs and a former neighbor."

Greetings were exchanged and Cissy promised to call the next day. The crush swept them toward their respective boxes.

Her disappointment with the theater arose from the impossibility of either hearing the play or following its plot. The theater remained noisy, the audience more interested in conversing with friends than in the action. Worse, the company's presentation of *Hamlet* had been edited out of all recognition. Shakespeare must be turning in his grave, she reflected as another scene jauntered off in an unexpected direction, introducing new characters at the expense of old and twisting the plot yet again.

But the stated purpose of the evening—introducing her to society—was admirably achieved. Their box overflowed with people at each of the intervals.

"Lord Rufton, how lovely to see you again." She smiled when he pushed his way through the crowd.

"Mrs. Mannering." He lifted her hand gracefully to his lips. "And why is Thomas not here this evening?"

"A small emergency delayed him at home," she explained yet again. "But he should arrive within a few days."

"How did you find Crawley?"

She shuddered. "Thomas can describe it far better than I. But things are slowly improving. You must visit and inspect our progress."

Rufton smiled. "I would be delighted. But we cannot converse here. Perhaps I could call upon you tomorrow?"

"I will look forward to it. There was no time to get acquainted at Sheldridge Corners."

Waite recalled her attention in order to introduce another visitor and Rufton slipped away.

"Caroline, this is your second cousin, Andrew Morris, Viscount Wroxleigh. Drew, my niece, Mrs. Mannering." He flashed a conspiratorial smile. "Do not believe a word he says as he has a well-deserved reputation for flummery."

"My secret is revealed," Wroxleigh moaned, theatrically smiting his brow. "How can my consequence survive such assault?" About thirty, the blond, blue-eyed viscount exuded the same powerful presence as Thomas. Noting the twinkle in his eyes, she concluded that Waite was warning he also shared a penchant for raking.

"Doing it too brown, aren't you, cousin? Perhaps it has long since succumbed," she teased as he raised her hand to his lips, retaining it considerably longer than protocol demanded.

"You wound me," he said, pouting.

"Is that possible?" she riposted with a twinkle.

"But of course! And you must make amends. Drive with me in the park tomorrow."

"Certainly, cousin," she agreed, stressing their relationship. A flicker of his eyes acknowledged the message.

"Alas, the interval draws to a close and I must return to my party. But I expect the full tale tomorrow of why you have hidden yourself from my sight all this time."

"You've not missed me a bit, my lord."

He laughed and departed as the second act began.

A moment later new arrivals entered a box across the way— Alicia and two well-dressed dandies. If the gown she wore to visit her modiste had been immodest, tonight's costume was little short of scandalous. Sheer silk clung revealingly to every curve, the neckline so low she was in danger of popping out each time she inhaled. A sapphire necklace dangled its pendant into the exposed cleft, further drawing the eye. Nor was she at all hesitant about leaning close to each escort in turn as she laughed at their sallies, offering an enhanced view even as her breasts brushed against their arms. Her behavior was far worse than that of the courtesans in the next tier. Even Lady Shelby—whom Uncle William had pointed out on arrival—acted the lady in public. But Caroline could understand Thomas's interest. Nearly every buck in the house avidly devoured her charms. And who could blame them?

Cissy and Lady Potherby both made morning calls the next day. Previously unacquainted, they took an instant liking to each other and the three spent a pleasant hour conversing over tea.

"What happened with Matt Crawford?" asked Cissy. For years he had pursued his self-appointed task of judging the behavior of the neighborhood young people—and not sympathetically.

Caroline laughed. "He returned home after the Little Season in a very agitated state, but whether from debt or disappointment in love or some other cause we never discovered. The night of Sir Robin's Christmas party he was quite melancholy, spending much of the evening in conversation with the punch bowl."

"Oh, dear," interrupted Cissy, "Matt never could handle wine."

"That much certainly hasn't changed," she agreed. "It wasn't long before he emerged very well to go. He grabbed Edith Hawkins and insisted that she waltz with him—despite the unfortunate fact that the music was a country dance." Cissy giggled. "They twirled dizzily into the refreshment room, his face turning greener by the second, until they crashed into a table. Matt landed flat on the floor with Edith sitting on his stomach and the punch bowl upside down on his very green face."

"What did he say?"

"Nothing. Two footmen dragged him hurriedly into the next room before he succumbed to his just deserts. He slipped off the next morning and hasn't been home since."

Shaking their heads over the excesses of young bucks, the three ladies recalled other ludicrous events they had encountered. From these, conversation moved on to the destruction wrought by Cissy's cat when a bird blundered into her morning room, to the condition of Crawley upon Caroline's arrival, and finally to the lurid and cluttered decorating scheme Lord Potherby's grandmother had imposed on the house. By the time her guests took their leave, Caroline's spirits were soaring. London promised to be quite enjoyable.

Lord Rufton called as promised, bringing with him another of Thomas's close friends, Jeremy Caristoke. The three had formed an inseparable trio since first descending upon Eton. Rufton was a stocky redhead of medium height whose most noticeable features were piercing blue eyes. It took but a few minutes to confirm her initial impression of his character. And Caristoke was much the same, though physically different—tall and slender with warm brown eyes set in an expressive face beneath a cap of brown curls. Both were interesting and witty conversationalists.

"So he bought some of Graylock's mares?" queried Caristoke when she had concluded a brief explanation of Thomas's plans.

"Four, as well as several from others."

"I quite long to see what the result will be from breeding them to that black stallion of his."

"Patience," urged Rufton with a laugh. "That must wait years."

"And perhaps longer if the Abbemarle curse passed to us," Caroline said, a giggle betraying her teasing. "Oh, dear. I was going to tell this so seriously."

"What curse could plague so recent a construction?" wondered Caristoke.

"Actually, Crawley is a replacement manor, the medieval monstrosity that preceded it having burned to the ground in 1710. We found old estate records that date back to the Plantagenets. And I believe a painting I discovered in an attic depicts the original dwelling. It would provide a perfect setting for a Radcliffe novel, all gothic battlements, turrets, blank walls, and cold stone."

"But what of the curse?"

"Why, Lord Rufton! Are you interested in ghostly phenomena?" she exclaimed.

"Oh, do call me George," he urged.

"And I am Jeremy."

"I am honored, gentlemen. As to the curse, the contemporary account of the fire suggests that an ancient curse was responsible, but we have been unable to find an account of what it might be. Did it attach to the land, the house, or the original family? Thomas's greatgrandfather acquired the estate from the Abbemarles after the present manor was built." Her eyes twinkled with mischief.

"Let me know if you uncover any information," George said with a chuckle. "My father's estate has half a dozen supposed ghosts, but I never encountered a real curse."

"Nor I," admitted Jeremy. "But what a dismal topic for a Mayfair drawing room."

"Thomas mentioned that you were well-read," commented George to change the subject.

"Yes, you have discovered my darkest secret. I admit to being a fearful bluestocking."

"You and Thomas must be well-suited indeed, Caroline," Jeremy observed. "He is exceedingly bright, though he always tried to hide the extent of his intelligence at school. But he absorbs a prodigious number of books."

"I have studied his library," she admitted.

They chatted about literature and laughed over memories of Oxford tutorials until it was time for the gentlemen to leave. Their visit provided a glimpse of yet another side of Thomas's character, she reflected as she changed for the promised ride in the park with her cousin. Anyone who could attract and hold the friendship of two such worthwhile men deserved her respect. Her husband was proving to be a complex character—witty, sensual, capable, intelligent, and protective of his friends. In fact, her only complaint was his continued obsession with Alicia that had so negative an effect on their relationship. If only they could return to the easy camaraderie of the early days. But such a wish would prove impossible any time soon. *Please let the future be better. Even indifference would be preferable to cold fury.*

Lord Wroxleigh called to take her up a few minutes later.

"Ah, your ravishing beauty would brighten the most dismal day," he exclaimed passionately as Caroline entered the drawing room clad in a peach muslin carriage dress and green pelisse. A chip bonnet trimmed in matching green was tied jauntily beneath one ear and sparked green highlights in her brown eyes.

"Fustian!" she snorted, eyeing his elegant blue coat, dove pantaloons, and mirror-finish Hessians with approval. "If you insist on Spanish coin every time we meet, I will be forced to avoid you, else I will become puffed with conceit."

"You are the hardest person to flirt with," he said, pouting as he escorted her to the door.

"You must not confuse flirtation with fantasy if you wish to retain your credibility," she chided him, shaking her head.

He laughed and led her outside. His equipage proved to be a perch phaeton painted dark blue with the wheels picked out in gold, pulled by a restive pair of matched bays. It took only a minute for her to relax in the knowledge that he drove nearly as well as Thomas.

"Is this your first trip to Hyde Park?" he asked as they drove through the gates.

"Yes. I've been in town less than a week, and you know what the weather has been like, cousin."

"Call me Drew, sweet Caroline," he murmured. " 'Cousin' is so respectable."

"Very well, Drew," she agreed. "Unless you need a reminder."

"You are being cruel," he accused playfully.

"Don't come the rogue with me or I shall be forced to forego your company," she warned, a note of steel underlying the words.

He remained silent for a full minute before turning a charming grin in her direction. "Agreed. I have an unaccountable urge to know you better, cousin. How can I wish to spend time with an unseducible lady?"

Caroline laughed. "Boredom?" she suggested. "Perhaps your life has become too predictable."

"Possibly. But I had best introduce you around lest people get the wrong idea." He hailed a passing curricle! "Ashton! Good day to you. Gerald, may I present my cousin, Caroline Mannering? She is Thomas Mannering's wife and just arrived for the Season. Caroline, this is Viscount Ashton."

"My lord." Caroline smiled. The viscount wore an enormous emerald on one hand that sparkled in the sunlight every time he moved.

"Is Mannering back then?" he inquired.

"In a few days."

By the time Ashton moved forward, Drew's phaeton was mobbed by others eager to meet her. Her head soon swirled with names, finally giving up on the task of attaching them to faces. Only three were of sufficient import to stay in her memory: dark-haired Sally Jersey, one of the feared Almack's patronesses; Beau Brummel, whose position as arbiter of fashion was yet unchallenged—Robert might lead the most flamboyant of fops, but the Beau's quiet elegance had a greater following and was far more pleasing to her eye; and Lady Beatrice, an elderly, purple-robed dowager who was the most feared gossip in Mayfair, knowing everything that occurred, most of it before the rest of the *ton*. With Drew's assistance, Caroline managed to navigate the conversational shoals without mishap and acquitted herself very well.

"Thank you," she said with a smile as they returned to Berkeley Square. "I would never have believed I could manage, but you make it easy."

"There is really nothing to park conversation," he disclaimed. "It is all hello and good-bye and repeating the latest gossip you learned from your servants and morning calls."

"I suspect I need to recognize faces and relationships first. Can you imagine repeating naughty *on-dits* to the wrong parties?"

Drew laughed. "Ah, yes. I had not considered that trap. But within a week I warrant you will have acquired enough town bronze to discard your fears. It has been delightful, my dear," he concluded, pulling his bays to a halt at Marchgate House. "I trust we will meet again soon."

"Undoubtedly," agreed Caroline as he handed her down, retaining her hand a moment too long. "But watch your step. One rake in my life is enough."

He sighed and turned back to his horses.

In the days that followed Caroline found herself caught up in the social life of the *ton*. Emily coached her on town conventions and accompanied her to several routs, a musicale, and a ball. Lady Marchgate and Eleanor sought her company for other events. She furthered her friendships with George, Jeremy, and Drew, and developed even closer relationships with Emily, Cissy, and Helena Potherby. She shopped, viewed the Elgin Marbles with Jeremy and the British Museum with George, drove again in the park with Drew and danced with them and with others. Helena and Cissy accompanied her to two lectures and a literary evening. Uncle William and Drew introduced her to other cousins. Her acquaintances multiplied as she accompanied Lady Marchgate on her daily round of visits or remained at home when the countess received callers. Thomas's mother had warmed perceptibly, no longer adopting her icy hauteur. Each morning Caroline shared breakfast and conversation with the earl, exploring any and all subjects as had been her wont with the squire. Their talks gave her a deeper understanding of Thomas, for he and the earl were much alike. If her friendship with her husband had not been nipped in the bud, they would now enjoy just this relaxed camaraderie. By the time Thomas arrived, she had carved a comfortable niche for herself in town and was welcomed everywhere with enthusiasm. But she had also learned more than she cared to about her husband's past.

It was at the Debenham ball. Her escorts this evening were Emily and Wembley. The viscount was an interesting conversationalist, applauding her efforts to employ veterans and describing a bill he was working on to provide pensions. But once in the ballroom, he switched to light social chatter and humorous commentary lest her reputation be besmirched.

She enjoyed the dancing immensely, still surprised at the number of men willing to stand up with her. Robert led her out for the second set, his conversation even shallower than Wembley's social chatter and she began to better understand Emily's critique of the *ton*.

"Lady Sheridan should never wear primrothe," he lisped as

they came together in the country dance. "She lookth like a lemon with that thick waist and apple green ribbons in her yellow hair. Delicious." He finished with an affected giggle.

Caroline smiled, unwilling to disagree. The lady did look rather sallow. And her gown in no way disguised a love of rich food in abundant quantities.

"I must say you look exquisite, Caroline," he continued, casting a connoisseur's eye over her embroidered ivory gauze atop a deep green slip, with slashed puff sleeves and green ribbon trim. The combination brought color to her cheeks and added green glints to her brown eyes. Dawson had threaded seed pearls through her hair, complementing the countess's pearl necklace.

"As do you," she murmured. His sky blue coat fit like a second skin. This waistcoat was embroidered in even brighter colors than the one he had worn to dinner, and his cravat appeared more elaborate.

A stir drew their attention to the entrance. Lady Darnley had paused, gathering all eyes before descending to the ballroom. A dozen dandies already jostled for position at the foot of the stairs.

"Like butterflies around a passion flower." Robert giggled. "Silly boys. The lady will eat them alive. Heartless."

"Would that everyone could see that," she murmured to herself.

"Don't tell me Thomas still hovers round the lady!" He sounded shocked.

"We shall see when he arrives."

"I cannot believe it. He would never behave so dishonorably. He would die first."

Caroline allowed the subject to drop, not wanting to either admit Thomas's obsession or contradict Robert's assessment. She danced sets with George, Jeremy, Uncle William, Drew, and several other gentlemen. Unused to attracting so much attention—her older sisters had always been the local beauties—she finally decided that her popularity arose from curiosity over Thomas's new wife.

Drew escorted her to dinner and kept her laughing with his droll wit and light flirtation. Emily introduced her to several ladies, mostly matrons in their twenties with young families.

An open set provided an opportunity to slip away to the retiring room to pin up a small tear in her hem. She paid no attention to the other occupants of the room until she caught Alicia's name.

"Why couldn't Lady Darnley stay home with her husband?" complained a pretty young miss. "With her around, the gentlemen look at no one else."

"Hush, Clara," admonished another. "Those mobbing her are

rakes, which is only fitting. She has undoubtedly bestowed her favors on most of them."

"Celia!" Caroline could not decide whether Clara's tone denoted shock or titillation.

"Don't pretend shock," chided Celia. "She's no better than she should be. Just pray she refrains from sinking her claws into decent gentlemen. She destroyed Mannering last year. And I had such hopes for him." She sighed.

"How? I had not heard that tale."

"She encouraged him to sit in her pocket most of the Season, allowing him to run tame in her house, waltzing three times with him at Almack's, even disappearing into Lady Debenham's garden for two whole sets. Everyone expected a betrothal. Then she up and accepted Darnley the next day. Mannering was devastated. Took to unrestrained debauchery. No one saw him sober for months. Squandered a fortune and blackened his reputation until few would receive him. Marchgate finally banished him to the country and married him off so he couldn't ruin his sister's come-out."

"Heavens!" exclaimed Clara. "But it sounds like you had a narrow escape. What if he hadn't been distracted?"

"True. He has not demonstrated any steadiness of character. But oh, those green eyes!" She sighed and returned to the ballroom.

Caroline remained for some minutes. Thomas's debauch sounded far worse than she had suspected. He had never hinted at ostracism. Would that still hold true? Alicia's conduct was easier to understand. Accepting and encouraging the attentions of a handsome rake would flatter her overweening vanity, but such a selfish chit would never marry without a title. He must be deeply smitten indeed to have ignored that. *And please let his oath that gaming and drinking are behind him be true.* Nor was she surprised that two young girls knew of Alicia's notoriety. Tales of her bedroom exploits were rife, eclipsing even those of Lady Shelby. That Thomas seemed ignorant of them was further proof of his blind obsession.

Would he ever recover? Or was obsession a Mannering family trait? There was Uncle Bertram, who had shut himself away in Crawley for forty years, reportedly conversing daily with his dead wife. And a cousin had fled the country to escape the consequences of obsessive gaming.

Several days later, she accompanied Eleanor to an evening of routs, the countess remaining at home with a migraine. Routs were the least enjoyable of the Season's social events. Invariably crowded, one spent half an hour in a coach trying to reach the door, another half hour in a line to greet the hostess, and a third fighting a way through the crush from one over-heated room to the next, greeting friends and exchanging *on-dits* before pushing a way out to continue to the next rout. No refreshments were served, nor was there music or dancing. They were an enormous waste of time.

Eleanor agreed.

"Why must we go to these?" the girl groused as they sat through yet another traffic tie-up near their third stop of a planned four. "I would much rather be at the Richardsons' soiree this evening."

"You know your mother would never countenance that," she reminded her. "The Richardsons are too fast for your first Season. You cannot take chances with your reputation. As to your first question, you know the answer better than I. If you do not appear at the events of important hostesses, your credit will suffer."

"Then why can you skip the most boring parties?"

"Because I'm married. That gives me more freedom. I am not restricted to the marriage mart. But I still must appear at social events. And even at Almack's on occasion. Now, straighten your shawl. We are at the door at last. I only hope it is not too hot this time. Did you see Lady Stafford at the Seftons? I swear she was on the verge of a swoon."

"I noticed. And Lady Castleton at the Delaneys. There must have been four vinaigrettes waving under her nose." She giggled and allowed the groom to assist her from the coach.

Surprisingly, they bumped into Drew in one of the rooms.

"What on earth are you doing here?" asked an amazed Caroline.

"God knows. I hate these things," he complained. "But Lady Fotheringay is related to my mother."

"It could be worse. This is our third stop tonight."

Drew laughed. "My poor Caro." They chatted several minutes until he suddenly broke off in midsentence. "Trouble's brewing," he warned quietly. "Hurry."

Eleanor had quickly tired of listening to their conversation and turned to a group of young ladies nearby. One of these was Miss Gumpley, also making her bows, but cursed with an acid tongue and lack of humor. She had not taken, in part because she couldn't keep her criticisms to herself. And the more unpopular she felt, the more she found to criticize. This time she attacked Caroline's association with a rake and Eleanor's acceptance of it. Too young to laugh off the words, Eleanor defended herself and her family in increasingly strident tones.

"Eleanor, we must pay our respects to Lady Seaton," Caroline interrupted, grateful that Drew had spotted the altercation before most were aware of it.

"Miss Gumpley, how charmingly you look tonight," murmured Drew seductively, raising her hand briefly to his lips and turning the full force of his eyes onto her. She froze in surprise, giving Caroline a chance to draw an unwilling Eleanor away.

"Watch your manners," she chided softly.

"But she said the most dreadful things," protested Eleanor. "How could I let such slander pass unchallenged?"

"Think of what your mama would say. By creating a public scene you lend credence to her words. Consider the source. With her reputation for catty untruths, her comments carry no weight. Now smile. Here is Lady Seaton."

Later that night she recalled the scene with a shudder for what might have been. *Thank God for Drew*.

Chapter 10

Thomas turned his curricle down Davies Street, heading for Berkeley Square. He was tired and out of sorts. Finding help for Jacobs had taken far longer than he had expected. In the interim, all the work had fallen on his shoulders. And thoughts of Caroline had plagued him since her departure.

Her suggestion to postpone their trip had been eminently sensible. Why had he spurned it? The words were out before he even considered them. Why? He had reached the same conclusion himself immediately after learning of the accident. And this time he could hardly accuse her of usurping his duties. It was unconscionable to send her alone to a city of strangers and a family she had never met. How often had his mother's hauteur intimidated even his most deserving friends? Robert was hardly an acceptable pattern card. Nor was the ninnyhammered Eleanor. However much he might wish otherwise, Caroline was his wife and needed his support. His recent behavior was unworthy of his breeding, as was his refusal to credit her accomplishments. The house had seemed cold and lonely since her departure. Not until she left had he realized how thoroughly her presence permeated the atmosphere of Crawley.

This was a clear case of pique. He had believed his occasional flashes of temper were behind him. The last time he had lost control of himself had been just before he had started at Oxford, though the incident still bothered him. Irritated beyond endurance by Robert's continued refusal to work on improving his horsemanship, he had dared him to ride Satan. He should have known better, of course. Robert could ignore taunting from everyone except him. The resulting injuries had haunted Thomas ever since. What damage might his tantrum have caused this time? There would be something. There always was. Shirking his responsibilities invariably called down punishment, and between Alicia and Caroline, he was building up quite an account with fate.

But his own behavior was only one of the problems that bedeviled him. How had his family responded to Caroline? Did she know how to conduct herself? He did not trust her. Not that she would deliberately embarrass him, but she was a naive, country girl, unused even to the society to be found in Banbury, let alone London. Her warm friendliness could lead her into trouble if she embraced the wrong crowd.

He shivered.

Then there was her wardrobe. Did she have any taste? Her current gowns left that question unanswered, but fear knotted his stomach. He should have accompanied her to the modiste the first time to see that she was properly turned out.

How was she filling her time? Acquiring books, certainly. And he had no complaints there. Unlike many men, he saw nothing wrong with intelligent females, perhaps because he was used to Emily. What else? Was she included in Eleanor's social rounds? But in the next breath he feared she would shame him in company.

She was so green!

And what had she told his family about their relationship?

"Thomas!" a sultry voice called.

He jerked his team to a sudden stop, gazing longingly at Alicia. Again he had been allowed no time to prepare for their meeting. Dressed in her favorite blue, she had just alighted from Darnley's town carriage.

"L-lady Darnley," he stammered, trying to force calm into his voice. "You look well. How is your husband?"

"No better, my love," she purred, stepping close to his curricle so the footmen would not overhear her words. She offered her hand and he had to press it in greeting.

The movement presented an unobstructed view down her low-cut gown. He bit back a groan as memories of her naked, writhing body assailed him. How could he have attacked her?

Alicia smiled. "But I am delighted you have finally arrived. It must have been dreadfully lonely without a wife, dowdy and plain though she is."

Her words confirmed his worst fears. Caroline's appearance was embarrassing him.

"You have met her?" he asked warily.

"Not formally, but she is everywhere about now that she has acquired a devoted cicisbeo in Lord Wroxleigh." A look of such understanding commiseration accompanied the words that Thomas had no doubt her insinuation was true.

It was long past time to take his wife in hand, he reflected grimly as he excused himself. Admittedly, he should never have sent her to town unaccompanied, but how could his high-stickler mother condone such behavior? He was grateful to Alicia for the warning, glad that someone cared for his welfare. Wroxleigh was the worst sort of libertine, an unscrupulous pariah who preyed on society's matrons. Had Caroline already welcomed him into her bed?

Behind him, Alicia licked her lips in satisfaction at the flash of anger in Thomas's eyes. Her attempt to drive a wedge between Thomas and his wife had worked even better than she had hoped. Not that she believed the chit offered any real competition, but Thomas had a rather warped sense of honor. Anything that would facilitate luring him back to her bed was desirable. She wanted him there. Regularly. His passion was everything she had expected. No one had come close to satisfying her since.

Fate plagued her. She had come to London in search of a title and wealth, not expecting to develop an overpowering lust for a man who had neither. The only child of a modest baron, she had long traded on her beauty and easily assumed innocence, growing up spoiled, willful, and self-centered, indulged in every whim by doting parents. She had early on mastered the seductive wiles that could bend men to her will. From her initiation into the pleasures of the body at age fourteen, she rarely bothered to control her passion, discreetly taking lovers and relying on her persuasive tongue to avoid any consequences. Rumor could be attributed to jealous rivals. Even Darnley believed her tale of a childhood riding accident that accounted for her unprovable virginity.

Her obsession with Thomas was as strong as his with her—on a purely physical level. Who would not be attracted to a man who worshipped her so devoutly? His passionate virility had beckoned her the moment they were introduced. But from a practical standpoint, marriage was impossible. Spurning his hand had cost her not a qualm. Convinced of the power she wielded, she knew he would grace her bed. She had rejoiced at his own nuptials once her surprise faded. In the world of Mayfair, a liaison between married partners was easier to conduct, and she could scarce contain her anticipation. His raging lust during their encounter at Graystone was all she had expected. Accepting that the experience would be the first of many, she had been furious to find him gone that evening. Not until she identified the dowd at Madame Suzette's as his wife had anger turned to hope. She owed his departure to his annoying code of honor, but she would soon convince him otherwise. Then victory would be hers.

Thomas climbed wearily down from his curricle and handed the ribbons to a footman.

"Welcome home, sir." The butler bowed formally, holding open the front door.

"Where is my wife, Reeves?"

"Mrs. Mannering is driving in the park today, sir."

"How about my mother?"

"Lady Marchgate and Lady Eleanor are also in the park."

He stifled a wave of disappointment. At least his mother would keep Caroline in order. He should have expected this, arriving as he had at the height of the fashionable hour, but it had been nearly a year since he had concerned himself with Mayfair's social rhythms.

"Thank you, Reeves. Am I in my usual room?"

"No, sir. You and Mrs. Mannering are in the silver suite."

Stifling his frustration, he turned upstairs. The clothing he had sent ahead was already there. Cramer had done well. The valet appeared almost immediately with bathwater.

A giggling Eleanor passed his door a short while later. He hurried his dressing, but Caroline had not yet returned by the time he finished. Pushing open the connecting door, he stepped into her room.

A servant was laying out an evening gown of soft rose sarcenet. His unannounced entrance clearly startled her.

"Who are you?" he snapped.

"Dawson, sir. Mrs. Mannering's dresser."

Guilt pricked him for not remembering that she must have a maid in town. At least someone had the sense to hire an experienced one. Perhaps Caroline was not embarrassing him as much as he had feared. Or had Dawson been hired because Caroline was making a cake of herself?

"I am Mr. Mannering," he introduced himself. "Has my wife returned from the park?"

"No, sir."

"But Eleanor is back."

"She did not drive with Lady Eleanor, sir."

"Then with who?" His temper was again perilously close to exploding. Alicia's hints echoed in his ears.

"I believe she is driving with Lord Rufton today, sir."

Paradoxically, the deflation of his fears left Thomas almost as angry. Why had George taken Caroline under his wing? George never took females driving in the park. Was she so uncontrolled that his friends were trying to protect him by monopolizing her time? *Devoted cicisbeo in Wroxleigh* . . . He shook away the words.

"Thank you," he murmured, remembering his manners as he stomped back to his own room.

Strangely, he felt bereft. Had he been looking forward to seeing his wife again? He thrust that thought aside. He could not miss her freckled face. But he needed to know what was happening. Now. She had not been raised to the *ton*. Nor had she any experience in the world of Mayfair. For an unknown, even the smallest mistake could bring censure and disgrace. How could he have sent her alone to London? She was greener than the greenest schoolroom miss.

Cramer appeared at the door. "Lord Marchgate wishes to see you in the library, sir."

Sighing, he complied. Was he about to be castigated for Caroline's lack of manners?

But the earl appeared relaxed, gesturing to a decanter.

"I trust you left Crawley in good hands," he commented once the initial greetings were concluded.

"Yes, I discovered a former cavalryman who is a wizard with horses. Jacobs will be incapacitated for at least another month, and it will be several more before his strength is restored, so Richards will have plenty to do."

"Caroline mentioned your program of hiring former soldiers. I had never considered it myself, but your successes interest me. Has she exaggerated their skills?"

"They have done wonders with the estate," admitted Thomas, his spurt of pleasure at his father's approval mitigated by a quickly suppressed reminder that the idea had been Caroline's. "And I could not ask for harder workers. There are limits, of course. Individually, several of the men cannot handle certain types of work. Ted, for example, has but one arm, so finds using an ax difficult. But as a team, they accomplish nearly as much as an equivalent number of able-bodied laborers."

"Perhaps I should look into hiring veterans at March Abbey," mused the earl. "Caroline claims we owe a great deal to those injured in their country's service, and I must agree. Wembley is working on some sort of bill. I will have to look into it. My support might improve its chances." He sighed. "I must admit that when she first arrived I was angry with you for callously dumping her in town without an introduction, but I quickly conceded that you knew best. She is a most capable lady, at home wherever she goes. You are fortunate in your wife."

"Thank you." He barely managed to speak through another wave of guilt, this time mixed with surprise. His father rarely passed out praise. And never when undeserved. Could she really be a credit? Was she managing to negotiate *ton* waters without mishap? The idea raised a flash of pride, quickly stifled. For lurking beneath was pain that she might not require his assistance. Ladies needed guidance and protection. A vision of Alicia rose before his eyes, reminding him of her helplessness in the face of parental insistence. He longed to stand as a buffer between her and a cruel world. Caroline never incited such thoughts. She was no lady.

They conversed for some time on Crawley and its problems. His father was well-versed in the latter. Caroline must talk of nothing else. Was there no end to her interference? Yet the earl spoke of her with respect and affection. Thomas's head swirled dizzily. She had wormed her way into the hearts of his family if his father's description could be trusted. Was she trying to drive a wedge between them and him?

Nonsense! The only complaint she could entertain was coming to town alone. She knew nothing of his other failings. If she had criticized him in her daily breakfast conversations, the earl showed no sign of it. And he was not a man to refrain from a deserved reprimand. If Caroline had already forgiven him for throwing her on the *ton* unprepared, she must be the sweetest lady alive. Her reports to his father were nothing but supportive.

Impossible! screamed his brain. Only Alicia had ever approached that ideal. Nor was he such a crass fool that he could fail to detect such virtues. Devil take the woman, what sort of game was she playing? And why? *Devoted cicisbeo* . . . Was she covering an affair?

The dressing bell sounded and he excused himself to prepare for dinner.

Caroline was seated at her dressing table when Thomas again opened the connecting door. In evening dress, he was a most elegant and handsome man, adhering to Brummel's tenets of sober colors, simplicity, and cleanliness. Snowy white linen set off his black evening coat and made his green eyes glitter even brighter than usual.

If only they could recapture their former friendship. Her daily conversations with Marchgate had triggered a longing to resume the similar discussions she used to hold with Thomas. Could he possibly have regained his composure during this separation? But she dismissed the thought as soon as it arose. Even if true, any rapport would not survive his next meeting with Alicia. And if he accompanied her tonight, they would meet. Lady Darnley seldom missed the more important balls.

"I see you have adjusted well to town," he commented coolly.

"Thank you, sir. How is Jacobs?"

"Recovering slowly. The new man, Richards, will remain permanently on the staff. Do you attend the Cofferton ball tonight?"

"Yes. Will you accompany us?"

"I believe so."

Caroline dismissed Dawson and rose to face him. Thomas stared. This elegant woman was his country wife? Soft waves framed her face, rising to an elaborate knot threaded with rose ribbon that matched the gown he had seen earlier. Its lines accentuated both her exquisite figure and her height. Nor had he previously noted her long, slender neck. She carried herself like a queen. The result was striking. Of course, she could never claim to be a beauty like Alicia, he hastily assured himself, guilty over admiring any other lady. But he could not repress memories of her passionate response on their wedding night. His groin tightened.

"Where did you get the pearls?" he asked, to divert his mind.

"Your mother loaned them to me since I have no jewelry of my own."

That was another duty he had ignored. Thomas stifled a new wave of anger, this time aimed squarely at himself. Nothing had gone right since the moment he abandoned honor to attack Alicia. He must pull himself together and carry out his responsibilities lest he call down further disaster on his head.

But dinner fed his pique. Every member of his family, including his foppish brother, accepted Caroline as an equal. Even his mother bestowed smiles and as much warmth as he had ever seen. He had worried himself sick for more than a fortnight, but she did not need him. This angered him more than anything else.

Born to one of the oldest families in the *ton*, convinced by the haughty countess and proud earl of his consequence, he was himself quite high in the instep. Not that he would ever admit such a fault. He had often gone out of his way to help others—steering young cubs around the shoals of London life; relaxing the fears of the less adept young ladies staging come-outs; aiding the needy. He even willingly sought advice from others. But he reveled in the acclaim such actions brought. He had been forced into marriage, a fact that inevitably stirred resentment. Yet Caroline offered some balm to this sore, providing satisfaction beyond the obvious. He had raised her above any station she could have achieved on her own. Only he could bestow such blessings on a mere vicar's daughter. In return he expected gratitude and reliance on him for guidance and protection. Her recent success cheated him of this magnanimous gesture and its accompanying acclaim. And it was his own fault. He alone had decided to send her to London without him. But the situation still made him angry. As did every proof of her acceptance, for none of their praise acknowledged his part in elevating an unknown.

"Thank you for letting Caroline come up to town early," bubbled Eleanor. "She has been so much help. And so much fun." She signaled acceptance to a footman who placed a quail on her plate.

"Yes," added his mother. "She has a knack for keeping Eleanor in line. And her chaperoning has eased my life considerably. Emily's Season was far easier."

Thomas nearly choked. Caroline sufficiently up to snuff to act chaperone? For his hoyden of a baby sister?

"And thuch exquisite taste in gowns," lisped Robert, transferring a minuscule nibble of lobster to his mouth. He had joined the family for dinner as soon as he heard of his brother's return. "She's all the crack, you know. Quite admired, indeed, even envied. Lady Beatrice bestowed the ultimate accolade just yesterday. 'You should follow Mrs. Mannering's example'—she was talking to the Delaney chit—'as she embodies all the virtues a young lady could want.' And how right she was."

Thomas nearly burst at Robert's allusion to a long-standing quarrel between the brothers. Alicia was the embodiment of all virtue. But both Robert and Lady Beatrice had long ago taken against her, wasting no opportunity to deride Thomas for his interest.

"Yes, you are quite fortunate in your wife, Thomas," agreed Marchgate, signaling for more wine as he dug into the crimped cod. Caroline blushed at the inordinate praise. "But what I want to know is when Robert plans to set up his nursery." He turned a rapier glance on his heir. "It is more than time that you do so."

"But I am barely seven-and-twenty, Father. There is no rush." Irritation marred his vacuous face.

"You are my heir and I want to see the succession assured."

The earl's implacable voice raised a flush on Robert's pale cheeks.

"As would I," added the countess.

"But there is no one I wish to wed," protested Robert.

Caroline saw Thomas's eyes narrow at this remark, but dismissed the horrifying suspicion that flared at his nearly imperceptible shudder. Why was she so attuned to his thoughts? Or was she?

"I expect you to look harder," commanded Marchgate, then turned the discussion to more pleasant topics.

Thomas banished thoughts of his brother. Much as he loved him, there were times his mere presence proved irritating. Just look at the fellow, sporting a jacket that probably required two assistants and twenty minutes to don. Caroline was problem enough.

Nor did his temper improve when they arrived at the ball. Before they even cleared the receiving line, they were assailed by acquaintances, all of impeccable *ton,* all eager to congratulate him on his wife. Manners demanded he accept their accolades, but he stumped off in high dudgeon as soon as they reached the ballroom. No insignificant country chit deserved such praise. Could she possibly survive this crush without humiliating him? He must watch her carefully, ready to intervene at any hint of trouble. He did, too, noting every smile, every gesture, every partner. Until Alicia arrived. Then he forgot all about her.

"Caroline!" exclaimed Cissy as the Marchgate party descended the stairs. "Who is the handsome gentleman?"

"My husband." She would have introduced them but Thomas was already striding away. "He only arrived this afternoon, and I fear the journey has tired him."

"Aren't you the lucky one, though."

"So it would seem," she murmured before deliberately turning the subject. "But you are beautiful tonight, Cissy. And you match the decor so perfectly."

Indeed, Cissy's gown of pink gauze over a silver slip could have been designed for this setting. Lady Cofferton had done up her ballroom in pink silk drawn into sweeping cascades by silver ribbons. Pink and white flowers massed in corners and around pink marble cherubs arrayed on silver pedestals.

"You are incredibly elegant yourself," responded Cissy, admiring the rose sarcenet gown caressing her friend's fine figure.

"Fustian! Have you seen Helena?" She lowered her voice. "I

found a new book she will want to read on the necessity of educating the lower classes."

"I would also like to read that. She is somewhere about, but I have not seen her to speak to as yet. This must be the worst crush of the Season." She was interrupted as Sir Nigel arrived to lead her into the set that was forming.

Caroline's own hand was solicited a moment later and she pushed serious topics aside, responding to her partner's chatter with lighthearted quips.

"I see Mannering is back in town," commented Drew as he led her out for the next set.

"Yes, he finally found a decent trainer." This dance was a waltz, her favorite when with her cousin.

"Does this mean I cannot accompany you again?" He pouted, his eyes a laughing contrast to his pursed mouth.

"You are ridiculous, cousin," she said, laughing in return.

He tried to pull her closer.

"Naughty, naughty," she chided. "You know the rules."

"I know the unwritten ones, as well," he murmured seductively.

"I suspect you devised some of them, but not with me."

"Well." His voice returned to normal. "You cannot blame me for trying."

"I suppose your reputation would shatter if you did not," she rejoined. "But neither can you blame me for refusing."

"How well you know me. How could the Morris clan produce anyone quite so proper?" He spun her in a dizzying series of turns.

"You forget that I grew up in a vicarage."

"That hasn't stopped many another."

"As you know from experience, I suppose. Wicked, wicked man." She shook her head in despair. "You are hopeless."

He laughed. "My besetting sin."

"Flirting is fun, but no more, Drew."

He heaved a deep sigh of dramatic frustration, but the twinkle in his eye gave him away. She giggled and they lapsed into correct social chatter for the remainder of the dance. When he finally returned her to Lady Marchgate's alcove, George already waited to lead her out.

"I hope Thomas is properly ashamed of himself for dumping you in town on your own," he commented.

"If so, he will never admit it and undoubtedly can twist any guilt into anger that I have managed without him," she conceded.

George started in surprise. "How well you know him! For all we are friends, I have never approved of that side of him."

"What prompts such behavior?" The dance separated them for several measures.

"I suspect his upbringing," said George thoughtfully when they moved together again. "I have known him since we were eight and often spent holidays at March Abbey. The countess is the most rigid of the high-sticklers, condemning any deviation from society's rules. She instilled a compelling need for convention and public acclaim, and a horror of offending others. The earl, on the other hand, believes fiercely in honor and achievement. Early on, he recognized Thomas's abilities. But in encouraging his development, he set standards that were nearly impossible to attain. And anything less was unacceptable. And he blamed Thomas for every problem connected to his behavior, even those things over which he had no real control. As a result, Thomas longs to be accepted, to conform, and to never make a mistake. So when things go wrong, he is the last to admit fault, instead using that facile brain to pin the blame on something else. For example, he spent Christmas with us one year and enjoyed showing off his skating ability—he's far more athletic than I. The acclaim he received went to his head and he started jumping over things—two chairs, a log, the warning sign marking the limits of safe ice."

"He fell in?"

"Exactly. He spent the rest of the visit grumbling that the sign had been placed too close to thin ice."

Poor judgment and arrogance. Caroline was silent as her feet automatically moved through the figures. George's analysis raised disturbing questions about her future. If Thomas could never admit a mistake, could be ever relinquish Alicia? Would he adore her forever, ignoring even blatant evidence of her unworthiness? And how did this affect her own prospects? He had compared her with obvious disfavor to his love. Could he ever alter his opinion?

But a ballroom was not the place for deep thinking. She recalled her surroundings, thrust the questions into the back of her mind, and deliberately set out to enjoy the evening. Reflection was more profitably accomplished in the quiet of her room.

"I swear you grow more beautiful each time we meet, Caroline," claimed Jeremy as he led her into a spirited reel several sets later.

"More Spanish coin?" She laughed, trying to hide her elation at the compliment. "You will turn my head with such blatant clankers. But who was that charming girl you were dancing with just now? I do not believe we have met."

"Hardly a girl anymore," he mourned. "My sister—another Caroline, by the way—now Lady Wormsley. She just arrived in town."

"Alas that so many of us share the name. It could become quite confusing."

He laughed, traded witticisms for the remainder of the set, and then introduced her to his sister and brother-in-law. Jeremy and Lord Wormsley fell into a deep discussion. The viscount was a long-faced man with a chronically dour expression, yet everyone in his vicinity spent an inordinate amount of time laughing.

"Caroline, that gown is even more fetching than I expected. Lady Wormsley, how nice to see you again." Emily's voice startled Caroline, who had not seen her approach.

"And you, Lady Wembley," Jeremy's sister countered.

"Is Thomas here?" Emily asked eagerly. "I can scarcely believe he finally made it to town."

"You might try that cherub by the card room. He and George were chatting there not long ago."

Emily bustled off and Caroline turned her attention to Lady Wormsley.

"So you are Thomas's wife," that lady continued their interrupted introduction. "I am thrilled to meet you and so very glad he settled down at last. I've known him all my life, you understand. He, George, and Jeremy were inseparable. I wanted to scream at him last year—" She abruptly stopped.

"Never mind. I know all about last year," Caroline soothed.

"Then you will understand the frustration those who cared for him felt watching that cat lead him around by the nose. Thank heavens he seems to have come to his senses."

"Yes," agreed Caroline thinly. If only he had.

"Hello, Caroline, Caroline." Helena broke into giggles at her greeting. "This is absurd," she choked. "When did you get back?" She stared pointedly at Lady Wormsley.

"Last night. How goes your school, Helena? You have not written in some time."

"Still only a hopeful future project. James is being a beast about lowering our consequence. Caroline"—here she turned her gaze on Mrs. Mannering—"has been collecting rebuttals to his objections."

"You also believe in educating the lower classes?"

"Yes. I started a village school at Crawley, having previously done the same at Sheldridge Corners. Fortunately Thomas approves." Or at least he did not actively oppose her, she thought wryly. She turned her eyes to Helena. "I found an excellent book containing compelling arguments in favor of education," she reported. Several minutes passed in discussion before Thomas appeared to lead her into the supper dance and the group broke up.

Thomas was riding an emotional whirlwind. Caroline was clearly relaxed, accepted by everyone, her behavior unexceptionable. The waltz with Wroxleigh was despicably indiscreet, of course, but he dared not make a scene. And aside from flirting outrageously with the man, she did nothing with which he could take exception. Nor did his mother seem concerned by the matter.

Far worse was the attention of his friends. They inundated him with congratulations, praise, and envy.

"Charming wife," declared Sharpton enthusiastically. "I don't blame you a bit for shabbing off early from Graystone. And she carries Waite's blood on top of everything else." The knowing leer that accompanied this last observation sent icy anger surging through his breast. What had she done to confirm that particular bit of breeding?

"You're a lucky devil, Mannering," another congratulated him. "Wish I'd seen her first. Always has a sensible suggestion for any problem but never makes a fellow feel foolish for not thinking of it himself."

"Welcome back," Jeremy said later in the evening. "Caroline's a gem. Why are all the beautiful, intelligent ladies snapped up by others? Elizabeth last year, Caroline this. Surely there is one out there for me."

Thomas was taken aback by such a description, but immediately discounted it. Anyone who preferred the redheaded Elizabeth Markham over Alicia demonstrated questionable judgment, for all he and Jeremy were close friends.

"Never thought I'd like a bluestocking," admitted George when they met at the punch bowl. "But Caroline is special. Don't get me wrong," he added, noting the martial light in Thomas's eye with interest, "There is nothing untoward between us and never could be, but I count her among my dearest friends. You are a far luckier man than you deserve to be, Thomas."

These and other comments rained on his head until he was ready to throttle her for cutting such a swath through the *ton*. Respectable females did not engender so many accolades. Especially among the bucks and beaus. Yet he could discover no evidence of misbehavior.

The Earl of Waite led her into a cotillion, and enlightenment struck. No wonder so many had mentioned her connection. He must have publicly acknowledged their relationship. Thomas ground his teeth. If Waite had sponsored her, he need not have worried about her acceptance. The present earl wielded tremendous clout. His cachet alone guaranteed access to the highest circles and placed her on a par with his own social status. The worry he had expended on her behalf was wasted effort, brought on, he now realized, by her own disclaimer of a lady's graces. Yet she appeared as adept as any other in the room. An unaccustomed spurt of pride surfaced as he realized that he owned something other men found desirable.

But all was forgotten when Alicia arrived. He had steeled himself for this meeting, so was able to continue his conversation even as he became aware of her presence, though his throat caught for a moment and his heart pounded until he was afraid Ashton would notice. She was breathtakingly beautiful.

He had thought long and hard about their situation since his return from Graystone. She might be his goddess, but honor was his god. And away from her disturbing presence, honor held sway. Never again would he repeat his disgraceful lapse. Nothing could alter the immutable fact that he loved her. But he would no longer wear his heart on his sleeve. Such conduct demeaned his honor. And there was Eleanor to consider. He could not ignore Alicia, of course. Aside from his own needs, any kind of cut would engender gossip and speculation. Only one course existed, though following the rules would stretch his will power to the limit. He would stay out of her orbit whenever possible, remain coolly polite whenever they met, never dance with her more than once, and make certain they were never alone together. Only thus could he hope to prevent unwanted *on-dits* and protect his heart from further abuse.

Thus, when she entered the ballroom, he continued chatting with friends, dancing with other ladies, and seeming, on the surface, to be as frivolously contented as any in the room. Yet he was constantly aware of Alicia's actions. He knew every smile and on whom it was bestowed, every partner, every laugh. Although it was a necessary part of socializing, he inwardly cringed to see her flirting with others, wanting only to spirit her away so they could be alone.

But his social mask never slipped.

He shared the supper dance with Caroline, not criticizing any of her previous partners—only one of whom deserved it—and demonstrating pride in his marriage. His smile never wavered.

"You look quite lovely this evening," he murmured, pursuing his role of satisfied husband.

"I have been pleasantly surprised with Madame Suzette's artistry," admitted Caroline lightly, somehow aware of his purpose. No warmth penetrated her heart at his words. "But there are many prettier ladies here tonight. And, of course, Lady Darnley is the most stunningly beautiful woman I've ever seen." *At least on the outside*.

"I understood Waite had cut your family off."

"The old earl did. But Uncle William disagreed, though he had no idea where we were by the time he acceded to the title. He has been quite helpful."

The brief set ended and he led her to supper. Conversation lagged as he mentally prepared for his upcoming country dance with Alicia. For once, he tasted none of the lobster patties, lemon ices, or other delicacies served at this well-catered ball. Nor did he note Caroline's silence. Or her strain.

His rigid control continued through the dance with Alicia. Thank God he had contracted for this set rather than a more intimate waltz. One more lesson to take to heart for future encounters. Each touch of her fingertips as he led her through the figures burned through his gloves. Her sensual movements offered enticing views of her neckline. His lips tingled with the memory of that soft flesh, his tongue craved again the sweet nectar of her mouth. Yet his countenance revealed nothing, his conversation bordering on stilted *ennui*.

"You look lovely tonight, Lady Darnley."

"Thank you, dear Thomas. This color does become me, as you have often noted. I rarely wear any other, particularly not those vulgar reds and roses so many seem determined to flaunt. Such ill-bred choices, do you not agree?"

"I doubt Lady Jersey would," he responded, nodding briefly at the dark-haired patroness, elegantly gowned in rose silk almost the same color as Caroline's sarcenet.

"Of course, she has both the coloring and the credit to carry off such a showy hue."

The figures briefly separated them, giving him a moment to regain his composure. And Alicia as well. Her uncharacteristically uncharitable comments showed how distraught she remained over their tragic circumstances. He had done her a grave disservice by courting her love.

"A sad crush this evening, is it not?" he noted as they came back together.

"Lady Cofferton would invite the entire upper ten thousand." Alicia's lips pursed into a pout. "Guaranteeing a squeeze makes her feel important, poor thing. Personally, I prefer a more intimate gathering. This crowd is unbearably hot. Do be a dear, Thomas, and escort me outside for some air." She slanted a melting glance upward through her lashes.

But he had himself well in hand. "That would leave the set short, as you well know, Lady Darnley." They separated once again for several beats.

"When the dance is over, then," she suggested, her fingertips burning into his own.

"I am promised for the next set. And it would be unseemly in any event," he reminded her sternly, resolutely turning talk to neutral subjects for the remainder of their dance.

Exquisite torture was how he had to describe that set. The most emotionally draining minutes of his life. He wanted to crush her in his arms and ravish her on the spot. Yet he could allow no more than a chaste touch between gloved hands lest he publicly dishonor them both and destroy Eleanor's Season, to say nothing of his mother's regard. How could he survive daily meetings like this? Yet not seeing her would be worse. The unwanted delay at Crawley had been unbearable. Aside from his fears over Caroline's behavior, every moment that kept him from Alicia's side dragged with excruciating slowness. Honor might tie him to Caroline, but he had no control over his heart. It had long since been in Alicia's keeping.

Caroline was also aware the moment Alicia arrived at the ball. She had feared this meeting, not knowing how adept Thomas was at controlling his emotions, but he conducted himself well and she offered up a prayer of thanks. Few would guess that his every nerve strained in Alicia's direction. But she knew. Even as they twirled through the supper dance and engaged in light social chatter, his mind and his eyes strained toward *her*. A pang pierced the rampart surrounding her heart and she thrust it down, deliberately thickening the barrier and distancing her mind. *Don't worry,* she assured her conscience. Her interest was only lest he lose control and disgrace them all. He made it through the evening without any overt slip, and she sighed in relief. None but George and Jeremy suspected his state of mind.

But he did not come to her that night as she had hoped he would. If only they had not shared that week of passion and friendship. His experienced ministrations had awakened needs she had not previously known, leaving an unfulfilled ache behind. She had never expected much for herself from life. But having once glimpsed Eden, she could no longer be content with the mundane world. Repressing a sigh, she finally dropped off to sleep.

The following week differed from the previous fortnight only in increased tension. Thomas still hovered, waiting for her to shame him. And she felt his turmoil each time he encountered Alicia. He played the social game well, spending his days in male pursuits and accompanying her to some but not all of her evening engagements. Nor did he attend every function Alicia graced. He carefully walked the line between acceptable behavior and personal desire, never betraying a hint that his infatuation still burned. But despite his demonstrated control, she never completely relaxed. *Please, don't let him disgrace himself.*

Her senses strained toward him as much as his gravitated toward Alicia. Caroline always knew where he was. And she was amazed by some of his behavior. No matter how many friends he chatted with, and no matter what other activities he pursued, he always found time to dance with several of the less popular young ladies who were making bows to society. She watched him use his charm to relax them and draw them into conversation. The effect of his attentions often lasted after his set, many of the girls delighting their subsequent partners with lighthearted quips. Even acid-tongued Miss Gumpley improved under his ministrations. Caroline never asked him what he said to them, but she had to applaud his kindness. In the same way, she watched him rein in excess spirits in some of the younger cubs, always doing it without bruising any feelings. If only he would return to caring for her in so tender a fashion.

Always conscious of Eleanor's reputation, Thomas fought to control his eyes, his voice, his yearning whenever Alicia appeared. And he succeeded in masking his feelings—except with his wife. Caroline was the only dance partner with whom he could never relax. She imperceptibly stiffened whenever he glanced toward Alicia. He had been a fool to think she would not have learned of his love. Any number of tabbies would have been itching to tell her. And it was hardly surprising that a chit from a vicarage would disapprove of his roving eyes. Anger stirred in him. She had no right to condemn him. Her own actions were not blameless, her very public flirtation with Wroxleigh far more blatant than his own painful encounters. He was so circumspect that no one else even suspected that his love remained true. Would that she would behave so well. His irritation surfaced as cold hauteur and an increased tendency to find fault with all she did.

Darnley never appeared in public, though rumor reported that he was no longer bedridden. Alicia accepted escort from any number of gentlemen, favoring none. If her flirting with Thomas was more blatant than with others, society did not comment. Her behavior had already placed her beyond the pale, but Thomas's unexceptionable conduct convinced observers that he had outgrown his infatuation. Marriage had settled him. His wife was well-received. No evidence of continued raking surfaced, so he was again accepted everywhere. It gave him a new grievance: Caroline's credit had rescued his own tattered reputation. His anger bumped up another notch. How long could he continue this travesty of a marriage? Something had to change.

Chapter 11

Thomas's mental state continued to deteriorate, plaguing him with unbearable discontent and frustration. Each day drew him further into an escalating emotional war. Bedlam seemed inviting.

His greatest battles still revolved around his passion for Alicia. Maintaining his distance grew harder each time he saw her. As did disguising his interest. He suspected that he might be happier if he did not love her. Certainly, life would be easier. But love was not an emotion that could be summoned or banished at will. Her own attentions undermined his effort to remain aloof, though he refused to cast blame on her enticing shoulders. Barely nineteen, she lacked the experience that would have enabled her to hide her love. And she was too young to understand that even the strongest emotional attachment could not excuse dishonor. Daily he cursed himself for losing control at Graystone, degrading her and hinting that wanton behavior was acceptable where there was love. But never would he admit that part of his unease stemmed from the unpalatable fact that her attentions were cloying. He preferred the role of aggressor in his dealings with the fair sex. With Alicia, he felt like prey.

Indicative of his dilemma was the night he attended a card party at Lady Beatrice's. Caroline had accompanied Eleanor to a ball which Alicia was also to attend, and he looked forward to a relaxing evening by himself. After several hours of whist, he wandered into the garden, seeking cool air to counter the dowager's overheated rooms.

Without warning, a soft hand caressed his arm and that beloved husky voice filled the darkness.

"Thomas, my love, I have missed you so. It has been two days since I last saw you. Surely you cannot have been avoiding me."

He froze. She was even lovelier than usual tonight, her blue gown pressed tightly against her by a cooling breeze, leaving the impression that she wore nothing beneath, though he discounted the thought. Only courtesans were so lost to propriety. He had long since convinced himself that overwhelming passion had erased all memory of removing the usual undergarments at Graystone.

"Of course not, Lady Darnley," he managed, removing her hand from his sleeve and stepping back a pace. Fortunately they were in full view of the door which tipped his emotional balance in favor of honor.

"The air is wondrously fresh. Can you believe how stuffy Lady Beatrice keeps her house? Though I suppose those ancient bones of hers can no longer tolerate chills." She glided down the steps into the garden and paused expectantly so he could join her.

"It is cool enough here," he declared, refusing to move away from the door.

"I expect you are as relieved as I to get away from home for an evening," she purred, sending him a melting glance through her lashes. "You cannot enjoy being tied to an insipid wife any more than I like catering to Darnley. He is too decrepit to be considered a man. Walk with me a while."

"No, my lady," he refused again, though his voice revealed his desire. If he left the light, nothing would keep him from ravishing her.

"But I need you." She pouted. "Life is so utterly dreary." Her tone conveyed exactly what she wanted. He banished a picture of the hordes of prostitutes that routinely accosted him outside the theater.

"Never again, my lady," he stated, keeping his voice firm. "You belong to Darnley."

"But what about Graystone?"

"That was a grievous mistake, as you well know. All I can do is plead forgiveness for dishonoring you so. But I will never again betray my honor or demean your integrity by ignoring your marriage vows."

He had returned immediately to the house, cursing fate. At times he thought this struggle between honor and desire would drive him mad, yet he was incapable of cutting her from his heart and his life. Perhaps he was already mad. Surely this mindless longing could not be normal. He tried to concentrate on his sworn duty to respect and care for his wife, but the thought only raised more guilt.

If he had glanced back, he might have received help in his dilemma. Anger suffused Alicia's face. "Damn the man's scruples!" she fumed. "And damn all honor!" Several minutes elapsed before anger abated and a new plan formed in her mind. He may

disdain bedding a wife, but what would he do when Darnley
died? She knew of several widows who had enjoyed his favors in
the past.

Caroline also haunted Thomas's mind, providing constant irritation. Everything she did annoyed him. Her friends were not
those he would have chosen for her—despite the uncomfortable
fact that two of her closest were his own best friends and one was
his sister. As in her redecoration of Crawley, her new wardrobe
demonstrated a flair for color and design. Admitting she was elegant and had become more attractive than he had thought possible
triggered new comparisons with Alicia that he had trouble suppressing. Guilt was his constant companion—for demeaning her
charms, for approving her looks, for failing to support her, for
wasting time worrying about her. George and Jeremy continued
to sing her praises.

She was aware of his obsession, stiffening imperceptibly whenever he looked at Alicia or vice versa. Each glance at his love
drove a wedge deeper into his marriage. The fact pained him, but
he could do nothing about it except fume at Caroline for her
awareness. A true lady would have remained ignorant and no
damage would be done.

But her worst offense was her determined dalliance with Wroxleigh. Thomas saw red every time he considered it, his fury
stronger than he could explain away by citing her disregard for
honor. Nor was it a matter of his eventual heir, though she had a
duty to provide a son who was undisputably his. Perhaps his
anger arose from sorrow that a basically decent woman was being
taken in by so unscrupulous a libertine. But that explained nothing—certainly not the pain that generally accompanied his
thoughts. And he had no proof. She and Wroxleigh were being
unusually circumspect. Not once had they disappeared into a garden together, or driven without her maid, or used even one of the
dozens of excuses he knew firsthand could cover a clandestine
meeting. Nor was there any rumor of their liaison, not even from
the lowest-minded devotee of scandalous gossip. Yet he was convinced they were more than casual friends. And pictures of them
in each other's arms rose before his eyes at unpredictable moments, even invading his dreams.

Nor could he be sure she met only with Wroxleigh. Alicia's observations echoed through his ears at unpredictable times.

"I see Harris has broken with Lady Tudbury," she commented
during a country dance, nodding toward that gentleman who was
deep in conversation with Caroline.

"Lord Ashby must be relieved that Hazelton is no longer pursuing his wife," she observed in passing. Hazelton was twirling Caroline through a waltz at the time.

Was Caroline following in Lady Shelby's footsteps? She had been a virgin that night at the Blue Boar. But what about later? Unbidden, the glowing faces of Vicar Stokes and Squire Perkins rose before his eyes as they hung on her every word at Crawley. Their names had occurred often in her dinner conversation. Had their relationship ripened into something beyond friendship?

The third antagonist in his internal struggle was Crawley. For the first time in his life he was doing something truly worthwhile. But Jacobs's accident threatened his progress. Richards seemed to be a talented horseman, but Thomas chafed at being away at this critical time. His active imagination conjured any number of possible disasters, each causing hours of trepidation before he managed to explain it away. Even the daily reports he received from Talbert could not relieve his anxiety. Nor was he likely to be home any time soon. Whenever he mentioned leaving, his mother found a more compelling reason for him to remain. She feared that society would misconstrue his departure. Finally he admitted that she would never countenance him returning before the Season ended. And having just regained his reputation, he could not risk reendangering it. He resigned himself to staying in town.

Another struggle arose from the rumors that abounded about Alicia. Not that anyone repeated them to his face. Everyone knew of his recent infatuation and though he appeared recovered, few were willing to test that theory. But he overheard several conversations at the clubs and at Tatt's, in which she figured.

Or did she?

It had started at White's two days after his return to London. Tired of yet another round of congratulations on his marriage, he settled into a high-backed wing chair and pretended to read the *Morning Post*. Other desultory conversations did not intrude on his thoughts until two newcomers entered the room.

"I hear she's insatiable," laughingly said a deep voice he did not recognize.

"Planning to try your luck, Robby?" queried a second. *Ashton,* identified Thomas's mind. "Don't do it. Stay away from wives. You'll live longer."

"Ah, but apoplexy has confined this husband to bed—alone—so he could hardly call me out. And I would be only one of many, after all."

Ashton laughed and turned the discussion to the upcoming races.

Thomas froze. They could not be discussing Darnley, could they? Of course not. Many husbands were bedridden. Apoplexy was common. And rumor had Darnley on his feet. He dismissed the notion and returned to his paper.

But two days later the suspicion returned. He was again at White's, again anonymously ensconced behind a paper.

"I heard she accepted Dobson's protection."

"Hardly protection. But she did invite him into her bed."

"Is she as hungry as rumor implies?"

"More so, I think. But what would you expect of one so young who takes an ailing husband old enough to be her grandfather?"

Thomas's hands balled into fists, crinkling the newspaper, but the speakers had already disappeared into the card room and did not notice. Again he assured himself that they were not discussing Alicia, but the effort was more difficult. Nor did it help that his body recalled every exquisite detail of just how insatiable she could be. Memory also played havoc with his image of her sweet purity, reminding him at inconvenient times that he recalled nothing beneath her gown but a thin shift, reveling in her sensuality, feeling again her stiffened nipples brushing against his arm . . . her questing hand sliding between his legs and . . .

He thrust the memory brutally aside and indulged in a brisk walk home through a heavy downpour. Rumors were bound to circulate about so exquisite a diamond, undoubtedly begun in a fit of jealousy by some spoiled chit who resented the competition. Or an envious cub who coveted her for himself. He failed to note that something deep in his mind accepted the idea that it was Alicia the rumor discussed.

The conversation at Tattersall's nearly destroyed him. He was examining a mare, with an eye to purchasing it for Caroline's use, when Devereaux and Millhouse entered. Both were long-standing libertines, without scruples, who often competed with each other for the favors of society wives.

"I'll leave you a clear field on this one, Bertie," said Devereaux with a laugh. "The lady does not appeal to me. I like my lovers willing and impressed, not insatiable and critical. Did you know she derided Atherton last week, claiming that only Mannering could satisfy her?"

Thomas stiffened in shock. Which courtesan dared banter his name about in such a fashion?

"What about her husband?"

"Maybe in his salad days," quipped Devereaux. "But that was long before that tease was born. Well, what should I do, Bertie? Do you agree this great beast was made for me?"

Thomas fought down nausea. The only married lady he had ever bedded was Alicia. *No!* screamed his mind. *You misunderstood.* Someone had tossed his name out in a fit of pique. Or perhaps the man in question was one of his cousins. He could think of several who weren't very particular. Or had one of his widowed liaisons remarried? By stretching his imagination, he produced half a dozen situations that could have generated that bit of conversation. But he did not find sleep until after dawn.

Nor did he buy the horse.

But by far his worst problem was guilt. He was very close to hating himself. For most of his life he had taken pride in upholding honor, feeding that pride every time he sidestepped temptation or another man faltered. Honor required loyalty to one's friends, fidelity to one's vows, and performing one's obligations without resentment. It was this last point that bedeviled him now. What were his obligations? One was caring for his estate—for five years he had ignored it, wresting money from it without putting anything back and allowing his tenants to live in deplorable conditions. Another was caring for his wife—he had all but ignored her for months, then thrust her into society unprepared, providing no help and no support. The most important duty was conducting himself properly at all times—yet he had assaulted Alicia, ignoring both her vows and his own. He must regain control of his life before he brought disaster down on all their heads. It was yet another reason he longed to return to Crawley. Perhaps there he could build rapport with Caroline. Somehow, he must set aside his love for Alicia. It was the only way he could find any peace.

In the meantime he was cursed with a very short temper. Cramer began to look back on the days of his debauch as utopian and even considered seeking other employment. The earl chastised him, particularly when he exploded at Caroline in the drawing room one night for the unpardonable sin of crying off a series of three routs in favor of accompanying Cissy to a musical evening. Even he had to admit that his reaction had been unjust and that shouting in front of the servants betrayed a lack of manners that was not to be tolerated. But an afternoon at Manton's listening to George extol Caroline's virtues, and Jeremy bemoan again how lucky he was to have her to wife had finally sent his temper over the edge. Nor had a month of celibacy helped. He still refused to satisfy himself elsewhere, but his frustrations and his uncertainty over Wroxleigh kept him out of Caroline's bed.

An excited Thomas entered Tattersall's auction ring, grateful for a chance to concentrate on business. A matched pair of chestnuts was up for sale and he hoped to purchase them for Caroline.

Not that she could use them immediately. They were young, half trained, and spirited. Her driving skills were still in their infancy. Both she and the horses would require several months of daily training before they were ready for each other.

"Mannering!" exclaimed a blond-haired captain. "I haven't seen you in an age."

"Hello, Hanson." Thomas smiled. "When did you get back? I thought you were on the Peninsula."

Captain Hanson shuddered. "True. And will be again in another month or so. I truly think we have Boney on the run at last."

"Are you acting courier these days?"

"No, just recovering from a scratch I picked up a couple of months back. Congratulations on your marriage, by the way. Your wife is a lovely lady."

"Thank you. But where have you been that I haven't seen you?"

"Out by Newmarket at that mill. Wonderful bout. You should have seen it."

Thomas ruefully shook his head, for he really would have liked to attend. "The price of settling down. I was already late getting to town because of estate problems."

"Your sister has turned into quite a charmer," observed the captain obliquely.

"Are you developing an interest in that quarter?" asked Thomas in surprise.

"Possibly, though your mother seems not to approve."

"Mother disapproves of everything and everyone. I wouldn't let it worry you." Though he could see why she might try to discourage Hanson. Military life was harsh at best, yet the captain was not a career soldier. With an estate of his own and a comfortable fortune, he would make an unexceptionable husband for Eleanor, and with similar natures that craved action and excitement, they were probably well-suited. "So tell me about the mill," he urged, turning the subject. "Was McKay as formidable as reported?"

"More so." Hanson embarked on a blow-by-blow description

that lasted well into the day's auction. Thomas's tacit approval went a long way toward settling his feelings about Lady Eleanor.

Thomas thoroughly enjoyed their talk, which soon ranged over additional topics, including a realistic assessment of the never-ending war with Napoleon. He kept one eye on the auction ring, buying a promising colt and two well-conformed broodmares, then remained silent as several riding hacks changed hands. He had still not found a horse for Caroline, but none in today's offering would do.

At last the bidding began for the pair he wanted. They were clearly the best horses up for sale and interest was widespread. The price rapidly approached his limit.

"Four hundred," he offered, hoping it would suffice. All had dropped out at three except Delaney's heir, young Lawrence. Barely eighteen, the lad had descended on London the week before, and was already eagerly sowing wild oats. Thomas smiled at memories of himself at that age. How simple life had been.

"I wonder if the cub has any sense at all," he murmured to Hanson as the boy paused to consider what to do next.

"Eight hundred," Delaney announced to a collective gasp from the crowd.

"Obviously not," replied Hanson in sympathy.

Thomas shook his head. "At least he is well to grass." What would Lord Delaney say when he learned his son had paid double their value for a pair of half-trained horses? Thomas smiled his capitulation. Perhaps he would have better luck next week.

That night everyone from Marchgate House attended a musical evening across the square at Lord Pressington's modest town house. Both London's newest singer and a well-regarded harpist would perform. As was customary, several young ladies would also demonstrate their skills, but such potential penance could not dampen Caroline's spirits.

Not until they arrived did she learn that the Pressingtons were Alicia's parents. As they approached along the receiving line, Lady Darnley began a *sotto voce* conversation with her mother, all the while staring daggers at Caroline. She began to feel uncomfortable. Nor did the smug smile that concluded their chat relieve her trepidation. But she soon relaxed. The vocalist was magnificent and the incident rapidly faded from memory.

"Thuch power and grace," commented Robert, accompanying her to the refreshment room during the interval. "And Mozart is so intense."

Caroline nodded. "I saw her last week in *Don Giovanni*, but I believe I enjoyed tonight more. I could hear." Her eyes twinkled wickedly as Robert broke into helpless giggles.

"You are certainly in looks tonight, Caroline," said Drew as he joined them. His eyes appreciatively scanned her figure. "But what have you done to send poor Hartford into a spasm?"

"Nothing, Drew. You look rather nice yourself. Have you broken many hearts lately?"

"Alas, no. I must be losing my touch."

"Any number of mothers would doubtless welcome such a disaster," she teased. "But do either of you know to whom we will be subjected in the next segment?"

Drew laughed, but shook his head.

"No more than three or four, I expect," offered Robert in consolation, his lisp less obvious this night. "There is still the harpist. I would guess Miss Bromley to start, for Lady Pressington is her aunt. And Lady Darnley to finish, though that is no problem. Her playing is lovely."

Mention of the fair Alicia dampened Caroline's enthusiasm, and reminded her of that odd, whispered exchange. But she hid her unease behind a social smile and turned the conversation to gossip, allowing Robert to regale her with the latest *on-dits*. Nor would she let her eyes drift to the strained discussion between Thomas and his idol across the room, though she sensed every minute of it, relaxing only when Thomas turned to speak with Eleanor.

They soon returned to their seats for the amateur portion of the program. Miss Bromley was indeed the first performer and acquitted herself adequately but without flair. Another niece, Miss Evelyn Pressington, performed next, with unfortunate results. Nervous, she floundered early in her sonata, her composure cracking badly when Alicia tittered. Caroline's temper flared dangerously. How could Lady Darnley tease her cousin in such a publicly cruel manner? Even Thomas appeared shocked. Poor Miss Pressington never recovered, concluding her performance in a crash of discords after a single movement. The applause was more appreciative of her decision to retire than of her playing.

Lady Pressington stared directly at Caroline as she rose to thank Evelyn, restoring her uneasiness. "I have heard claims that Mrs. Mannering is a gifted musician. Not having heard her play, I would take this opportunity to remedy that deficiency. Mrs. Mannering?"

And how had she heard that? wondered Caroline, unable to

imagine Thomas bragging about his wife to his lover. Then she caught a glimpse of Alicia and nearly burst out laughing. The Incomparable's face radiated malicious gloating. Knowing that Caroline grew up in a vicarage and was unfamiliar with the *ton,* she plotted to embarrass her by revealing her lack of accomplishments. Caroline stifled an unchristian spurt of glee and smiled at her hostess.

"My pleasure, Lady Pressington." She thought quickly as she seated herself at the keyboard. The pianoforte was of excellent quality, with a full, rich sound she had admired all evening. And in perfect tune. Spurning the music sheets piled on a nearby table, she chose instead a recently published sonata by Herr Beethoven, his *Pathétique* in C minor, and instantly lost herself in the notes.

Thomas sat spellbound as Caroline moved from the somber introduction to the passionate *allegro.* The music grabbed his heart, pulling the emotional strings first one way, then another. Not since he accidentally overheard her practicing the first week of their marriage had he listened to her play. Nor had he believed that a single piece of music could unleash the power, majesty, or poignancy captured in this one. Within moments, he found his spirit soaring among the clouds. His frustrations faded into the background, leaving him in charity with her for the first time in weeks.

Caroline allowed the final flourish to die away before lifting her hands from the keys. It always took a moment to return to the world, particularly after a piece with which she felt so closely attuned. The gathered audience must have felt the same way, for stunned silence continued a moment longer before she was engulfed in applause, accolades, and appreciation. Only Alicia refrained, her eyes blazing in fury.

"Encore!" shouted a male voice and the cry was quickly taken up.

"Only one," she agreed when Lady Pressington repeated the request.

This time she chose Beethoven's gentle *Für Elise,* letting the notes slide across the room, binding her listeners in a seductive spell of love and peace. They exhaled in a collective sigh of loss when the last note died away.

"Remarkable talent," breathed Drew as she passed his chair.

"Thank you."

"Exquisite!" Robert beamed. He had missed none of the by-play. "You certainly rolled up her catty ladyship."

"I wish I could play half as well," mourned Eleanor.

Thomas remained silent, his face a study of awe. But he turned a smile on Caroline that sent her heart racing. She remembered that smile.

Lady Darnley chose to play a challenging Scarlatti sonata. Caroline listened for some time before she identified the source of her disappointment. Though an excellent technician whose fingers executed the most difficult passages with ease, Alicia's performance did not engage the senses.

Her mother had been right. *You must throw your heart into your music, Caro,* she had constantly admonished her during her years of instruction. *Think your way into the notes. Live there. Feel what the composer was feeling. Imagine what he was thinking. Only thus can you ever hope to engage your audience.*

And it was true. Heartless Alicia felt no connection with either composer or opus. All emotion was missing. She might as well have been playing scales.

Thomas was also puzzled over his lack of response. But he finally discovered an excuse. Beethoven wrote for the pianoforte, taking advantage of its full, vibrant tone and exceptional dynamic range. Scarlatti had written for harpsichord. Any lack in Alicia's performance was due to the composer's restricted medium. Satisfied on an intellectual level, he nevertheless encountered no difficulty restraining his applause to the brief acknowledgment politeness demanded for any performer. The audience was on the move toward the refreshment room while Alicia's last chord still echoed. No calls for an encore greeted her. Thomas refused to question either the situation or his own satisfaction over the turn of events.

He could not approach Caroline through her crowd of admirers and chose not to approach Alicia, whose face resembled a thundercloud. He instead turned to food and a new round of congratulations from friends and acquaintances that he wholeheartedly echoed.

Even the harpist proved anticlimactic.

Chapter 12

Caroline perched on a chair near the drawing room door, trying to avoid spilling tea on Lady Marchgate's carpet as she fought to confine her laughter to a ladylike chuckle that would not attract the attention of Eleanor's callers. Drew could be so droll.

"You impossible man," she chided, once she controlled her mirth. "How dare you embarrass me like this?"

Drew adopted a hangdog expression with eyes sad enough to induce sympathetic tears in the hardest heart.

"How can I forgive myself for so distressing you," he intoned in a sepulchral bass.

Caroline giggled. "Stop that. Now sit down and behave like the gentleman you are not."

"Ah, a mortal wound!" But his eyes were laughing and he sat. "Who would have thought I would discover a lady with whom I could be friends? You've added a new dimension to my life, Caro."

"Fustian. There are any number of females who would enjoy friendship with you, cousin," she declared. "But you will have to pull your brain out of bed to discover them. To say nothing of the rest of you."

"That's asking a lot, coz." He laughed. "I daren't take you driving again for a while or the tabbies will gossip, but what about an early morning ride tomorrow?"

"All our horses remain at Crawley."

"That is not a problem, sweet Caroline," urged Drew, letting his voice resume its usual seductive cadence. "I can mount you whenever you wish."

Caroline shook her head in exasperation. "Thank you, but not tomorrow. I have other plans."

"Spurned again!" he exclaimed dramatically.

"Oh, do be serious, Drew," admonished Caroline. "Eleanor's ball is tomorrow night and I really must help."

"Of course." He rose to take his leave.

*   *   *

Fists clenched, Thomas continued upstairs. He had passed the drawing room just in time to overhear Wroxleigh's promise to mount Caroline and her breathless acceptance. Between his own history of flirtatious double entendre and his chancy temper, he immediately assumed they were arranging an assignation. Fury engulfed him, more intense than ever. The approval he had felt at the musicale had not lasted the evening, being blasted to shreds when he spotted her with Wroxleigh, their expressions demonstrating a closeness of spirit he had rarely witnessed.

It was time to do something about her escalating affair. She was his. He expected adherence to the same code of honor he himself espoused. That meant no dalliance. If he could refrain from bedding the woman he loved, she could certainly forgo a casual affair with a heartless, teasing rake like Wroxleigh! He would never live down the ignominy if her actions became public. Imagine Thomas Mannering unable to satisfy his wife! He must speak to her.

But she did not return upstairs and when he questioned her whereabouts, Reeves informed him that she and Jeremy had gone to Somerset House to view paintings. Such independence ill became a lady. He longed for Alicia's clinging helplessness. It was past time they held a serious discussion about propriety. But she was still out when he joined George at his club for dinner.

Caroline had been delighted when Lady Marchgate asked her, shortly after her arrival, to assist with the preparations for Eleanor's ball. Never having attended such a function, let alone planned one, she looked upon the experience as training for her own future entertainments. And the amount of work involved astonished her. Under the countess's tutelage she learned the nuances of guest lists, precedence conventions, seating for the formal dinner preceding the ball, catering arrangements, wine choices, decorating, and a thousand and one other details. The logistics of hundreds of coaches converging on a single spot swirled through her head. Then there was the problem of accommodating five hundred guests, combining rooms to form a ballroom, setting up card rooms, refreshment rooms, retiring rooms, cloak rooms— the list went on and on. Servants, musicians, candles, flowers. Her head spun. But she rapidly discovered that her talent for organization created order out of potential chaos. And by the day of the ball, the countess had dropped all pretense of formality. The two were fast friends.

Standing in the receiving line, she graciously welcomed each new arrival while striving not to detract from Eleanor's come-out. The Marchgates had insisted that she receive, placing the final seal of approval on her introduction to London society, although the ball itself was solely in Eleanor's honor. After only a month in London, she was amazed at how many of the guests she knew.

Thomas stood beside her, his easy social smile firmly in place, but inwardly he seethed. He had found no opportunity to speak to her about Wroxleigh. Nor did he know what he would say when he did confront her. His lapse at Graystone still haunted him. Could he condemn her without confessing his own fault? His thinking was becoming so muddled that he was no longer sure he could trust his own judgment. And that was dangerous for it invariably led to failure. Every time it happened, someone got hurt. When he had dared Robert to ride a horse he could not control, Robert had nearly broken his neck. When he had stupidly decided to flaunt his expertise on ice, he had nearly drowned.

He stifled a shudder at another memory he had not thought of in years. Even at twelve, he should have known better. His actions had been both reckless and dishonorable. During a long break spent with George's family, conversation had turned to ghosts, specifically to the gentleman who supposedly appeared each Midsummer's Eve in Blatchford's oldest wing. George's sister, Mary, had openly scoffed at the legend, deriding the boys as fools for claiming to believe it. In response, Thomas had delivered an impassioned defense of the spirit world, daring her to confront the spectral visitor for herself. But he would have done nothing else if George had not discovered a secret passage that very afternoon. It opened near the Elizabethan wing, its existence too provident to ignore. And so he had succumbed to temptation. On Midsummer's Eve, as full dark fell, a slender gentleman dressed in the doublet and hose of an Elizabethan courtier stepped from a seemingly solid wall to confront Mary Mason. She screamed and fled in panic. But Thomas's glee turned to horror when she tripped on her hem and tumbled down a flight of stairs, breaking her leg. As servants converged on the spot, he threw honor to the winds and faded back into the secret passage, never telling a soul about his part in the debacle, though guilt assailed him for years afterward.

Why had the memory surfaced now? Was his conscience castigating him for ravishing Alicia? Or was he in danger of initiating

some new disgrace? His pain and anger over Caroline's liaison
with Wroxleigh was nearing the explosion point, as was his frustration. Was he on the verge of again doing something stupid?

His temper worsened as the evening progressed. Caroline
talked even less than usual as he led her into the opening dance.
Nor could she hide an involuntary flinch as his hand touched hers
unexpectedly. It was the first time she had ever demonstrated that
she found his presence repulsive, and it confirmed his suspicion
that she was seeking satisfaction elsewhere.

For Caroline, Thomas's presence constituted a burgeoning
problem. Daily she watched him flirt with countless women,
charm self-conscious maidens, advise green cubs, and converse
intelligently with worthy gentlemen. He demonstrated a character
she could only admire, except with herself and Lady Darnley. Despite his aloof expression when in Alicia's company, Caroline
could feel his desire. She was aware of every look he bestowed on
his idol and every longing glance when he believed himself unob-
served. And despite his parody of being an infatuated husband
when in her company, she could feel his frustration behind the ice
wall that stood between them. How could he continue to dance attendance on a self-centered, manipulative baggage like Lady
Darnley? Did the man not have ears? Tales of Alicia's scandalous
behavior were so ubiquitous that even innocent maidens knew of
her exploits. Yet he continued to adore her. Why was Caroline the
only one aware of his obsession?

She had no answers and refused to acknowledge the pain resid-
ing in her heart. She concentrated on her own circle of friends,
her own social calendar, her own interests. Aside from an occasional dance together, she spent no time in his company. But the
hour standing shoulder to shoulder in the receiving line had been
pure torture. The passions he had aroused remained unfulfilled,
tormenting her nights. Nor could she expect the future to differ,
she reminded herself when her body strained for contact with her
husband. But it took time to reexert control. When he accidentally
brushed his hand against hers as they took their places for the first
set, she flinched at the heat. His lips twisted in distaste with the
contact, obviously regretting their hasty marriage and wishing
that it had never taken place.

As assistant hostess, she could not spend her evening entirely
carefree, but she found time for her friends. Her performance at
the Pressington musicale still engendered a surprising amount of
comment.

"You never cease to amaze me," swore George as he spun her

through a waltz an hour later. "But I demand a chance to hear you play at the earliest opportunity. You've no idea how I regret not attending that musicale."

"I believe the situation has been exaggerated," she protested with a laugh. "But sometime soon you can judge for yourself."

"Lady Darnley is still seething," he reported. "She never could tolerate coming off second best."

"Actually," confided Caroline, "she planned to thoroughly embarrass the country nobody by maneuvering me into floundering in public just before her own polished performance. If looks could kill, I would still be stretched across the Pressington pianoforte."

George burst out laughing, nearly tripping them both.

"Dear God, I wish I had been there! What a remarkable miscalculation. And such an utterly fitting revenge. How was her performance, by the way?"

"Technically brilliant but heartless and emotionally dead," she said succinctly. "Very like the lady herself."

"Too true. How did Thomas react?"

"He seemed almost satisfied," she murmured in surprise. "I must have misread his face. He has not mentioned it since."

"Interesting," was George's only comment as the music swirled to an end.

Caroline left to check the refreshment room for potential problems. Robert claimed a set upon her return.

"Thuch a lovely gown, my dear," he began as usual. She was clad in ivory lace over dusty blue silk.

"Thank you, Robert. And you present your usual sartorial splendor." His coat tonight was bright green, his breeches yellow, and his waistcoat embroidered in every color of the rainbow, an appearance that brought to mind Helena's descriptions of her grandmama-in-law's lurid decorating. She nearly giggled.

The dance separated them.

"Do you think Brummel and Prinny will make up their quarrel?" he asked when they next came together.

"Has something new occurred?" she wondered. "The last I heard, the Beau had slighted Lady Fitzherbert."

"Oh, yes," tittered Robert. "The Prince is furious, for Brummel has now disparaged his choice of snuff."

"Goodness. I would hardly expect such a considerable breach to be healed this Season. Would you?"

"No. Perhaps next year."

Again the dance separated them.

"Mother is most appreciative of your help with Eleanor's ball," he said sincerely later on with no sign of his usual lisp.

"I have enjoyed it immensely," she admitted. "And I expect I will bless the experience one day."

"She is calmer now than after Emily's come-out, despite her winter illness. I am grateful." Intelligence simmered in his usually vacuous eyes. Had Emily and Thomas underestimated his abilities? Just because he was not bookishly brilliant, one could not assume stupidity. Did he employ an emptyheaded demeanor to avoid competing intellectually with his siblings?

"Thank you for a most gracious compliment." She smiled, dipping into a curtsy at the end of their dance.

Supper proceeded smoothly and Caroline was able to relax, enjoying Drew's wit. They shared a table with the Wembleys and Captains Felton and Harrington, home from the Peninsula to recover from wounds. For once Drew abandoned his ingrained flirting, engaging in a lively discussion on the prognosis for the war following Napoleon's disastrous retreat from Moscow the past winter. From there, conversation turned to Wembley's efforts on behalf of veterans, and then to dissecting Byron's latest, *The Giaour,* which all had actually read in its entirety. It was the most entertaining exchange she had enjoyed in London.

But most of the time, her duties as assistant hostess kept her busy. The ball was a sad crush, made insufferable by the unusually warm evening. She lost count of the ladies overcome by the heat. Even some gentlemen were affected. She was helping yet another dowager to find a cooler place in which to recover when she came upon an agitated Lady Marchgate in the hall.

"I will take care of Edna," the countess declared. "But would you please check with the caterers and discover why the punch bowl has been allowed to empty? We ordered plenty. Even the heat cannot have depleted the supply."

"Immediately." But it took nearly half an hour to resolve the contretemps that had arisen between the Marchgate servants and the caterer's staff.

Thomas's suspicions and that snippet of conversation with Wroxleigh goaded him into watching Caroline more than usual this night. Not even Alicia held his thoughts for long. His stomach tightened as Wroxleigh led her out for the second set, eliciting smiles and far more animation than she had accorded him. Anger increased when the notorious viscount also shared the supper dance with her. And anger turned to fury late in the evening when he could locate neither of them in the ballroom. Nor were they in the refreshment room.

Caroline had just dismissed Dawson for the night when a glowering Thomas pushed open the connecting door and raked her with a cold stare.

"Is something amiss?" she asked calmly. She knew of no problem that could be blamed on her, not that Thomas would let that stand in his way. Despite the pretense of cordiality he generally adopted, he now looked as icy as he had in the worst days at Crawley.

"Why were you gone so long this evening?" he demanded.

"After supper? There was a problem with the caterers."

"Surely Mother should have seen to it, if such a thing really happened," he snapped.

Caroline's brows drew together, his blatant disbelief fanning her own anger. "Your mother asked me to handle it as she had her hands full with Lady Blakeley. Or are you unaware that the lady took ill?"

"And I suppose it was coincidence that Wroxleigh was absent from the ballroom for the same length of time?" Sarcasm dripped from every word.

"Yes, if he was. What are you implying?"

"I imply nothing. I am telling you. Leave Wroxleigh alone. I don't want to see you near him again."

"How dare you dictate my friends, Thomas," she sputtered. "How dare you! You gave up any right to run my life when you chose to ignore me and sent me to town without so much as an introduction."

Fury threatened to strangle him. "Enough! I should have known better than to marry one of Waite's brood. Be warned. I am wise to your game, wife. But I will not be cuckolded by anyone, least of all by that unprincipled libertine. Are you aware that you are nothing to him but another conquest? He specializes in seducing dissatisfied wives."

Caroline's fury at his unwarranted charges loosened her temper, particularly in light of his own disreputable past and continuing obsession with Alicia. "You are incredibly stupid if you believe such ridiculous fantasies," she snarled. "Or are you attributing your own failings to me? Does it excuse your behavior if others are worse? Your reputation is hardly spotless, nor can I assume that tales of your exploits are confined to the past. But at least you admit I have cause to be dissatisfied!"

Thomas abandoned any curb over his temper, grabbing her by the shoulders and shaking violently. "So," he spat as she struggled to escape, landing a punch in his stomach, "my pious vicarage wife has claws. You have remained far too long in town. It has not improved your character. No one ever implies I leave them unsatisfied."

"Arrogant fool!" she hissed. "Conceited toad! How long has it been since you paid the slightest attention to my needs? Dissatisfied doesn't begin to describe this wife, sirrah!" She shoved against his chest, trying to break free of his grasp.

"How dare you!" he roared, green eyes flashing fire as he batted her hands aside. Jerking her closer, he crushed his mouth across hers, temper goading him to brand her as his own. She parried his tongue, their furious fencing suddenly transforming to a sensuous duel as each became aware of the moist heat and velvety texture of the other.

Passion exploded, blinding them to all else. His hands tore frenziedly at her bedgown, while hers frantically attacked his nightshirt, both intent only on shredding the barriers that separated them.

His loins tightened painfully as her bounteous breasts burst into view, exquisite twin globes that had haunted his dreams for months. He shoved her onto the bed, his mouth already closing about one rigid peak, his tongue lapping greedily at its tip. His fingers clutched its mate, stroking, kneading, driving her into writhing ecstasy, her moans a siren's song that banished all thought.

Her body tingled as sparks ignited every nerve. It had been so long. So very long. She pulled him closer, arching into his touch, her hands clawing desperately at his back, her mouth working on anything within reach. Her legs twined about his, stroking up and down, reveling in his masculinity. His mouth swooped to hers, his plunging tongue plundering her depths even as his hand sank into her nest of curls. She screamed, shudders convulsing her body.

Need exploded through him. Urgent need. Jerking her hips to meet his own, he frantically sheathed himself, pounding her mercilessly into the bed, agony building as she locked her legs around his hips to pull him deeper. Again he fastened lips to her breast, suckling until her taut nipple teased the roof of his mouth, sending new fire racing through his veins. His rhythm accelerated, thrusting deeper and deeper, building tension, concentrating it . . .

Her teeth sank into his shoulder as a shattering climax engulfed them both, more intense than ever before, a cataclysmic explosion rending flesh from bone that went on and on and on. . . .

Utterly drained, they drifted in darkness for an eternity before opening their eyes. Brown met green like clashing swords. For with satiation, memory returned. And anger. And pride. Neither would admit to enjoying this night.

And nothing had changed.

Thomas sat up and glared. Both her nightclothing and his had suffered irreparable damage in their mutual onslaught. "You are mine, wife. You will not permit Wroxleigh to hover around you again," he ordered coldly.

"I will choose my own friends, sirrah," snapped Caroline, just as coldly. His continued intransigence hardened her heart. "As you choose yours. Does Darnley ring the same peal over his wife concerning you?"

"How dare you compare me to a vile seducer like Wroxleigh! I have never been in the habit of bedding other men's wives!" But his voice wavered on the last word. The Graystone bookroom shimmered before his eyes, along with the remembered sensation of light fingers caressing his length. Pain suffused his face before he fastened his social mask in place.

She saw that flash of agony. And understood it. Turning her back, she pulled the coverlet to her neck lest her own pain be remarked. Her fingernails dug into her palms as she fought to hold tears at bay. Arrogant, odious wretch! How lowering that he believed her capable of such deceit. But even if he were right, how dare he hold her to standards he himself flouted!

Her apparent rejection cut deep into his heart. An unexpected urge to explain pushed his hand out to her in supplication before anger again took control. Why should he justify his one lapse to someone guilty of far more crimes? Her attack on his expertise still rankled. Sliding to the floor, he slammed out of her room.

He sounds jealous, whispered a voice in her mind through the reverberation of the door. *Fustian*, she replied, lips quivering. *He is merely dictatorial, suspicious, and odiously possessive, even of that which he does not want*. The last thought shattered all control.

Her muffled sobs lasted until dawn.

It took a decanter of brandy to put Thomas to sleep.

Chapter 13

A nearly sleepless night left Caroline lightheaded and slightly nauseated, but she hid her indisposition and accompanied the countess on her morning rounds. Their first stop was Lady Beatrice's mansion where several callers were already ensconced in the drawing room.

"Lady Martha Fitzgerald and Sir Jason Bromley were caught in a most indecent embrace at the Dumbarton soiree last night," reported Lady Debenham, her voice hinting at envy.

"I presume a betrothal announcement will be in tomorrow's paper," commented the purple-robed Lady Beatrice.

"Hardly surprising," Lady Stafford put in. "He's been living in her pocket for weeks."

"Could they have planned it?" murmured an ample matron swathed in puce. "Her father has been vacillating over granting approval for the match. Despite Sir Jason's fortune, he is merely a baronet."

The company discussed this possibility for some time while Caroline sipped tea and nibbled on lemon wafers and seed cake. She had not partaken of breakfast, fearing to face the astute earl who would certainly have noted her sleepless night and deduced that she and Thomas had indulged in a rather nasty fight. Which they had, of course. Recounting that scene, even in memory, would have sent her into fresh tears.

In retrospect, she never should have married him. The lack of any pretense of affection doomed them from the start. Nor had he been truthful, despite his words at the time. In the confusion of the moment she had allowed his charm to overrule her usual good sense, condemning them both to this charade. She should have brazened out the possible scandal. After all, what was the worst outcome? Loss of her position, leaving her back at the vicarage. She would have survived. Instead, she was trapped into life with someone who resented her very existence. And her fortitude was rapidly running out. But she could not yet see a solution.

"Lord Darnley passed away last night," reported Lady Beatrice, preening that she was the first with the news. Her voice recalled Caroline's attention to the conversation.

"Probably just as well," commented Lady Stafford. "He could not have been happy confined to bed."

"I wonder . . . Will his wife observe mourning?" a malicious voice asked.

"She certainly has made no secret that she cares nought for the man," agreed another.

"Scandalous behavior," condemned a third. "I will not receive her. My dear Lisa's reputation could be ruined by contact with the woman. She is little better than . . ." She halted abruptly as she recalled that innocent maidens were present.

Two matrons started a murmured conversation detailing what each had heard of Lady Darnley's exploits and the growing estimate of how many gentlemen she had welcomed. Caroline tuned it out, pondering how this would affect her own situation.

Disastrously.

Already regretting their marriage, Thomas would now have further cause to resent her. Alicia was free. Though convention demanded at least a year of mourning for a deceased husband, Lady Darnley would hardly adhere to such an empty gesture.

Nor did she believe that Thomas could resist his passion for the woman of his dreams. Despite his denial that he bedded wives, he had obviously made an exception for Alicia. Now that she was a widow, he would have no cause to restrain himself. Such a liaison could only drive the wedge further between them, for Caroline now represented the only barrier between Thomas and his heart's desire. He would not only curse her existence, he would also curse the fate that forced their union only months before Alicia was free to marry him herself.

Talk had now moved into the normal channels of who had driven with whom in the park, which couples had slipped into the gardens the evening before, and how much money had changed hands at the tables. Caroline and Lady Marchgate rose to leave. Already new callers had arrived to be greeted with the latest news.

Two more calls elicited no additional gossip. The same stories graced everyone's lips. Speculation was rampant on how Lady Darnley would greet widowhood. Many welcomed the news of a mourning period. It would allow them to drop her from their guest lists without offering a direct cut. Scandalous though it was, her behavior had not quite reached a point demanding ostracism. Darnley had maintained enough credit to protect his wife.

Thomas learned of Darnley's demise directly from Alicia. He had hardly finished his breakfast—a meal that sat heavily in his stomach after a night of anger and brandy—when a footman brought him a scented note. He stared at the words for a long time, thought suspended as his mind fought to make sense of the message.

The viscount's death was hardly unexpected. What surprised him was Alicia's request that he assist her in arranging the funeral. What should he do? He would like nothing better than to see her, spend time with her, aid her in her time of need. But prudence demanded that he avoid any contact, particularly alone in her home. She was in deepest mourning and could not properly entertain any but relatives. He was a married man, not available to indulge his desires. For the first time Caroline hung like a gigantic millstone around his neck, pulling him into the bowels of hell, away from the life-giving sun. He hated the trap he was caught in. But he worshipped honor above all else. At least he wanted to. But it was so difficult . . .

Alicia needed him. Not because she grieved, though she was undoubtedly saddened at Darnley's passing. But she faced so many difficult decisions. No lady should have to cope alone. He could ease her confusion so easily. Could a friend not help a new widow understand the complexities surrounding death? How else could he demonstrate his love in an acceptable way?

Not acceptable, not acceptable, murmured his conscience in reply. The duty fell to Darnley's heir. And that man was in town and available. Pain gripped him for an opportunity lost but his will never wavered.

Moisture clouded his eyes as he penned his reply, offering condolences and recommending that she consult the new Lord Darnley. He dispatched a footman with the missive, then forced his feet to Jackson's for his regular sparring practice. He could allow no hint of his true feelings to show nor interrupt his routine. But melancholy blanketed his spirits even as he laughed and joked with his friends.

Life limped on. Thomas concealed his struggles when in public, but made little effort to hide them at home. He rarely spoke to Caroline, confining himself to terse comments when unable to avoid silence. Confused dreams tormented his nights. No details remained, but he slept poorly, developing a haunted look around his eyes.

Caroline determinedly pursued her own interests, rising early to ride in the park with Drew or Jeremy, enjoying London's intellectual offerings with her bosom bows, and continuing the round of parties and other entertainments in the evenings. She made her debut at Almack's—agreeing with Emily afterward that it had to be the most insipid stop on the social circuit—and thoroughly enjoyed the Warburton masquerade, an annual event open only to those of the highest *ton*. The only improvement was not having to watch Alicia's nightly flirtations as that lady was, for the moment, observing mourning.

She had given up all hope of a rapprochement with Thomas. Darnley's death had crystallized his anger, for the first time graphically pointing out his situation. Without her, he could marry Alicia. She could see it in his eyes whenever he looked at her. The unwanted encumbrance . . . the thorn in his side . . . the locked gate separating him from heaven. . . . She concentrated on his coldness, trying to forget the friendship they had found at first, to ignore the charmer he so often acted for others, to block out memories of his passion. It did no good to consider what she could not have.

She entered the library one afternoon, seeking a book, and was surprised to find the earl sitting at his desk.

"Pardon me for disturbing you. I did not know anyone was in here."

"I was not working," he disclaimed immediately. "And you are welcome at any time, as you well know."

"Thank you."

He examined her face before continuing. Her eyes showed evidence of restless sleep and unhappiness tightened her mouth. Mentally cursing his son, he decided to stick his oar into the water.

"Has Thomas been ignoring you?" he asked bluntly.

"No more than usual." She looked at her father-in-law in surprise, then realized that Thomas's antagonism had been more apparent since Darnley's death. Naturally the earl would have noticed.

"Is there some problem that could benefit from discussion?" he pursued.

So be it, she decided. "You know very well what the problem is, my lord. Lady Darnley."

He sighed. "I was not certain if you were aware of that situation."

"I have known of his feelings since the first week of our marriage," she admitted. "But there is nothing to be done but allow his obsession to run its course." That it might never do so was something she was not prepared to voice, though with Thomas's history, she feared it would prove true. And given his state of mind, there was little chance he would turn to her even if it vanished.

"He actually told you?" exclaimed the earl in surprise.

"Of course not, but he talks in his sleep."

"I will speak with the boy," he declared, lips compressed into an angry line. "He must be made to realize what a disservice he is doing you by his continued intransigence."

But she immediately threw up a hand in protest. "No, please do not mention the subject. It would only make matters worse."

He raised his brows in surprise.

"You know how obsessed he can be," she tried to explain. "And despite what you just said, you also know how poorly he will greet interference. Why else did you wait eight months before intervening last time?"

"You know about that?" He sounded surprised.

"He mentioned your conversation and conditions for bailing him out as part of his effort to convince me that marriage was our only alternative. You won that round, but I would never accept odds that you could repeat the feat. Thomas throws his heart into everything he does, but only in the case of Lady Darnley is he truly obsessed. I am sure you know how unworthy the lady is."

He nodded.

Caroline went on. "By all accounts she is celebrating widowhood with an orgy of self-gratification. Sooner or later Thomas is bound to discover that. He cannot remain blind forever. In the meantime, interference can only cause disaster.

"And what can you condemn? His behavior? His *behavior* is everything that is proper. Were he to cut Lady Darnley, the *ton* would have a field day. Likewise, pretending to be barely acquainted would convince the tabbies of a passionate affair. He has managed the precise touch of old friends who have moved on to new interests. Nor has he sought her out since Darnley's death."

She paced the room while he watched in respectful silence.

"And can you condemn a man's thoughts? His desires? What man can control another's mind? Can you force your ideas into a fixed pattern, preventing all other notions from intruding? Of course not. Nor can you force another to accept truths he is unwilling to concede. He would resent the effort, creating a rift between you. Even if you convinced him of her true character, the resentment would remain. But I doubt even you would succeed. Opposition would make him cling more tightly to his beliefs. We can only pray that his own common sense will discern the truth. And you must admit that he is hiding his feelings well. None but his closest friends know of his turmoil. If we distress him at home, he may lose that self-control and disgrace the entire family. We must be patient. This is a problem Thomas will have to work out for himself."

The earl frowned as he pondered her words. Several minutes slipped by in silence.

"You are right, my dear," he finally agreed. "As long as his public demeanor remains controlled I will not interfere, though his treatment of you is beyond shabby."

"Yet he needs an outlet. Better me than someone public." How had she uttered such rubbish with a straight face? But a moment's thought pointed out its truth. The only respect he accorded her was honesty. Would she really prefer feigned affection?

"He does not deserve you. I only hope that some day he will realize what a jewel he has in his keeping."

"Nonsense. I am no paragon, but I expect we will muddle along somehow. If you will excuse me, I must change. Eleanor wishes me to accompany her to Lady Debenham's."

She slipped out of the library, anxious to reach her own room before any trace of tears filled her eyes. If only the earl had not decided to raise this subject! The situation was becoming unbearable, for Thomas's scorn and antagonism embedded a hundred pins under her skin every day. Nor did she understand how that could be. Granted, she did not like to see anyone caught in an impossible coil, but that did not explain her frustration.

Have you formed a tendre for him? asked that voice. She froze in horror. *Never, never, never!* What a terrifying thought. Handsome he might be (green eyes blazing with passion floated momentarily in her mirror), intelligence she would grant him, but he was the most stubborn, odious, thick-headed wretch alive. Yet why else did her heart leap when he entered a room? And why could his rare smile quicken her breath? Tremors shook her and she forced the thought brutally aside.

She summoned Dawson to help her change. Fifteen minutes later she accompanied Eleanor and Lady Marchgate across the square.

"My dears, the most delicious story!" exclaimed Lady Debenham before they had even found a seat. "Brummel held a celebra-
tion at the Argyle rooms last night and Alvanley arrived in the
company of the Prince. But Prinny has not forgiven that last
slight. He administered the cut direct."

Several ladies gasped.

"Whatever did Brummel do then?" asked Lady Scarfield.

Lady Debenham smiled in glee. "Why in a bored drawl asked,
'Alvanley, who's your fat friend?' "

"The cut sublime!"

"Prinny will never forgive this!"

Caroline ignored the exclamations. Her conversation with the
earl still echoed in her mind, threatening her control. What was
she to do about her marriage? The way things were going, she did
not see how she could last until the end of the Season. Controlling
her emotions grew more difficult every day. Treacherous tears
fought to free themselves. She was rapidly becoming a watering
pot. And that would never do. She forced her attention back to the
drawing room.

Lady Beatrice was announced.

"I know all about Brummel's latest," she proclaimed immediately. "Far more shocking is young Delaney's behavior."

"What is that scamp up to now?" wondered Lady Stafford. His
escapades had amused Mayfair's drawing rooms since his arrival
some weeks earlier.

"Hmph! This is no oat sowing," sniffed Lady Beatrice. "He has
revealed himself as an insufferable *voyeur* with a sad lack of
decorum."

Gasps filled her pause.

"Why, early this very morning he burst into his aunt's bedroom—while that poor lady was in complete *déshabillé*—bold as
brass, without even knocking! Startled her out of her wits. Her
hysterics nearly brought the house down. And did that induce the
boy to leave? It did not! Just stood there, staring at her and grinning."

"Good heavens! How awful for Lady Feldham."

"Has she recovered?"

"What did they do to Delaney?"

Lady Beatrice drew a deep breath, pleased at the reception of
her news. "That boy should be sent back to school immediately.
He has certainly forfeited the right to be received. And what
about his sister? Twins are so alike. I would never risk a son of
mine on her stability."

"That might be true of identical twins, but hardly boy-girl."

"Yet if his rearing was so slipshod, can hers be much better?"

"They are Irish, after all. One cannot expect rigid decorum."

"That is absurd! They are just as capable of behavior as you are. But Lord Delaney has ever been a loose screw. Hardly a desirable pattern card."

The Marchgate party rose to leave when custom demanded despite the continuing analysis.

They were walking back to Marchgate House when Caroline's heart nearly stopped. She was trailing behind the others, who were rehashing Brummel's conduct, when she chanced to glance down Davies Street. Thomas was standing on the doorstep of number fifty-five. As she watched, the door swung open to reveal Alicia, scantily clad in her favorite blue. As Thomas stepped into the entry, one of her hands slid up his chest in an intimate gesture of great familiarity. His hands grasped her arms as the door closed.

Caroline fought to control her face, grateful that Brummel's escapade meant her companions were paying no attention to her or their surroundings. The stabbing pain and nausea that nearly doubled her over was accompanied by a blinding flash of knowledge, equally upsetting.

She had committed the greatest folly of her life.

She had fallen in love with her husband.

Somehow she responded with social chatter as they returned to the house. She even reached her own room before nausea overwhelmed her, followed by a cloudburst of tears. How was she to conceal her feelings? And how could she continue to live with his antagonism?

Thomas daily sank further into despair. Nor could he devise any way to alleviate his suffering.

The facts of his life remained unchanged. He loved Alicia and she loved him. Events had conspired to separate them, leaving them both miserable. Honor prevented him from comforting her. Honor also demanded that he be loyal to Caroline, respecting her and caring for her. But respect was difficult considering her affair with Wroxleigh. She spent so much time with the man that tongues had to be wagging, though no one had yet dared repeat the tale to Thomas himself.

His fury over her presumed infidelity was out of proportion to their situation, but he did not stop to wonder why. Examining his reasoning might disclose poor judgment or some other lapse in honor that he was unable to face. It always led to disaster, and he wanted no more blood on his hands.

He hardened his heart to Caroline, refusing to discuss her with his friends and terminating any conversation that included her name. He remained polite to her in public, but could no longer hide his anger in private. Their predicament was all her fault. She should have made a firmer effort to remove him in that mail coach. Instead, she had allowed his attentions to continue, had even accepted them. Her behavior alone convinced their fellow passengers that they were wed. Without that, he would now be free to marry Alicia. Had she deliberately set out to snare him as an alternative to governessing?

He conveniently forgot that without Caroline, he would have long since been shackled to Miss Huntsley. Yet despite his anger, honor prevented him from seeking solace elsewhere. How it would end he could not tell, nor would he allow himself to consider the future. Enduring the present was agony enough.

Alicia sent another plea for help, begging his assistance to straighten Darnley's tangled affairs and reminding him of her undying love. After a lengthy battle with his conscience, he again refused, suggesting that she seek advice from Darnley's solicitor or man of business and reminding her that the new Lord Darnley was now responsible for the estate. He congratulated himself on avoiding a *tête-à-tête* and basked for most of a day over his achievement. But by nightfall he was again miserable. Alicia haunted his dreams, nightmares actually, in which she, Darnley, and Caroline writhed in confused chaos.

Only those restless nights controlled his simmering rage. He rarely awoke before noon, unaware that Caroline rode most mornings with Wroxleigh. Even Cramer refrained from passing along that information. It would have shattered what was left of his temper.

Alicia's third missive presented an unsolvable dilemma. She again requested his presence, this time on the pretext of offering Darnley's horses for sale. Would Thomas appraise their value? He could have his choice from the stables. She would accept any offer he cared to make.

He vacillated for a full day. Prudence demanded that she send them all to Tattersall's. Yet he could certainly buy directly from Alicia for less than he would have to pay elsewhere, while paying her more than she would receive after Tattersall's deducted its fees from the selling price. And Darnley was Graylock's cousin. What were his stables like? Could he meet her in the relatively intimate environment of the mews without disgracing himself? It had been nearly a week since he had last set eyes on her and desire was growing with each passing hour. Knowing she was so near made it worse. Finally, he succumbed to temptation and sent off a note agreeing to present himself that afternoon for the purpose of inspecting her horses. *Please let the stable be full of grooms.*

Steeling himself, he knocked on her door, having walked the scant two blocks to her home on Davies Street. Shocked when she answered in person, he successfully held his composure.

Dressed in a thin silk dress of pale blue, she turned exquisite violet-blue eyes to his, her expression communicating better than words how lost and frightened she was in this time of crisis. One hand slid up his chest in mute appeal and she pressed herself close.

"I am so glad you will help me, my love," she murmured. "I need you so badly." Her other hand pushed the door closed before reaching up to caress his cheek.

But Thomas had not spent the day preparing for this encounter for nothing. "No, Alicia," he groaned, self-control firmly in charge. He gently removed her hands and set her firmly away. Tears trembled in her eyes. She lowered her hands to her sides, sliding them provocatively downward, cupping her breasts and molding her hips. His body responded instantly, but he ignored it, drawing a ragged breath to steady his pulse.

"We have had this discussion before, Lady Darnley," he declared firmly, pleased that no tremor marred his businesslike voice. He could not blame her for her lapse. She labored under considerable stress. Was it any wonder she would turn to the man she loved for comfort? "I will not dishonor you by placing you in so compromising a position. Nor will I dishonor myself by ignoring my own marriage vows. Please detail a footman to show me the mews so that I can look at those horses you wish to sell."

Anger swept her face, clearly visible for several seconds before she recovered her mask of lost vulnerability.

Thomas spent an hour examining horses. None met his current needs. Besides, the associations would play havoc with his mind whenever he saw them. Not trusting either his own control or Alicia's, he dashed off a note declining to make any purchases and recommending that she dispose of them through Tattersall's. He sent it with her footman and turned his steps to White's. Poor Alicia. So confused. And so unaware of propriety's demands. Except for her forced marriage, she had rarely met defeat. It was to be expected that she was a bit spoiled. Someone of her talents and beauty could hardly help it. But it did make his own lot harder. He must be the conscience for both of them. If only he had not won her heart. Controlling himself would be easier if he did not have to consider her love.

Caroline recovered quickly from her bout of tears. She must not let her feelings show in public. Nor could she consider the future until her emotions were better controlled. Besides, Drew was due to take her driving.

But evidence of distress could not be completely banished. Drew took one look at her face and turned his phaeton toward the quieter confines of Green Park. He also signaled his tiger to leave as soon as they were out of sight of the house.

His flirtatious banter continued until they were quite alone, then he set himself to discover what disturbed his favorite cousin.

"You look under the weather today. Are you sleeping all right?"

"As well as can be expected," she responded obliquely.

"Ah," he replied suggestively, then continued with exaggerated mourning, "Mannering is one lucky fellow. I think I'm more than half in love with you myself."

"Fustian," she snorted, responding as usual to his teasing. "You confuse friendship with love. If you didn't waste all your time pursuing new conquests you might find someone who could be both a friend and a lover."

"Like you and Mannering?" But he halted abruptly at the pain that flashed across her face. Though his bantering words were those he used to great effect with other women, an element of seriousness underlay the claim. He cared deeply for Caroline. And he now knew what before he had only suspected. She was very unhappy. Nor was there more than one possible cause.

"Is he still making an ass of himself over Lady Darnley?" he asked quietly, pressing her hand in silent commiseration.

She could no longer maintain the pretense. But Drew would never hurt her by using her confidences to fuel further rumors. Her face crumpled and she nodded. Tears threatened again to spill over.

"Oh, my dear cousin, I am so sorry." Drew snubbed the ribbons and pulled her head against his shoulder. "Cry it out, Caro. You need to." He continued to cradle her until her weeping stopped, ever alert for any sign of observers, silently cursing a man who could overlook a jewel like Caroline in favor of a scheming slut.

"I'm sorry, Drew," she apologized sheepishly when she finally pulled herself away. "I'm afraid I've ruined your coat." Accepting his silently proffered handkerchief, she blew her nose.

"Glad to help. You love him, don't you?"

"I fear so," she admitted. "And I really did not need that particular complication just now."

"Do you want me to seduce the lady and show her up for what she is? You must know her reputation by now."

"I'm well aware of her reputation, thank you, but it would do no good. Thomas is obstinately blind when it comes to Lady Darnley. And he would never forgive me for interfering. No, Drew, all I can do is trust that sooner or later he will admit the truth. Then he might possibly stop blaming me for standing between him and marriage to his heart's desire."

"What a bloody fool!" he exploded. "Pardon my language."

"No need. I have often thought the same. But obsession is a form of madness, falling outside all bounds of sense or reason. There is nothing to be done."

Drew flicked his horses into motion while she straightened her hair. Nothing could improve her eyes, which were red and swollen. She could only pray that they met no one she knew.

Fortunately the daily promenade was at its height in Hyde Park and she was able to slip into the house without encountering anyone but the footman at the front door. Sam would say nothing. Summoning Dawson, she set about the daunting task of hiding all traces of agitation and preparing for an evening of fun and frivolity at the Staffords' ball.

Governessing looked better and better.

Chapter 14

Life continued, despite Thomas's turmoil and Caroline's despair. The hardest part, she found, was pretending in public that all was well between them. It gave her a better understanding of what he faced each day, and she tried to make the charade easier for him. Aware of the importance he placed on public opinion, she worked to maintain the fiction that they were a loving couple. But at the same time, she had to hide her true feelings from Thomas. This was one situation in which honesty was the worst policy.

His disdain was obvious, from his stilted conversation and cold, clipped voice to the way he recoiled from any physical contact. Nor was she any happier. His touch affected her like no other, but the resulting shivers knifed her heart rather than stoking her passions. How long could this continue? She did not know. At some point they must air their feelings. Neither of them could stand the strain much longer.

She was descending the stairs for breakfast one morning, intent on appearing relaxed and content, when it happened. Two footmen carried a settee along the corridor. It was a heavy piece and both strained with the effort. Suddenly, one of them fell, grunting in pain and surprise. His end landed on the top step, throwing the other off balance so that he lost his grip. The settee hurtled downward, bouncing from step to step, with Caroline squarely in its path.

She screamed.

Grabbing the rail with both hands, she flung herself atop it. And just in time. The settee bounded past, bruising her thigh before crashing to the floor below.

Footsteps pounded as servants raced to the scene.

Caroline shakily regained her feet and turned her eyes from the wreckage below to the crowd above. The footmen wore identical expressions of horror, which immediately changed to relief when they saw that she was unharmed. Thomas also stood rooted at the top of the stairs, but his face bore a different expression. Horror was there, but mixed with—disappointment?

Convulsed in shudders, she sank to the steps and dropped her head into her hands. Surely it was an accident. Thomas derived too much pride from his honor. He would never consider jostling a footman into dropping that heavy settee to sweep an unwanted wife to her doom. Would he?

Would he?

She thrust the suspicion away, but it continued to lurk. Without the warning provided by the footman's groan, she would now be sprawled on the floor below. How convenient if she simply disappeared from his life. Alicia was no longer tied to Darnley.

No!

She forced her mind away from an accusation, convinced that Lady Darnley would never consider marriage to an untitled younger son. Especially one who lacked a fortune. Such a match would force her to discard her own title, would negate the only possible reason for her first marriage. *But did Thomas know that?* He had misjudged her from the beginning and showed no sign of revising his impressions.

He reached her side.

"Are you all right?" he asked stiffly, offering a hand to help her to her feet.

She cringed from his touch, ostentatiously inspecting her dress for damage. A tear in the hem was all that was visible, though her thigh throbbed painfully.

"I believe so," she responded shakily, then grabbed the railing to pull herself up, again ignoring his proffered hand. Touching him would shatter her precarious control. What would she do? Cling to him in tears? Hurl accusations at his face? Neither was desirable. Turning abruptly away, she forced her feet back to her room.

Thomas watched her go, confusion raging. His emotions had undergone so many convolutions in so little time he could not decide what he felt. He had been just behind the footmen when one of them caught a toe on the edge of the runner and fell. But he was not close enough to catch the fellow. Horror paralyzed him as the settee hurtled downward, followed swiftly by relief that she was safe, then by the unworthy thought that if she had died, he would be free to go to Alicia. That engendered anger at himself which immediately became fury at the footman for unwonted clumsiness. But the worst of it was meeting Caroline's eyes a moment later. Clearly she suspected him of initiating the accident.

The realization hurt. And he was aghast that he could ever wish injury on another. The momentary thought of freedom had filled him with joy.

How had they come to this pass? What had he done to deserve this coil? He had married her without love, to be sure, but he had tried to treat her with respect. *Respect?* mocked his conscience. *Betrayal. Unjust condemnation as you vented your frustrations on her. Revulsion and neglect.* He shook away the voice, but could not ignore the message. One by one he examined his actions over recent months. His conduct was appalling.

He sank to the step Caroline had just vacated, burying his head in his hands.

He had spent four months angry at his wife. Why? Because she was not Alicia. The one thing over which she had no control. Was he to blame her for fifty years because she was not Alicia? Of course, there were other things. Her interference in Crawley's operation, her independence, her nauseating competence.

But further thought surprised him. Her efforts with Crawley no longer bothered him. Somehow he had come to accept and even applaud the work she had started. Her willingness to step into whatever role needed filling provided insurance whenever he was absent from the estate. And never had she tried to usurp his own position, insist on her own views, argue against his decisions, or interfere when he was present.

Nor was her independence something he could honestly condemn. True, a man liked to feel protective of his women, but Caroline never made him feel less than a man. And until today she had never refused his assistance. Some of her independence had been forced by his own actions. He cringed over the memories. He had fled Crawley with no thought to the estate problems he left behind, then stayed away longer than necessary. He had callously tossed her into the *ton* without so much as an introduction. A clinging, helpless chit would have broken under the strain and embarrassed him and his family. Instead, she was a credit to both.

And could he condemn competence in a female? Emily was equally blessed, something he had always pointed to with pride. Did he really want to go through life with a wife who was unable to accomplish the simplest task without making a mull of it? Wasn't that one of the complaints against Miss Huntsley that caused him to welcome Caroline's hand in the first place?

In retrospect, he had indeed treated her badly. On the other hand, their relationship was not so simple that he could forget the past, beg forgiveness, and live happily ever after. Two stumbling blocks stood in the way.

The first, of course, was Alicia. No change in his perception of Caroline could alter the fact that he loved Alicia, nor could he banish the companion desire that it was she to whom he was married. Never before had he accepted second best, and facing a lifetime married to a woman who fit that description was daunting.

Nor could he forgive or forget Caroline's association with Wroxleigh. Despite warnings and outright orders, she continued her liaison with the fellow. What should he do? Catch them together and call Wroxleigh out? Accept being cuckolded as fitting punishment for his lapse with Alicia and allow the affair to run its course? He did not know, and having no answers angered him as much as her conduct.

Sighing, he turned his footsteps upstairs. His first duty was to apologize for his unfair judgments and find a way to mend their relationship. Perhaps they could recapture the friendship they had shared during that first week together. How badly shaken was she? Had the settee struck her?

But he never saw her. Dawson informed him that Caroline was resting and would accept no visitors. Hurt at being thus labeled, Thomas left for his usual rounds of sparring, shooting, and visiting his clubs. Appearances must be maintained. Never would he allow the *ton* to suspect that all was not well with his marriage.

Caroline spent the morning resting. Her leg was bruised and scraped, but not seriously damaged. However, she refused to sleep after a nap ended in nightmare. Again and again that flash of disappointment twisted Thomas's features. In her dream he pushed the settee down on top of her, then followed with other forms of mayhem when his scheme failed. Awake, she refused to believe him capable of perpetrating such a crime. *You should not take chances,* whispered the voice. She thrust the thought aside, not wanting to even consider the possibility. Yet she let Dawson turn him away a second time, rather than face him with her mind in turmoil.

What should she do? Her attitude toward their marriage had changed. She paced her room restlessly, trying to decide just what she wanted. *Love . . . And pigs will fly,* she scoffed. *Be reasonable!* All right, she loved him. But that deplorable situation was not responsible for the change.

She paused to peer into her mirror. She was different. Not just the hair and the fashionable clothes. Not even the improved social graces. The whole image had changed, right down to the core. And with it, her view of Thomas had also changed.

She had originally agreed to marriage out of desperation, expecting nothing beyond friendship and more security than she could have found as a governess. Believing Thomas to be well above her touch, she had determined to serve him faithfully without demanding anything in return—a role combining the duties of housekeeper and mistress. Fool! How could she have denigrated her own worth so thoroughly?

But London had improved her self-image, beginning with her appearance. She was not the plain dowd she had considered herself after a lifetime of comparisons with her beautiful sisters. Nor was she beneath the touch of the polite world. Her two grandfathers were an earl and a baron, a more exalted lineage than many of the *ton* could boast. Her mother had taught her the skills needed to hold her own in the drawing rooms and ballrooms of Mayfair. And she had acquitted herself well. If anything, her credit now surpassed his.

Never again would she consider herself either the lesser of two evils or a millstone around his neck. Nor should he. She had allowed him to retain those images far too long. It was time to abandon her passive role and fight for a place in his life and affections. No longer was it possible to remain in the background while he worked out his problems for himself.

The battle would not be simple, she admitted, dropping onto the bed and staring at the canopy. Obsession was a formidable foe. And his inability to acknowledge errors in judgment would compound the problem. Her words to Lord Marchgate still held true. Under head-on assault Thomas would dig in his heels and cling ever more tightly to his mistakes. He was not a man to be coerced into anything. Nor would she want him to be. She despised men who lived under the cat's paw. Instead, her campaign must approach through the back door, taking advantage of every opportunity to support or assist him. Her presence must become an integral part of his life, essential to his well-being. But her behavior must remain matter-of-fact. Never again would she play the role of servant. Nor would martyrdom help. And no matter how difficult, she must never criticize either Alicia or his behavior. If ever she succeeded in breaking Lady Darnley's hold, she must put the past behind them and never refer to it, even if he did not turn his support to her. *Can you really manage that?* asked the voice. It was a question she hoped never to have to answer.

She resumed her normal schedule in time for afternoon calls

and attended a ball that evening. It would not do to advertise the mishap.

"How lovely you are tonight, Caro," exclaimed Robert, leading her into the first cotillion. "We go well together." Indeed, her blue silk was the identical shade of his jacket, though she would never have donned anything like his lemon waistcoat, gaudily embroidered in acanthus leaves and bluebirds. He sported a new style of cravat.

"Is that one of your own designs?" she asked.

"Yes, a variation on the Oriental."

"Exquisite."

"Thank you. Did you hear about young Delaney's latest scrape?"

"A bit, though no one seems to know why he was there. Lady Beatrice imputes the most scandalous motives."

"She would. But he was merely saving the poor woman."

"Oh? From what?"

"My dear, thuch horrors!" His lisp intensified with the affected words. "His youngest brother had to come to town for a few days—visiting the tooth drawer, I believe."

"Poor chap. How old is he?"

"Just eight. He didn't like the idea at all, as you can imagine, so he brought along a few items with which to amuse himself. One was a baby hedgehog."

"Oh, dear." Caroline giggled—she had had plenty of experience with young boys and their pets.

"Oh, dear, indeed. The poor thing escaped, as one must expect of such creatures, and turned up in Lady Feldham's bedroom—when the poor lady was barely awake. She succumbed to hysterics. Young Lawrence was the first on the scene."

She giggled once more. "I take it Lady Feldham has little use for small animals."

Robert tittered. "Very little. She was standing on a chair, one hand clutched to her bosom, the other shaking out her skirts, her eyes in danger of popping out. The terrified hedgehog succumbed to its own hysterics, cowering on the hearth, rolled up in a little spiny ball, only its tiny black eyes peeping out. Lawrence collapsed against the wall, laughing too hard to rescue the beast."

"Laughter would hardly be appreciated under such circumstances."

"How right you are. By the time Lady Feldham's dresser arrived, she was screeching at him to stop staring and take himself off. The hedgehog had summoned the courage to escape out the door, and Lawrence was in a pickle."

She was having a difficult time restraining her own laughter. "And what of his brother?"

"Back home."

"Sans hedgehog?"

Robert giggled and nodded. "The poor creature has not been seen since. Much to Lady Feldham's horror."

"The poor lady must be having twenty fits every day," she choked.

The music swirled to a close and Robert raised one hand to his lips before escorting her to join Emily and Helena. "Delightful, as always."

"Has Lord Potherby accepted your school plans?" she asked Helena as Robert departed.

"He has yet to agree, though he is no longer protesting. I must thank you for talking with him that day."

"Were you really able to persuade him?" asked a surprised Emily.

"It was nothing," demurred Caroline.

"Fustian. He has been a different man since," explained Helena. "Caroline presented all the appropriate arguments, wisely citing observations of Lord Waite and your parents rather than her own experiences. I have heard nothing about consequence since, though I suspect he is discussing the idea at his clubs."

"Things were easier once I discovered that Waite was a neighbor and had been a close friend of his father. He should find little support for his top-lofty objections. Even those who disagree with education seldom cite consequence. And he so readily adopts changing agricultural methods that he is bound to agree in the end." Unless someone scared him silly with fears that education would lead to insurrection.

"I hope so," murmured Helena as their partners approached for the next set.

"What is bothering you tonight?" Jeremy asked at supper. "You seem unusually quiet."

Caroline sighed in resignation. Was she really that easy to read? Her close friends always seemed to know what she was feeling. Drew's unexpected perception had been disconcerting, though he was right to think she had needed a good cry.

"Nothing serious," she tried. "I suffered a slight mishap this morning and am a little stiff as a result."

"What happened?"

"A footman tripped, sending a settee tumbling down the stairs, narrowly missing me."

"Good heavens! Are you all right? How could such a thing occur?"

"I am fine, Jeremy, but the details are a bit hazy. Thomas left just afterward so I do not know precisely how it all came about."

"He was there?"

"Yes."

But Jeremy must have noticed something in her expression, because he frowned. "You cannot believe that he had anything to do with it."

"Of course not," she denied, but her voice wavered.

"He would never consider such a thing."

"That's what I keep telling myself," she declared. "But you know how things stand with him. He considers me a millstone now that Alicia is free."

"He is a fool to continue adoring her when he has you," snorted Jeremy. "But obsession is blind. To some extent I can sympathize with him. Though the fair Alicia never appealed to me, I too fell in love last Season."

"What happened?"

"She turned me down. Claimed I did not know her at all. And she was right. Infatuation had blinded me to her real character. I saw only what I wanted to see. She wasn't at all like I believed. She married Wrexham last summer and is ecstatically happy by all reports. Produced an heir just last month. It's too bad Thomas has not learned the truth about his inamorata, for I cannot believe he sees her clearly. I don't suppose you could tell him."

"Surely you jest!" exclaimed Caroline, chuckling at the idea. "How can a wife approach her husband to inform him—strictly for his own good—that the woman he loves is a scheming, selfish, bad-tempered harridan, who has probably enjoyed the favors of more men than he has women in his long career as a rake?"

"Is she really that bad?" Jeremy laughed in turn.

"See? Even you don't believe me. Yes, she is." And she described the scene at the modiste's and several similar occurrences Emily had related. "And you cannot be ignorant of her reputation, though somehow Thomas remains so."

"Good Lord!" gasped Jeremy. "But surely he will discover her true nature."

"Perhaps, if given enough time. But his brain ceases to function whenever she is around, and he never questions his devotion otherwise. Nor can I imagine him ever admitting to a mistake in judgment. He possesses a stubborn single-mindedness that sets a goal, then pursues it relentlessly without ever again questioning whether it is worthy or whether he still desires it."

"Too true," sighed Jeremy. "He has ever had that problem. I can remember when we first came down from Oxford. He bought a horse at Tattersall's. Beautiful animal, but about as sound as a house with dry rot. Immediately obvious to everyone else, of course, but would he agree? No. Even after he replaced it with that black stallion he rides now, he never admitted that the original was a mistake. Always claims he switched because he wanted a horse he could put to stud."

"Maybe there is hope, then." Caroline surprised him with this observation. "He may not have admitted the mistake, but he obviously learned his lesson. Everything he owns now is prime blood."

This conversation restored at least some of her hope for the future. If she remained patient, Thomas would learn for himself what Alicia was really like. She would never expect him to apologize for his behavior or even to admit that he was making a cake of himself over someone unworthy. But he would eventually turn to her. She had to believe that.

In the meantime, she continued her own social schedule, accepting Thomas's public attentions in the spirit in which they were offered. He had mellowed, seeming less icy, though she did not believe that the fundamental problem had eased. She was unable to find any way to pursue her goals at home, but maintained her optimism. Something would turn up.

"Hello, Thomas," George called when his friend wandered into White's one afternoon. "How about sharing a bottle over a couple of hands of piquet?"

"Only a couple?" asked Thomas, dropping into the opposite chair.

"I have to visit my tailor. Usual stakes?"

He nodded.

George frowned. "You look a mite down today. Problems?"

Thomas shrugged, but no one was close enough to hear. Picking up a deck of cards, he began shuffling. "I've made a royal mess of my life," he admitted while George cut. "And I've been unfair to Caroline—you see, I can admit mistakes."

George remained passive with an effort.

"But it seems too late to make it up to her. She hardly ever speaks to me these days."

"That doesn't sound like Caroline," protested George. "She is not the type to hold a grudge, and a more forgiving nature I have yet to meet. What did you do to her?"

"Nothing!" But his voice lacked conviction. "I really did not instigate that accident, you know."

"What accident?"

"She didn't tell you? She came close to being killed last week." At George's gasp of surprise, he related the details of the mishap on the stairs. "I cannot believe she suspects I caused it, yet she is so distant these days, and her eyes wonder."

"No, I too cannot believe she harbors suspicions," agreed George. If anything, she was madly in love with her undeserving husband. "Yet your behavior could suggest such a thing to a less scrupulous mind. We both know where your heart lies and so does Caroline."

"God, what am I going to do, George? Some days I truly believe I am mad." He ran a hand through his hair in frustration.

"Perhaps you need to distance yourself from the lady," suggested George with great daring. "Then you can evaluate the situation with an open mind. You might discover she is an ordinary beauty rather than a goddess." He dared hint no further for anger already suffused Thomas's eyes. How could the man remain so blind? George wondered. Rumor credited her with three regular lovers and innumerable casual liaisons. Since Darnley's death there had been a steady parade of gentlemen through her room. He knew courtesans who entertained less. But he had to admit that Thomas would be the last to hear such stories. Few people dared mention Alicia to him.

He let the subject drop and examined his unpromising hand. He had not seen anything this bad in months. Drawing the full complement of five replacement cards changed nothing. "Have you seen any good horses lately?"

Thomas's expression lightened as he considered his own hand. "Not since young Delaney bid such an exorbitant amount for the pair I wanted. I hope the lad has a good trainer. They were barely half broken."

"I don't know about his groom, but he has to be the most cowhanded driver I've ever laid eyes on. They spent Christmas with us if you recall. While his twin sister batted her lashes at me, he was out ditching a dogcart pulled by a placid pony along a wide, dry lane."

"You can't be serious. Caroline could drive better than that after one lesson, and she had never sat on a box before." Pride threaded the words, raising another speculative glance from George.

"If the horses are as green as you say, we'd best pray he doesn't drive them in town."

"What is he doing in town anyway? He cannot yet be eighteen. I would have thought he was still in school."

"What a miserable hand!" George tossed his cards down. "I concede. He was sent down for some prank or other. A pig in the bagwig's rooms or a bear in the belltower—something like that."

"Were we ever that young?"

"I seem to recall a tale concerning a certain tutor and two goats. Of course, the perpetrator was never discovered. Cut." George had been busily reshuffling.

Thomas laughed in remembrance. "Not to mention the unsolved mystery of how the hedgehogs got into Wrexham's boots. Who are you backing at next week's races?"

They discussed horses while playing out the next hand.

"Damn," muttered Thomas as George won the last trick. "I should have discarded the diamond."

Hold that thought, begged George, but he dared not voice the command aloud. "You still take the day. That first hand was a killer." He tossed down a couple of coins and excused himself.

Setting out at a brisk walk, George traversed St. James, heading for Bond Street. Was Alicia's hold finally beginning to slip? This was the first time Thomas had admitted that his treatment of Caroline was both shabby and undeserved. George hated seeing two of his closest friends at loggerheads, especially when they were so well suited.

But his cogitations ceased when a terrifying spectacle greeted his eyes. A high-perch phaeton careened around the corner, its seat precariously balanced a good six feet above the ground, two wild-eyed chestnuts in the traces. No whip would drive so fast along a crowded street, he realized just before he identified the driver.

Lawrence Delaney.

"Bloody hell!" he exclaimed, already darting toward a door to protect his hide from the inevitable disaster. He dared not shout a warning. The horses were barely under control as things stood.

Perhaps the lad would escape unscathed.

He prayed.

But fate had other ideas. A cat tore out of an alley, a yapping terrier on its heels. Shouts rose as the creatures threaded the crowd.

The instant din proved too much for Delaney. His horses bolted in terror. Sawing on the ribbons merely swerved them toward the sidewalk, overturning his phaeton and pinning several pedestrians beneath the wreckage. Delaney landed against a brick wall, one leg broken and his head concussed.

"Somebody fetch Dr. Mantry," shouted George, as he ran to help.

It took the efforts of six gentlemen before the horses were finally under control.

Chapter 15

Caroline always enjoyed paying afternoon calls with Emily. It was far more entertaining than making the rounds with the countess, for Emily patronized young matrons.

"Did you see Miss Fielding's face last night?" Emily pursed her lips as her town carriage rumbled along the cobbled street. "If ever anyone looked thoroughly kissed! That girl had better learn to control her countenance if she plans any more assignations in the garden."

"Meaning that one should not allow a gentleman to make improper advances unless one can appear cool and bored afterward?"

"Something like that. She can probably get away with it this time, but if it happens again, she will be thought fast. Did you hear about Lord Packford and the pigeons yesterday?"

"Not only heard. I was there, and nearly fell out of Jeremy's curricle I was laughing so hard and trying to remain ladylike about it. You know how puffed Packford is."

"Lord, yes. He makes Mama seem positively plebeian. And his cravats rival Robert's."

"Not anymore. He was sauntering along with his nose in the air, face twisted into that pained expression he adopts in the mistaken belief that it radiates boredom—I swear, he looks more like a colicky babe than anything else."

Emily giggled.

"Well, there he was, pointedly ignoring those whom he thought socially inferior, when along came a flock of pigeons."

Emily burst into laughter.

"At least ten of them," continued Caroline, giggling in turn. "Big, fat pigeons. One by one, they swooped d-down and s-soiled his c-coat. You should have seen his f-face! One of them hit his n-nose!" And she succumbed to hilarity, only a desperate grip on the strap keeping her in her seat.

Tears rolled down Emily's cheeks and she pulled out a lacy

handkerchief, dabbing at her eyes in a hopeless attempt to stem the flow. Caroline followed suit.

The carriage pulled to a halt before Stafford House and a footman let down the steps. Quelling their laughter, they composed their faces into social smiles suitable for afternoon calls and descended.

Stafford House was elegantly appointed, Lady Stafford favoring the regency style with its simple lines and rich colors. The butler led the way upstairs to the drawing room.

"Well, he may be more circumspect, but young Mannering is still hanging out after that shocking Darnley wench. Lady Sefton saw him calling on her just the other day," boomed Lady Beatrice.

"Given their respective reputations, it is not to be wondered at," agreed another. "He has ever been a rake and she is certainly no better than she should be."

"Lady Wembley and Mrs. Mannering," intoned the butler as they arrived in the doorway.

"Welcome," said Lady Stafford. Not a single social smile hinted that they had been discussing Thomas moments before. Greetings were exchanged and Caroline found herself sitting next to Lady Beatrice.

"And what has that husband of yours been up to lately?" probed the dowager slyly. "I have not seen him for several days."

"We attended the Harris ball and the opera, but mostly he is pursuing horses and finding it most frustrating." The best course was to confront the gossip, offering an explanation for that most public call. Hopefully Lady Sefton's view had not included Alicia's intimate caress. Caroline firmly pushed her own searing memories aside.

"Tattersall's does not have any horses that meet his needs," she continued. "Have you ever heard of such a thing? Nor has he been able to find what he wants from private sellers. Westhaven has three colts but none are suitable for hunting. And Lady Darnley asked him to evaluate her late husband's stable before she puts it up for auction, but he declined to buy. The viscount had a deplorable eye for horseflesh, surprising in one so closely related to Graylock."

"You will not find it surprising by the time you reach my age," snorted Lady Beatrice. "Men will never seek advice, having such exaggerated opinions of their own abilities."

"True, though that has never been one of Mr. Mannering's failings. He has often consulted Graylock and others to ensure the success of his own venture."

"Sounds like a man of unusual sense." Her voice could not hide surprise at this conclusion.

"I have found him so, and the last year has matured him to a remarkable degree. Fortunately."

"You know about last year?" prodded Lady Beatrice.

"Of course. He made quite a cake of himself. Little boys . . ." She ruefully shook her head. "He is horribly embarrassed to be reminded of how silly he was. But at least the lady was beautiful. I'd hate to have a husband who had turned mooncalf over an antidote." She offered her lies with a perfectly straight face. Thomas might rue the day he was forced to marry her, but the least she could do was protect his reputation. It was the only way she could express her love. And his credit could not stand another beating. Without a title he would never recoup a second time.

"Lady Horseley," intoned the butler, again appearing in the door. The new arrival greeted those already gathered, two earlier visitors took their leave, and the footmen again passed refreshments.

"There has just been a shocking carriage accident over on St. James," Lady Horseley announced. "Young Delaney lost control of that new team of his and overturned his phaeton."

"Goodness!" exclaimed Lady Stafford. "Was anyone hurt?"

"Delaney broke his leg, according to Lord Ashton. He came on the scene just after it happened and helped calm the team. And apparently a couple of others were knocked down."

"Wembley has often decried that boy's driving," declared Emily. "What is his father about to allow such pranks?"

"Lord Delaney was no better," put in Lady Beatrice. "I recall similar incidents from his own youth. He once ditched your father, Lady Stafford."

The hostess giggled at the thought.

"Yes," added Lady Pembroke, "and there was quite a commotion when he was refused membership in the Four-in-Hand Club. He swore it was due solely to his Irish background, unwilling to admit that only top sawyers are accepted and he could never hope to qualify."

"At least if young Lawrence is laid up with a broken leg, we will be safe on the streets," commented Lady Stafford. "That phaeton of his would be hard for even a good whip to handle. Boys should be barred from driving such vehicles."

"And his horses were barely trained," Caroline added. "Mr. Mannering had hoped to buy them with the idea that a year of work would turn them into a reliable team. But Delaney offered an exorbitant price, nearly double their value."

"Cubs will ever behave recklessly." Lady Beatrice sighed dismissively. "Remember the scrape Albright drove into three Seasons ago?"

"Of course. Ran his carriage into the Serpentine during the afternoon promenade. Miss Severton had hysterics for days and never forgave him. Until then we all thought they would make a match of it."

"That's nothing compared to Shelford's mishap back in '04," contributed Lady Stafford. "He was visiting my brother's estate that summer and lost control of his curricle. Bounded over lawns, through Mama's garden party, knocked over two tables, and landed in the pond." Several ladies laughed. "Fortunately, no one was injured, but he was so embarrassed that he spent the rest of the summer working on his driving and now belongs to the Four-in-Hand Club."

Emily caught Caroline's eye and rose to leave. Behind them, the discussion recalled other exploits of cow-handed young men.

"I hope you successfully killed that story about Thomas," Emily said with a sigh when they were seated in her coach.

"Surely you don't believe it!" exclaimed Caroline, detecting a hint of fatalism in Emily's voice. When no answer was forthcoming, she snorted. "For heavens sake, Emily, think! As careful as Thomas has been, can you imagine him waltzing up to the front door at three in the afternoon if his call was not innocent?"

Emily relaxed into a smile. "Put like that, you are right. Even in his worst obsessive trances, he has never lost all signs of intelligence."

"And she did request his analysis of her stable. Dawson got it from Cramer who saw her note." Of course, what else might have occurred during that visit was not to be considered in company.

"I wonder if young Delaney will learn anything from today's mishap."

"That he needs driving lessons, one could hope."

"Or that he should consider becoming a fop. Robert cannot handle anything more spirited than a plow horse, you know."

"Really? What do Thomas and your father think of that?"

"Father sighs and refuses to discuss it. Thomas would never criticize him. He is very protective of Robert. And he may recall how much work it took to turn himself into a whip. The summer he was thirteen, he spent hours driving every day. He sustained three wrecks and two runaways before he mastered the art."

"Goodness, I cannot imagine Thomas losing control of a horse."

"Not any more. But skill at his level requires much practice. Like you and the pianoforte, I imagine."

"Of course," she agreed, much struck. "It is to be hoped young Delaney realizes that."

"Too bad Thomas never had the money to support coaching. He drives better than most Four-in-Hand members."

"Agreed, but that cannot be helped just now. Perhaps when the stable proves profitable. It would certainly enhance his image."

"True. Are you attending Lady Jersey's soiree this evening?" asked Emily as the carriage turned into Berkeley Square.

"Yes, and then we plan to move on to the Stokeley ball."

"I probably will not see you, then. With Wembley out of town dancing attendance on his aunt, I am accompanying the Staffords. We go to the Warrington rout first and then on to Lady Jersey's."

As soon as the door opened, Caroline knew something dreadful had happened. Reeves's face was gray and his butler's mask could not cover his shock.

"What is it?" she queried sharply.

"There has been an accident—" His voice quavered and he stopped to swallow before continuing. "Lord Hartford was gravely wounded."

She gasped. "Where is her ladyship?"

"Retired."

From the shock, or worse? She hesitated to ask. Reeves appeared ready to collapse.

"Where will I find Lord Marchgate?"

"The library." Trepidation overwhelmed her. Who was with Robert?

Fearfully, she tapped on the door, entering though there was no response. The earl was slumped in a chair, head in his hands. His very posture confirmed her suspicion.

"Is it true?" she asked gently, kneeling before his seat.

Haggard eyes scanned her face. "Robert is gone," he choked.

"How?"

"Carriage accident on St. James."

"I heard, but there was no indication that any but young Delaney was injured," she protested, not wanting to believe it.

"Three others were pinned under the wreckage," he managed, though his voice cracked badly. "Two were unhurt. Robert received a blow to the head. He never regained consciousness."

"I am so sorry." Her hands gripped his in silent commiseration, feeling guilty at how lightheartedly news of the mishap had been treated at Lady Stafford's. Nor could she believe that Robert was actually dead. Despite his silliness, she liked him very much.

"What can I do?"

"Portia will need you when she wakens," he said. "Her maid gave her a strong dose of laudanum. Perhaps you could find Eleanor." He ran his fingers absently through his hair, further disturbing it. "I cannot think clearly just now."

"That is to be expected," she murmured soothingly, noting a brighter glint in his eyes that showed how close to tears he was. "Is Thomas here?"

"Not to my knowledge. Footmen left to find him and Emily, but I do not know if they were successful." His voice cracked again.

"I will see to the immediate duties," she promised and left him to his grieving. Her heart went out to the earl, knowing he would grieve the harder because he had secretly believed his heir to be unworthy of the title.

The footman sent to locate Thomas had not yet returned, nor had the one dispatched to Wembley House. Robert's body was upstairs, with the housekeeper supervising the laying out. Eleanor was in her room, huddled in a chair before the fire, her face puffed from a lengthy bout of tears.

"Are you all right?" she asked gently.

She hesitated a moment, then threw herself into Caroline's arms, tears again flowing freely. "It's all so horrible," she sobbed. "How can he be gone?"

Caroline held her and rocked her, encouraging her to talk and offering condolences. What emerged between sobs was a tale of shock and distress. Eleanor had never been close to her oldest brother as the ten-year age difference was an insurmountable barrier. By the time she was born, he had left for school. And he spent many holidays with friends. Yet his death affected her deeply. Perhaps it was the suddenness, or the realization that someone sauntering along an elegant street could be cut down without warning. But the reminder of life's uncertainties shattered her security.

And then there was her anger. It was as much a product of shock and misery as it was a reality. For Robert's death also marked the death of her Season. As soon as the funeral concluded, the family would retire to their respective estates. Even country entertainments were banned during deep mourning. For a girl in her first Season, this constituted personal punishment rather than respect for the deceased. Her reaction was understandable, yet Caroline hoped Eleanor could hide her feelings. Neither of the Marchgates needed this additional burden.

"Go to sleep for a while," she urged when Eleanor had at last aired her distress and come to terms with it. "It can do nothing but good. And there is nought you can do just now. But your mother will need comfort when she wakens. You must be strong and in control."

She pulled a chair close to the bed, vowing to stay until Eleanor slept. But she could not deaden her own thoughts.

Had Thomas been located yet? She had heard no one come in, and the footman must have had time to search all the usual places. Where was he? She forced the image of Alicia's house on Davies Street from her mind. The idea of him making passionate love to another while his brother lay dying was too horrifying to contemplate. But if he was anywhere near his club that day, he must surely have heard the news. Emily had described him as protective of Robert. What hell was he enduring now?

A new thought surfaced and her eyes widened at her own slowness. Thomas was now Viscount Hartford and the heir to the earldom. What difference would that make to his life? With an increased allowance and his future prospects, he might have further cause to regret their hasty marriage. Would it affect his attitude toward Crawley? The derelict estate no longer represented his entire fortune. Perhaps he would welcome a return to London and resumption of the frivolous waiting game indulged in by most of his peers.

Sounds of arrival drifted up from the foyer. Eleanor was finally asleep. Caroline slipped quietly from the room, hoping it was he.

Emily paced the drawing room, tears streaming down her face. She raised pained eyes as Caroline entered and quietly shut the door.

"Is it true?"

She nodded.

"And we were laughing . . ." But she could not complete the sentence.

Caroline understood. She had faced the same horror when she realized the details of Robert's death.

"We could not know," she declared. "There is no reason to feel guilty. And he did not suffer. He did not even have time to feel pain." She led Emily to a sofa and handed her a glass of sherry.

"How are they taking it?"

"Your father is in shock, grief numbing most of his senses. He will go through worse when that wears off. Your mother is asleep, under a heavy dose of laudanum. I have not yet seen her. Eleanor is also asleep, after a long cry. She is shocked, terrified, and also angry over the cancellation of her Season. Guilt will rescue her from airing that reaction to your parents. And she knows I will listen when she needs to talk. Thomas has not yet returned."

"He will take it hard," said Emily, dabbing ineffectively at her eyes. "For all their differences in character and understanding, he and Robert were very close. He always protected Robert, helping him out of scrapes and shielding him from the contempt of those who maligned his silliness. At times he almost appeared to be Robert's father. There was that much difference in their abilities."

"I hope this does not trigger another bout of drinking," Caroline said with a frown.

"I doubt it. But he will not return home until he can control himself. He has always cared deeply about appearances. Displaying emotion is not considered manly in his circle. I remember when he was fourteen. He had a favorite dog that followed him everywhere. One day it wandered into a pasture and was killed by a bull. Thomas was heartbroken. He disappeared and did not return until dusk the next day. Papa was furious, though he understood as well as I did. But Thomas never mentioned Charley again."

"I hope he does not do that now. How many months would it take to submerge a brother's death?"

"We shall see." Tears again filled her eyes. Caroline pulled her close and let her cry on her shoulder. Her gown was becoming soaked with salt. Eventually, Emily pulled away and blew her nose. "Thank you. I think I am empty enough now to speak with Father."

"He is in the library. Shall I have a tea tray sent in?"

"Not there. But I would welcome one in here later." She drew a deep breath and resolutely left the room.

Caroline followed. She must consult with Reeves and with the housekeeper. To say nothing of the cook. So many details needed immediate attention. Was there mourning stationery for the death notices or would she have to send a footman out? What about clothing? And funeral arrangements. Which decisions were important enough to require her to disturb the earl? Which could she make on her own to ease his burden?

Thomas was still sitting in White's when George suddenly reappeared at his side.

"That was a fast trip. Was your tailor otherwise occupied?" But a closer look at his friend's face wiped the smile from his own. "What is it, George?"

"Young Delaney tried out his new team, hitched to a high-perch phaeton of the less stable variety." His voice wavered.

"Oh, my God. What did he do?"

"Broke his leg in the ensuing crash." He hesitated, searching for words and finding none. "There were other victims, including one fatality."

Thomas blanched.

"Your brother."

"No—" But George's expression eliminated all possibility of jest.

"Let me see you home," he offered gently.

"No," protested Thomas again. "I cannot face—"

"Then come with me." They had to get out of White's before word spread. Thomas could not hold up under the sympathy he would be offered. And it would be embarrassing all around if he did not.

In a fog, Thomas allowed George to lead him away. They quickly traversed the block to Albany.

"I must leave," said George as he unlocked his door and pushed him inside. Thomas needed to be alone. "I still have to visit my tailor. Help yourself." He pointed to the brandy decanter.

Thomas's mind was still groping with the enormity of what had just occurred. He had lost friends before. A close one had died at Badajoz a year before; another in a hunting accident just after coming down from Oxford. But losing a brother was far worse. And to have an accident cut him down as he walked along St. James Street seemed almost blasphemous. Protecting his brother had been a lifelong activity, dating to their earliest years. Robert was a little simpleminded. He could not help his lack of understanding, nor his unsuitability for the more masculine pastimes.

But he had found a niche in Mayfair's world of fashion and gossip, creating a life that kept him happy. And now he was gone. Gone . . .

Despite his resolution, tears welled and sobs tore at his throat. *Thank God George was so understanding.* He gave in and wept. . . .

Had hours passed. Or days?

Thomas splashed cold water on his face, finally able to exert some control over his emotions. Memories had flooded his mind, each new picture triggering a new round of tears. Robert excited over his first trip to London. . . . Robert ecstatic when acclaimed a tulip of fashion. . . . Robert decorating Marchgate House for Emily's come-out. . . . Robert giggling in his affected way over the latest scandal. . . . The snowy Christmas when the eleven-year-old viscount had squealed like a toddler as they whizzed down the Abbey's hills, tumbling into snowbanks at the bottom. . . . The night their father had prodded Robert to take a wife, to assure the succession. . . .

Shock collapsed Thomas back into his chair. He was now Viscount Hartford.

What would this mean for his own future? Financial security. It would be far easier to restore Crawley, and he would one day have the Abbey. And with the backing of a title and fortune, his stables would lose any taint of dabbling in trade.

Alicia will be furious at passing me over, whispered a voice. How absurd! She regretted their position as much as he, but neither of them had contributed to it. Her parents had forced that match on her.

He forced his mind back to Crawley. His allowance would not cease at the end of the year. In fact, it would substantially increase, allowing more scope for his stable. And he would have to study the Marchgate estates. Not that he would take an active role in managing them, but it was imperative that he fully understand his future inheritance. For another result of today's tragedy was a better appreciation of just how uncertain life could be. He needed to prepare for any eventuality. And that meant making an honest effort to repair the breach with Caroline. One of his duties would be providing an heir. Immediately. The next in line was an unscrupulous, spendthrift cousin.

George returned, stepping noisily through the door to allow him time to compose himself.

"A footman has been searching for you for several hours," he reported. "Are you ready to return home?"

"Yes, I must. Father will need support. And I hate to think how Mother and the girls are taking this."

"You are all right?"

"I believe so. Thank you, George."

He headed for Berkeley Square, emotions in check, mind divorced from reality. It hardly surprised him to find Caroline firmly in charge. Nor did he find her management irritating. In fact, he had known she would take care of everything until he was able to return and see to things himself. That certainty had given him time to come to terms with his own shock and grief.

He dealt with his parents and his sisters without breaking down. Caroline orchestrated the meetings so that he first spoke to each separately. She had arranged a cold collation in the breakfast room, allowing everyone to eat when and if they wanted, without pressure. Emily told him of all that Caroline had accomplished, praising her tact and her compassion. His parents each expressed gratitude for her presence. Eleanor seemed unnaturally reticent, offering commiseration but displaying no emotion on her own part. Recalling Emily's comments, he suspected Caroline was responsible for sparing him the expected outburst. Not until he steeled himself to view Robert's body did his composure again slip.

The wound that had killed him was on the back of his head, so he looked perfectly normal. His valet had dressed him, his cravat as stiff and perfect as ever in life, his hair curled in deliberate dishevelment around his face. Tears again filled Thomas's eyes despite his efforts. Not even the sound of someone entering the room could stop his wracking sobs.

Soft hands grasped his arms and led him to a settee in the corner.

"Cry it out, Thomas. No one else will come in," murmured Caroline, pulling his head down onto her shoulder.

Amazed at himself, he willingly complied, not caring that she saw him at his vulnerable worst. He did not stop to consider why he would feel that way, desolation sweeping all thought aside. His arms moved around her and he again let his overwhelming loss control his actions.

Caroline said nothing. She would not intrude on his grief. But neither could she leave him alone at this wrenching time. He needed warmth and comfort, but no words. Words required thought in order to respond. His grief placed him beyond thought.

She smoothed a hand over his hair and gently massaged the stiffness from his shoulders.

"I am sorry," he finally choked as his sobs abated.

"It is nothing." She watched as he pulled himself upright, satisfied that he was again in control. He still needed to commune with his brother. And that was best accomplished in private.

Chapter 16

Oh, God! Make it not be true!

Thomas buried his head in the pillow, unable to decide if sleep or rising offered the least pain. His few hours in bed had been endless torture, round after round of memories, tears, and nightmares. But the day promised equal torture without the purge of emotion.

Despite viewing Robert's body, he could not accept the finality of his death. Nor could he banish blame. Somehow he should have protected him better. Surely there was something he could do to change the outcome, to recoup his loss. But he knew there was not. Despite all his efforts, despite his lifelong resolution, he had failed.

Robert had always needed protection. Never bright and lacking the athletic ability that might have incited approval in his peers, he had been the target of malicious bullies from the moment he arrived at Eton. When Thomas started school the following year, he discovered the treatment meted out to those who did not conform. He was appalled. Taller and far more athletic than his older brother, he quickly demonstrated that he would tolerate no more attacks.

Robert found Oxford easier, for by then he had a reputation for incipient dandyism, his expertise with wardrobe and cravat inspiring envy among those boys less adept. And his physique, a handicap to a sportsman, was marvelously suited to displaying elaborate fashions. His mind, unable to grasp the complexities of Greek or Latin, could recall any tidbit of gossip and retell it humorously. He soon earned a name for *on-dits* that equaled Lady Beatrice's. Indeed, many preferred Lord Hartford, for his stories always carried his characteristic touch of humor rather than her acid condemnation.

Tears again welled and Thomas buried his face in his pillow. The memories marched inexorably through his mind. Games . . . scrapes . . . lessons . . . holidays . . .

But no memories could hold at bay the ultimate horror: Lawrence Delaney bursting into St. James behind the team of untrained chestnuts. If only he had bought the horses himself. Trained, they would be worth even more than Delaney had paid for them. How could he justify giving in so easily to an inept cawker? A few hundred pounds could have saved his brother's life. It was another example of his own failed judgment. His childish prank had broken Mary's leg. His abandonment of duty had killed his brother. He should never have allowed such wild horses to fall into such inept hands. Was this his punishment for mistreating Caroline?

The question arose from one of his nightmares in which he was pilloried in Hyde Park during the fashionable hour, while his three failures mercilessly mocked him. He had failed to protect his brother. He had failed either to win Alicia's hand or to respect her new position. And he had failed miserably with Caroline, creating a breach that might never be healed.

His admiration for his wife had grown markedly since he had admitted wronging her. For the first time he considered her with an open mind. Her handling of the household since Robert's death was masterly—comforting his father, initiating the rituals of mourning, relieving the earl of all but the most important decisions; preventing Eleanor from disrupting the family with hysterics, leading his flighty, selfish sister into acceptance and even a recognition of how her own behavior could harm others; and supporting Emily, who swore she could not have dealt with either herself or their father without Caroline. And her presence at Robert's bedside had helped him as nothing else could. Nor was anyone else in a position to run the house. His mother was prostrate, unable to make the simplest decision. Robert had always been her favorite child—a situation that he had never openly admitted but which he accepted in the same spirit he accepted his own protection. *How could he survive with Robert's blood on his hands?* His lapses were growing more serious. Never before had he been responsible for a death.

He forced his mind back to Caroline. Underestimating her abilities made him feel foolish. He owed her much more than the condemnation he had heaped on her since their marriage. In a few days they would return to Crawley. He would use it as an opportunity to start over. They must build a relationship they could comfortably live with for the rest of their lives. If that meant consigning Alicia firmly to the past, then so be it. A brief pang stabbed his heart at this decision, but he felt none of the wrenching agony he would have expected. Thank God, numbness had finally descended. Emotions under control at last, he rose to face the day.

The earl was already in the breakfast room when Caroline came down. Given the disruption of their lives, she had not expected company. Nor did he appear capable of accomplishing much this day. Dark circles underlined his eyes and emphasized the grayness of his skin.

"Good morning," she murmured, helping herself to eggs and ham. He nodded a response without speaking. At her signal Reeves departed, closing the door behind him.

"Caroline," he finally began, but his voice cracked on the word, his fork absently pushing eggs and kidney around his plate.

"Would you like me to leave? Grief is often better expressed alone."

"No, my dear. I need to talk and Portia is too distraught. Robert was always her favorite." His voice broke on the name and it took a moment to reclaim his composure. "I fear I favored Thomas."

"And now you feel guilty?"

He nodded.

"You should not. Much as a parent would like to love all their children equally, such an ideal is generally beyond a mere mortal. Thomas is much like you, just as Robert favored his mother. The preference was to be expected. But you never treated him badly. If anything, I suspect you eased his way a good deal."

"Yet I frequently rued his position as the elder," admitted the earl. "It is that which I cannot accept now."

"You blame his death on your wish that Thomas succeed you? But that is blasphemous," she chided gently. "You are not God that your preferences, however secret, can change the destiny of another. Nor is your position so exalted that God would strike down a life to satisfy you. Do not allow guilt to overpower the natural grieving of a parent for a child, lest bitterness follow. I will tell you the same thing I must tell Thomas—for he will also shoulder guilt for this tragedy. Robert's death was an accident to which neither of you contributed. In human terms, there was nothing you could have done differently that would have prevented it. In heavenly terms, his span of years was appointed by God and ran its course." She smiled. "Perhaps the angels had need of a fashion arbiter with a delightful sense of humor."

The earl smiled wanly at her small jest, but her words blanketed him in comfort, lifting the guilt that had weighed heavily on his shoulders since word arrived of the accident. He turned his thoughts to what else she had said.

"Why would Thomas feel guilty about Robert's accident?"

"To begin with, he is much like you. But specifically, he tried to buy that pair of horses when they came up for auction at Tattersall's. Young Delaney won the bidding by offering an exorbitant price. But Thomas knew they were half trained and knew that Delaney was a deplorable driver. He will convince himself that it was his duty to pay whatever was necessary to keep the team out of incompetent hands. Failure to carry out that duty makes him responsible for the injuries and death that resulted."

"What fustian!"

"I agree, but logic rarely wins arguments over emotion."

"Especially with Thomas."

Both sighed.

"I will have to speak with the boy, I suppose," continued the earl. "Thank you for your help. Portia could never have managed without you."

"It is nothing. She has suffered a great shock. But she will recover in time. As will Eleanor and, despite what she believes, her life will not be irrevocably ruined by skipping the rest of her first Season."

"You will continue as yesterday?"

"Yes. If you will excuse me, I must respond to the condolences. Are there any you wish to see to personally?"

He thought a moment, then listed half a dozen names and she nodded. "Portia will send her own responses in time," he added so that she could include this information in her notes.

They parted company in the breakfast room doorway, the earl heading to his library, Caroline toward the drawing room to discover what new messages had arrived since she had retired.

"A visitor, my lady," Sam announced as she crossed the hall.

She continued for two steps before she realized the footman was addressing her. She had a hard time remembering she was now Viscountess Hartford.

"Who?" she asked. It was still too early for callers, and mourning precluded any but relatives.

"Lord Wroxleigh," he reported. "He is in the drawing room."

"Thank you, Sam." She nodded graciously. As her cousin, his presence was unexceptionable, but she sent for Dawson to preserve the proprieties.

Drew stood before the fireplace, his face radiating concern.

"Caroline, I am so sorry this tragedy disrupted your first visit to town." His eyes raked her appearance.

Dressed in an old gown of dark brown, her vitality suppressed by sadness and grief, she again appeared the dowd Thomas had first thought her. Nor true mourning, of course, but there had not yet been time to acquire the prescribed black. Madame Suzette would arrive after luncheon with a selection of appropriate clothes.

"Thank you, Drew," she acknowledged, her eyes suspiciously moist. "I was surprised at how much this affected me—nothing like the rest, of course. But he always seemed to be such a happy man. It is difficult to find him gone, and so suddenly."

He handed her a handkerchief, ignoring her sniffs as he continued speaking. "Yes, this does force us to consider the uncertainties of life. None of us is immune to fate."

"But why does it have to strike down someone so harmless?" She at last gave way to her own tears, as she had not permitted herself to do around Robert's family.

Drew pulled her into his arms and encouraged her to cry. "You needed that, did you not?" he observed when she had finished. "I suppose you have been playing organizer and confidante for the family."

"Who else is in position to? I am far less emotionally involved."

"Just don't submerge your own needs too far, Caro," he urged, releasing her and straightening his cravat. "I admit I too will miss him. London will seem duller without his colorful presence and humorous tales."

They chatted for several minutes and then Drew rose to go. Even for a tenuous family connection, his call could not be properly prolonged.

"If there is anything I can do, please let me know," he offered in farewell.

"Thank you, Drew. You are a true friend. I expect we will return to Crawley soon, so I will not see you for a while. Take care."

"And you." He briefly kissed her hand and departed.

Caroline turned to the task of sorting notes.

Half an hour later, she was again interrupted, this time by the Earl of Waite. She straightened her hair, then asked that he be shown into the drawing room.

"Welcome, Uncle William." She seated herself and gestured

for him to do likewise. Reeves set a tea tray at her elbow and withdrew.

"My condolences on your loss, Caroline," offered Waite as she handed him a cup.

"Thank you, Uncle. How suddenly things change."

"Yes, which brings me to my reason for calling. It is more than time that I visit your parents, my dear. I am on my way to Sheldridge Corners now. Have you any messages?"

"Actually, I had just finished a letter when you arrived. I thought it best if they heard of this tragedy first from me."

"I will gladly carry it for you. Are you bearing up?"

"Yes. Though I liked Robert and feel his loss, I did not know him well enough to suffer as his immediate family must."

"How is Edward?"

"Devastated. As is the countess. Would you like to speak to him?"

"If he wishes."

Caroline sent Sam to apprise the earl of this request, then retrieved her letter from a pile awaiting his frank and handed it into her uncle's keeping. Instead of the expected summons, Marchgate himself appeared at the door. She tactfully bade Waite a good journey and left the friends alone.

Alicia greeted news of Robert's death with fury which a night of reflection did nothing to mitigate. If she had succumbed to their mutual passion and accepted his suit, she would now be Viscountess Hartford, someday to become Countess of Marchgate with access to the riches that went with that title. To say nothing of unremitting access to Thomas's lovemaking.

Instead, she had cold-bloodedly accepted the guaranteed viscountess title and wealth Darnley controlled. It had taken a week of tantrums and pleading before her parents had allowed the connection, but her determination won in the end. She had always won whatever she set her heart on.

But fate had played her false. Darnley turned against her early in their marriage, much to her satisfaction. His aging body and limited stamina could never begin to satisfy her needs and his defection left her free to sample the lustiest bucks in town. Not until his death did she learn the ramifications of his rejection. His will left her nought but her own dowry—a mere ten thousand pounds—and use of Darnley House for but a year. Invested, the money would produce an annual income of a few hundred pounds. Adequate if she retired to a country cottage and spent little on clothes. Impossible given her extravagant tastes and addiction to *ton* pleasures. Nor could she count on her parents. Her father's disgust over her escapades was clear.

She was still coming to terms with her dilemma. Within the year she must find a new husband. Yet capturing one seemed impossible. Only Thomas still believed her pretense of sweet innocence. In her quest for satisfaction she had badly overplayed her hand. Never expecting to wed a second time, she had made no attempt to preserve her reputation. But she would die before casting lures at a cit. Such people were beneath contempt. The future loomed as a terrifying choice between country obscurity and abandoning all pretense to society for life as a courtesan.

If only Thomas was not married! His devotion and blind adoration made him a perfect match. He would instantly accept her hand and count himself lucky in the process. But Caroline stood in the way. Again the country vicar's chit had bested her. That humiliating musicale still haunted her nights.

Her breakfast tray crashed against the wall.

Thomas moved through the early days of mourning in a fog. Only three images remained in his mind: Caroline offering silent comfort and support when he had broken down beside Robert's body; his fury when he learned of Wroxleigh's blatantly improper call, particularly the report that they had been shamelessly embracing; and Caroline, swathed in mourning, head bowed over the casket. Black did not suit her.

Yet as he analyzed his conflicting emotions, confusion reigned. He should have felt utter humiliation at breaking into tears in front of her. But he didn't. Despite the hours in George's rooms, he had needed the release. And Caroline's presence actually helped. It was as though he had transferred some of the pain onto her shoulders, easing his own burden. Nor was he ashamed of such a display. She would never criticize him or think less of him for such weakness. Nor would she mention it to others. How did he know that? He had no answer. Yet the certainty remained.

He watched her move confidently around the house, directing the servants, making arrangements, soothing Eleanor, comforting his mother, supporting his father, a rock in a sea of grief, the one anchor that kept them all from drowning. He had badly underestimated her worth and felt more than a bit foolish as a result. But oddly enough, the feeling engendered no anger. Her appearance was very like the dowd he had first met rather than the elegant society matron she had become. Yet he could no longer think of her in those terms. She had forever changed. He wondered at this new perception. Was he beginning to care for her just a little? Not love. That emotion was reserved for Alicia, whatever steps he took to remove her from his life. But his spirits rose whenever she entered a room. And he thanked fate for providing a mate he could rely on.

On the other hand, her continued association with Wroxleigh infuriated him. Even his new tolerance would not extend to accepting that. Oh, he could understand how she might have begun their liaison. But it must cease. How could he bring this about? He had already tried the direct approach without success. And given his own negligence and mistreatment, any further demands would meet the same fate. Even if she agreed with his reasoning, she might ignore him out of sheer pique. Perhaps he should do nothing while in London. They would return to Crawley within the week, as soon as he finished the painful business of settling Robert's affairs. Once they were home, he would begin anew to forge a partnership with Caroline. If they could rediscover their aborted friendship, perhaps then they could discuss Wroxleigh. She would have little need of an affair at that point. At least he hoped so. Visions of those two together haunted his nights, forcing his other nightmares aside. *Dear Lord, please help us find a way to live with each other.*

It had rained continuously since the evening of Robert's death. Almost as if heaven itself mourned him, reflected Caroline. She was busy enough that she had barely noticed the weather. Nor had she been accorded much time for thought. Which was just as well. Robert had been almost a caricature fop, but he possessed a sweetness that was very endearing. Remembering him raised a lump in her throat, but she dared not break down. Everyone else's composure was too fragile.

Finally, two days after the funeral, the rain ceased.

She rejected taking a turn around the square. Such a public appearance would not accord with accepted mourning practice, particularly in such a popular location. Sunshine brought all of society outdoors. Carriages clustered around Gunter's and dozens of people wandered through the square. Sighing, she settled for several turns about the Marchgate garden. Though not extensive enough to allow any real exercise, she could at least benefit from fresh air. And they would return home very soon. Crawley beckoned invitingly.

The garden glowed in a rainbow of colors, spring flowers

massing before shrubs feathery with new growth. High walls separated it from adjacent houses, providing privacy, their only break a decorative iron gate leading to the mews. The height muted the noise from the square, allowing her to relax as though in the country.

What would returning home accomplish? Thomas had been deeply affected by Robert's death. Would this change his perceptions of Crawley? Of Alicia? Of her? Reminders of mortality sometimes forced people to take stock of their own lives. She could only hope that such an analysis would benefit him.

She had surprised several indecipherable looks in his eyes over the preceding days. Was he finally seeing her as she was? Or was he cursing her existence? Without her, Alicia would be his, for Lady Darnley would accept marriage now. He held a viscount's title with a promise of an earldom in the future. His financial position was secure, again with the promise of great wealth. And he still offered both good looks and passion. A lady of Alicia's propensities would appreciate both.

She shook her head. Such thinking served no purpose. Instead of considering failure, she should be planning how to further her own cause. She hoped she had made a start. He seemed to appreciate her efforts to spare his family in their time of grief. They would remain at Crawley throughout mourning. Even if he lived in the stables from dawn until dusk, there should be ample opportunity to spend time together. Perhaps they could rediscover their early camaraderie. She would make a concerted effort to earn his respect. And this time she would have additional weapons at her disposal.

As he started down the stairs for breakfast, Thomas spotted Caroline just ahead of him. Even though neither left the house these days, they rarely met. Irritation flared, for she seemed oblivious of his presence. He quickened his pace to catch up. But in his hurry, he overstrode the next step, throwing himself into a fall. He lunged for the railing, grasping it with one hand, but the other caught Caroline between the shoulder blades, pitching her forward. Still fighting to regain his own balance, he was unable to catch her.

She screamed.

Caroline was lost in thought as she headed for breakfast. As much as she hoped and prayed for a rapprochement with Thomas, it seemed so impossible. Nightmares had tortured her sleep.

Again and again she relived Alicia's greeting when Thomas had appeared at her door. Nor did her imagination stop there, filling in the details of a passionate encounter of epic proportions. What hope was there for her own paltry dreams? Yet what options did she have? A wife was but a piece of property, wholly at the command of her husband. She was obligated to live where and how he ordained, suffer whatever treatment he meted out, and perform whatever services he demanded. She owned no property, could instigate no divorce proceedings, commanded few legal rights.

Someone touched the center of her back and pushed. Hard.

Screaming, she pitched forward, gripping as tightly as possible with the hand that had trailed down the railing, flailing wildly with the other. One foot slid off the edge of a step, but she managed to regain her balance without falling. Heart pounding she turned to see who wished her ill.

Shock froze her soul. Thomas stood calmly, three steps above her, his face completely blank. But his eyes blazed with guilt. And with something else she refused to name. *Hatred,* whispered the voice.

So it was true. Obsession had won, even over honor. Only freedom would satisfy him now. Stifling a sob, she fled to the breakfast room.

Thomas had barely gained his balance when Caroline caught herself. Guilt over his carelessness paralyzed him, but when she turned her eyes to his, he was overcome with self-loathing. She clearly believed the push was deliberate. How could he have brought them to such rampant distrust? Despite his treasured honor, his touted ethics, even his chivalry, manners, and good sense, his treatment of his wife—the one person he had vowed to God, no less, to honor and cherish—was so appallingly callous that she accepted without question the conclusion that he sought her death. But he could not blame her. The conclusion was wrong, but his behavior was abominable. He was the worst sort of cad. *How could he ever atone?* Wearily, he plodded back to his room.

He went out that evening for the first time since Robert's death. Not publicly, of course. He dropped by George's rooms to bid farewell to his closest friend. Jeremy was also visiting.

"My condolences," offered Jeremy solemnly.

"Thank you." The morning's shock had receded, blending into that gray fog that had protected his emotions for the past week. It permitted him to carry on a normal conversation, even about Robert.

They spent the evening sharing memories, first of Robert, then of past escapades and mutual friends. George's brandy was good, a late supper better, and Thomas stayed until nearly dawn, relaxing in the warm friendship and support, maintaining a parody of his customary demeanor without too much effort.

But his mind churned, quite apart from the discussion, rehashing the details of his marriage. By the time he collapsed into bed, he had decided that postponing the confrontation with Caroline until they reached Crawley was unacceptable. He would speak with her first thing in the morning.

Caroline awoke with the dawn, too restless to go back to sleep. A week tied to the house was finally eroding her composure, and a night of confused dreams left a pounding headache. Donning a black gown, she wrapped a cloak around her shoulders and slipped into the garden. Much as she would have preferred the square, she could not flout convention. Besides, anyone she met this time of day would likely be a gentleman staggering home after a long night, and she did not wish for such an encounter.

She was no longer convinced that Thomas's push had been deliberate. Surely, if he had intended death, he would have first removed her hand from the railing. He had never been stupid. This hope was supported by a glimpse of him crossing the foyer after lunch, limping as though his right ankle was badly sprained. He had not seen her, so was not faking. Had he slipped on the stairs, regaining his balance as he crashed into her? She clung to this picture, using it to erase that blaze of hatred that had flared in his eyes.

Fog clung to shrubbery and trees, turning the garden into a forest of ghostly images. She paced the enclosure for nearly an hour, mind churning in nauseating circles. She loved Thomas. Thomas loved Alicia. Alicia loved Alicia. And anything in breeches. How could she induce Thomas to discover that fact so he could turn his attentions elsewhere? If she destroyed his image of Alicia, would he hate her forever? Yet his current resentment was just as bad. It was time to chance his wrath. Nothing she did now could possibly make things worse. So how could she expose Lady Darnley? Denounce her to Thomas's face? Challenge him to discover the truth for himself by watching the mews gate to Darnley House? If Alicia was half as active as rumor reported, but a few hours should convince the most determined skeptic.

The light gradually brightened, but the fog remained, casting a shroud of mourning over the garden. She shivered as its icy fingers penetrated her cloak. It was more than time to return to the house. But nothing was settled. She allowed herself one last circuit.

As she approached the gate to the mews, she spotted another early riser on the other side. He had donned a hooded cloak against the foggy chill so she could not see who he was, but he seemed to be staring directly at her.

Her mouth opened to bid him good morning, but no sound emerged.

His right hand clutched a pistol. Taking careful aim, he squeezed the trigger, the sound echoing hollowly through the fog.

Caroline reacted instantly. Twisting sharply to the right, she dove for a thick hedge and rolled behind it. The bullet whistled past her shoulder, putting a double hole through a fold of her cloak. A muttered curse rent the morning calm, the voice clearly belonging to the London slums. Footsteps rapidly retreated along the mews.

Carefully working her way behind the hedge until she was out of sight of the gate, she concentrated on control, refusing to dwell on what had just occurred. Stealthily she slipped from tree to shrub to bench, forcing calm, forcing quiet, forcing blankness into her mind. Her back tingled, expecting attack at any moment. Her head was in constant motion, twisting this way and that as she scanned the fog-shrouded landscape for other assailants. Every misty shrub assumed a sinister cast. The five minutes it took to reach the door stretched like five years.

When she finally reached her room, she collapsed, shaking so hard she could barely turn the key in her lock. Then she threw herself across the bed. *Why?* screamed her brain. Her eyes saw nothing but the black hole of the gun barrel. Sobs tore through her throat and she wept for a long time.

The attempt was deliberate. That much was abundantly clear. The assassin first identified her, then took careful aim. Who would wish her dead?

"No!" she protested aloud. "I will not believe it." New tears welled. She fought them down, pacing the floor in agitation. Was this not exactly what she derided Thomas for? Allowing love and desire to cloud his reasoning so that even blatant evidence was ignored or explained away? Two accidents on the stairs. A shooting in the garden. He had been away most of the night—ample opportunity to arrange such a thing. Yet she could not believe him responsible. He lived for honor. And if he chose to kill an unwanted encumbrance, he would never hire another to carry out the act. He had been asleep in his room when she returned to the house.

Another possibility came to mind. She clung to it as to a lifeline.

Thomas might not be responsible, but what of Alicia? She could not accuse her openly, of course. But who else existed with the slightest motive for terminating her existence? Every sense accepted *her* guilt. She relaxed into a smile. Could she use this attack to further her own cause?

Hopefully, she explored this possibility. If nothing else, it distracted her mind from the horror of that pistol shot. The longer she considered the situation, the more certain she became. It did not take long to develop her strategy.

First and foremost, she must remove from town without delay. If Alicia wanted her dead, this morning's failure would not prevent a second attack. She would pack a small valise and order out the carriage immediately. Dawson could pack the remainder of her clothes to be sent down when Thomas joined her. And she would have to reward Dawson for her faithful service. Perhaps the earl could advance her enough. Caroline's reticule was woefully empty just now.

She would not wake Thomas before leaving. If he was— No, he was not guilty, she reminded herself sharply. She would leave him a letter containing an explanation of the morning's events.

No longer did she face having to make a direct accusation. The shooting might be enough by itself to force him into seeing Alicia for what she was. He could come up with no other suspects either. Dawson should pack her cloak last, allowing him to examine it.

She descended to the breakfast room.

"What!" The earl nearly choked on a piece of bacon when she baldly announced the murder attempt.

"I fear it is true," she calmly repeated. "And I have no doubt who was behind the plot." A wave of horror convulsed his face, and she hastened to reassure him. "No! Thomas would never stoop to such depths. You know that as well as I do. I am convinced a certain unnamed female conceived this action."

"My God, I'll see her transported for this," he swore viciously.

"No, you will not," countered Caroline. "Do you want to plunge us all into scandal? Society would never believe Thomas was not involved. Let him handle it. He will settle things without publicity. Please do not meddle unless he requests it. This might be the one thing that will force him to confront the truth. Since I emerged unscathed, I am actually delighted at this turn of events."

He frowned for several minutes in thought before his brow smoothed. "Very clever, Caroline. What do you plan to tell him?"

"Nothing in person, believe me. Prudence dictates that I leave immediately for Crawley. I cannot risk another attempt. The carriage will be here in fifteen minutes. I left a letter for Thomas describing the attack, but naming no names and assigning no blame. He should be able to reconstruct the plot without further assistance. And will accept it more readily if he does so."

Marchgate nodded. "Is there any evidence you can offer to aid his thinking?"

"My cloak. It contains two holes. I will leave it in my room."

The earl blanched. "You must take Worth for protection," he insisted, naming his head groom. "He can return later. Thomas will need to borrow a coach for baggage, as his only other conveyance is his curricle."

"Thank you."

They discussed the details of her forthcoming journey while she finished breakfast, then bade each other a fond farewell and she slipped away into the fog.

Chapter 17

Caroline arrived at Crawley in midafternoon, weary from the emotional strain to which she had been subjected for so long. The entire journey had passed in agonizing memory and unanswerable questions.

Though convinced that Alicia was responsible for the morning's attack, she could not completely banish a nagging suspicion that Thomas might be involved. Or might condone his idol's actions. Obsession obeyed neither common sense nor prudence. Would he accept a *fait accompli* without delving too deeply into how it came about? Could that convoluted brain somehow twist Alicia's attack into a justified action? Though she was convinced that his conscience would eventually rebel against such horrors, the immediate outlook was definitely uncertain. Nor could she forget the disappointment that had flickered across his face after the first accident or the hatred that blazed following the second. He may not have initiated either action, may not even have entertained the idea of eliminating her, yet he was not slow to recognize what it meant to his future.

But she loved him. No suspicion could alter that. Unbidden, her thoughts moved ahead through the years. Could she share his house if he stubbornly continued adoring Alicia? Sadly, she could not. The constant pain would destroy her. Love would turn to bitterness. Anger would eat at her soul. It would not take long for mutual recriminations to destroy them both.

How long could she endure the present situation before she gave up all hope? A month? A year? If Thomas remained adamant, would her efforts turn his course? She shook her head. Even if her hopes proved true, he might not redirect his attentions toward her. Suspicions of Drew would cloud his judgment.

Wearily, she gave up. Unless Thomas acknowledged Alicia's true character, there seemed no hope for their future. So she was back to her initial problem. How long should she wait before removing from the scene? And where would she go? Sheldridge Corners was not a possibility. Not only was it unfair to her parents, but she could not tolerate the sympathy she would receive from her family. Perhaps the present Lord Cummings could help. There were several aunts and elderly cousins who might be willing to take her on as a companion. *This is the last chance. Give me the strength to leave if it fails.*

The carriage pulled to a halt and she composed her features into a calm mask.

"Welcome home, my lady," greeted Peters at the door. "Is his lordship not with you?"

"No." She smiled. "Again I must apologize for not warning you of my arrival. But with the funeral behind us, I simply could not remain in town. Lord Hartford will follow in a few days, as soon as he winds up his brother's affairs. But the journey has wearied me. Dinner on a tray in my room will suffice for tonight, Peters."

"Shall you need Sarah, my lady?"

"Yes, please, and a bath. The house looks lovely. I see the new covers are installed in the drawing room."

"Last week."

"Wonderful. You and Mrs. Peters have done well."

She climbed to her room, relaxing for the first time in days. Despite the amount of work yet to be done, she could not but feel content in her own home. The idea of leaving tore at her heart, but unless Thomas recovered from his obsession, she would have no choice.

A bath improved her outlook and she lay down for a nap, sleeping soundly until a nightmare intruded late in the afternoon.

She had been cornered in the Marchgate garden by the cloaked killer, reliving that awful instant when the realization that he was going to shoot had paralyzed her legs. Only when she established that her assailant could not be Thomas had she been able to move. Her attacker was much too short.

Sleep was now impossible. She donned an old cloak and wandered toward the lake, again pondering the events leading to her flight from London. The nightmare would fade in time. No one could survive such an attack without residual terror. It would continue at least until Thomas returned. His attitude would determine how long it would remain. If his obsession continued, the dream would intensify. If he repudiated Alicia, it would fade quickly. If he set his idol aside but retained her image, she did not know what would happen. But until then, she must concentrate on estate duties.

The rest of the day flew past in a flurry of activity. She met with Jacobs, who introduced her to Richards. Jacobs's leg was much better, allowing him to walk with the aid of a cane. He could not yet stand for any length of time, but should soon be riding for short periods. Another hour passed with Talbert. Estate conditions improved daily. Planting was complete. She was surprised at the difference in the gardens and grounds. Deadwood and overgrowth were gone. Many garden plantings were too damaged to recover and had been removed. She must plan replacements. *If she stayed*. But even with bare spots, the grounds began to do justice to the manor.

These activities kept her thoughts at bay. But an evening at the pianoforte failed to do so. She could not connect with the music. Nor could she reach any real conclusions. Fears, plots, options, and longing swirled through her head, unaffected by the most challenging pieces. There was no one with whom she could discuss her problems. Drew might have offered sound advice, but he was beyond reach. She could not air her difficulties with anyone local. Not even the vicar. She had to protect Thomas from rumors.

There *was* a vicar who could help, of course. Her fingers crashed in a dissonant cluster on the keys. Vicar Cummings, her own father, would listen and understand her problems, and he knew enough of London society from his own youth to offer realistic advice. Was Uncle William still there? Could she bare her soul to her father without advertising to Waite her rift with Thomas? Possibly. Particularly if she could make it appear her stop was a side trip between London and Crawley, taken because the Marchgates had departed, but Thomas's business was incomplete. After all, he would not return for some days yet. She would be back at Crawley before his arrival. It was perfect.

Peace at last descended over her spirit. Issuing the necessary orders for an early departure, she composed a brief note explaining her absence in case Thomas returned early, then went to bed.

Thomas awoke to a mild headache from George's brandy and the familiar fog that had plagued him since Robert's death. Another day to be endured, one that must start with a confrontation. Hopefully, he was right to believe that Caroline would welcome this discussion. He sat up gingerly, not yet ready to face Cramer.

A folded paper propped on the washstand caught his eye, Caroline's copperplate on the outside. Cold fury washed over him as he read.

Thomas,

I leave for Crawley immediately. Between accidents and attempted murder, London has proven unhealthy. There is no need to rush your business. Worth and Larkin can ensure my safety.

Disturbing your sleep can serve no purpose, so I will content myself with reporting facts. As I walked in the garden just after dawn, a hooded and cloaked man stopped at the mews gate. After watching me closely for some time, he removed a gun from beneath his cloak, deliberately aimed at me, and fired. He immediately raced away. I was unable to discern his direction as heavy fog distorted the echoes of his footsteps.

This time he missed, but his care and deliberation convince me he will try again. I refuse to offer him a chance to succeed. Flirting with death is not my style.

I am making no accusations, Thomas. You care nought for me, as I well know. But I cannot believe you are so lost to honor that you would stoop to murder, even to rid yourself of an encumbrance that must daily grate on your soul. Yet the fact remains that someone desires my death. I will not remain a target.

Caroline

He hated her.

Not only did she stand in the way of happiness with Alicia, she was a leaden burden. *An encumbrance that must daily grate on your soul. . . .* She certainly understood his dilemma. But how dare she imply that he might kill her?

He paced the room, fists clenched in anger. In spite of her disclaimer, she must believe it. Why else would she leave without even waking him? He had every right to know immediately of the shooting. And she had no business making decisions on her own. He should decide whether to send her home.

He again read her infuriating missive. *Stoop to murder . . .* She had even relinquished her good sense. Did she have no understanding of honor? Were she ten times as bad—nay, a hundred times—he would never harm one he had pledged to care for. How could he ever accept her after this outrage? He should have found a way to marry Alicia. *She* would never suspect him of infamy!

His mental bluster continued for some minutes before he admitted in surprise that it was, in fact, bluster. His pacing abruptly stopped. Did he really hate Caroline? He carefully smoothed the crumpled note. Taking a deep breath, he pushed aside the anger at her sudden departure, ignored her hints at his involvement, and reread the message.

Shorn of his emotional response, her words struck terror in his heart. He shuddered. By no stretch of the imagination could the incident be an accident. Was it an attempt to scare her? Injure her? Or was she correct to suspect deliberate murder? Icy shivers marched down his spine.

Who would want to kill Caroline? He rejected the obvious answer, and more forcibly rejected it again, but it would not go away. *Someone desires my death. . . .*

Grimly he summoned Cramer. Twenty minutes later he strode toward Davies Street, with an open mind for the first time in more than a year.

Memories assailed him from the moment he accepted the unthinkable as a possibility. Images he had long ignored smote his conscience, their juxtaposition revealing truths he had never wanted to believe. A cold hand grasped his heart, squeezing tighter with each blow—

Alicia wantonly pressing against him, hands tearing at his clothes as she begged for his body, explicitly spelling out precisely what she needed, demanding satisfaction but giving nothing in return. No wonder he had come away from the encounter confused and disappointed. Passion was to be shared. But there had been no pretense of sharing. Once his control had snapped, there was nothing but pure, selfish lust. . . . Caroline in their first week of marriage, her inexpert hands eager to learn how to please, discovering ways to arouse him that even he had not known. . . . He groaned.

Alicia's catty compliments, sly innuendo, spurious sympathy, and vicious put-downs of Caroline, worded, he now saw, to fan his anger and draw him closer to her side. . . . Caroline's unfailing graciousness and refusal to denigrate anyone, even acknowledging without sarcasm that Lady Darnley was the most stunningly beautiful woman she had ever seen. . . .

Caroline urging him to employ ex-soldiers. . . . Alicia sneering at an outstretched hand and pointedly avoiding its legless owner. . . .

Alicia clad in gowns that, he now admitted, could only be described as scandalous. . . . Caroline's demonstrated good taste, even the wreckage of Crawley exhibiting charm once her elegant touch was imprinted on it. . . .

The flashes of anger he had never dared identify that crossed Alicia's face at the slightest opposition to her will. . . . Caroline's unfailing good temper. The only time he had ever seen her lose control was the night of Eleanor's ball. And his provocation had been extreme. . . .

Alicia's selfish, grasping greed. She was much more than the slightly spoiled miss he had admitted. . . . Caroline quietly supporting his family, demonstrating without fanfare the most caring, sharing, loving heart he had ever encountered. . . .

The musicale. Alicia's face had changed from gloating to fury. . . . He nearly burst into laughter as he recognized the plot and Caroline's perfect revenge.

Someone desires my death. . . .

How could he have believed Alicia to be perfect? He no longer loved her. The truth stabbed him so painfully that he stopped dead on the street, nearly collapsing in shock.

Oh, God! He had never loved her.

Bedazzled by beauty, overwhelmed by lust, he had created her character out of his own desire, attributing every virtue to her credit. And ignoring every hint of vice. Another wave of shock set him trembling as with an ague. Caroline embodied nearly every aspect of that created image—and more.

How could he have been so stupid? Another truth slammed through his brain. Alicia had seduced him at Graystone—deliberately and knowingly. Amazement battled chagrin and anger. With all of his own seductive arts, perfected over years of practice, how could he have failed to recognize the same wiles turned against him?

His friends had tried to warn him. Jeremy had more than once prosed on about the dangers of infatuation, describing how he had mistakenly attributed many virtues to Elizabeth that she did not possess. Yet, arrogantly sure of his own judgment, Thomas had never entertained the suspicion that he was guilty of the same mistake. And then there was George, suggesting he remove himself for a period of contemplation. His own voice echoed across their last card game—*I should have discarded the diamond*, and George's piercing stare . . .

He reached Alicia's house and knocked on the door. In his present mood, he allowed the butler no chance to deny him entry but settled into the drawing room, expecting a lengthy wait, while knowing that she would eventually meet with him. The room was garishly decorated in the latest Egyptian mode. He shuddered in distaste.

For the last time, he recalled every meeting with Alicia, from their introduction at Almack's until he had called to examine her horses two weeks before. Shorn of editing, the pictures unrolling through his mind appalled him. When had she chosen to abandon her place in the polite world? Before her first trip to London? After she accepted Darnley? When he had unexpectedly surfaced at Graystone? Or had Darnley's fit triggered her rebellion? He could not relinquish a fear that he was somehow responsible for her fall from grace. If that were true, he still owed her something. Though never again could he even like her.

Removed a gun . . . Deliberately aimed . . . Fired . . .

He squeezed his eyes shut, trying to erase the image. What was Alicia's goal? Injury as revenge for the musicale? Or the wealth and power that belonged to the Countess of Marchgate? Did she really believe that he would marry her if Caroline died? . . . How could she believe otherwise? He had as good as told her that only Caroline kept him out of her bed.

He shuddered.

The connecting door between the drawing room and an adjacent morning room was slightly ajar. Someone entered the morning room, banging the hall door closed.

"What happened to your eye, Rosie?" a voice exclaimed in shock.

"Nothin'." The muttered response was sullen.

The newcomer snorted in disbelief. "The truth, girl! Nothing would surprise me, you know. I suppose it was *her*. How bad is it? Do I need to take steps to protect you? You would hardly be the first who needed rescuing." Cloth rustled and a chair scraped.

"You know what her ladyship's been like this past month," capitulated Rosie. "Expected to lure Mr. Mannering into her bed long ago as besotted as the fellow is. His refusal fair drove her mad."

Thomas stifled a gasp, gritting his teeth through another wave of anger. How many others knew of his stupidity? The entire *ton*? Servants were the source of much of Mayfair's gossip.

"True. She threw her breakfast tray at me yesterday. And poor Clara turned up with a swollen jaw last night. I wish I knew how to find a new position without the reference she is bound to refuse me. Ten years serving that bitch and nothing to show for it but threats and abuse."

"Oh, Giddings, it's sorry I am to be remindin' you."

Thomas now recognized the newcomer in the next room. Giddings was Alicia's abigail and had usually accompanied her mistress during the Season he had courted her. Rosie was undoubtedly a housemaid.

"Forget it. Nothing will ever change her, and somehow I will escape. I always thought she made a mistake insisting on wedding for a title and money, believing the one she lusted after would fall into her bed anyway. Her parents should never have given in to her tantrums and allowed it. I nearly died laughing when his lordship cut her off with a pittance. He saw through her pious act that first week. What could she have expected, as experienced as he was? Called her a tart to her face, kicked her out of his bed, and informed her that any brat she produced would never be recognized. Put it in his will, too. And left her nothing but her own dowry. If she can't snare another husband soon, it's off to a country cottage for her ladyship. Serves her right for being a bad-tempered shrew."

Giggles.

"Shush. If Potts hears us, we're both in for it. He fair dotes on her."

"Right you are, Rosie. And her temper is none too good just now. Mannering refused to bed her after all. Cited his honor. You should have seen her that day. Lucky you were off. But she's been livid since he turned up heir to an earldom. If she'd played her cards right last year she'd be wed to him all nice and tight. But she's arranged to rid him of that inconvenient wife of his. That ought to earn his gratitude. He can't like being tied to such a common wench when his heart belongs to her ladyship. Now let me look at that eye."

"But that's why she's in such a temper this morning. The attempt failed . . . Ouch!"

"Shush . . . Somebody's coming . . ."

Thomas normally abhorred eavesdropping, but this time he was grateful. The maids' chatter removed his last shred of obligation. She had tricked him from first to last, pulling the wool over his eyes to an extent he would not have thought possible. All his worries over her nonexistent love were pointless. He felt a fool—a furious fool—not an emotion likely to prompt conciliation or forgiveness. His eyes glinted as coldly as green ice when the drawing room door opened.

Alicia made a grand entrance. Dressed as usual in a blue gown with a neckline that barely cleared her nipples, she exuded sexuality. But this time he felt nothing. She looked like a cheap tart and he frowned in distaste.

"Thomas, my love," she purred. "Just the person I most wanted to see."

"I very much doubt that, Viscountess Darnley," he snapped coldly. "I can no longer address you as 'Lady,' you see. Your criminal activities have stripped you of any right to such a title. In case you have not yet heard, your attempt to murder my wife this morning failed."

She gasped. "But what can you possibly mean?"

He pushed her hand aside as she tried to caress him. "I mean, you scheming jade, that Caroline is safe. And she will remain so. I guarantee that if the slightest harm befalls her, no matter how accidental the circumstances appear, I will see you in Botany Bay for the remainder of your natural life. From there I have no doubt you will descend straight to hell."

This time he slapped her caressing arm aside, hard enough to leave an angry red welt on the skin.

"I am no longer affected either by your admitted beauty or by your very practiced wiles, Viscountess," he declared in a menacing tone. "Nor will I ever again willingly spend time under the same roof with you. Your selfish, wanton behavior and your despicable plotting have erased any desirability you may once have possessed. If you wish to ever grace even the lowliest drawing room in Mayfair again, you had best retire to the country for a few years and hope that your escapades become sufficiently dulled by time that you might be offered a second chance."

Alicia's mouth hung open in shock. Completely ignoring her, he turned on his heel and departed. Behind him the sound of smashed glass echoed along the street.

Would Caroline accept his change of heart? He pondered that question as his feet dragged in the direction of Berkeley Square. His behavior for the past year had been abominable, especially since his marriage. Could she forgive him? Or had he alienated her affections for all time? Not that he expected love from his wife, just as he did not expect to fall in love with her. But she was an intelligent and comfortable lady, someone he badly wanted for a friend and partner. Especially a bed partner, he admitted, remembering those few nights early on when they had shared a bed without anger. But would she welcome him back there? The gnawing fear was never far away. Had she given herself to Wroxleigh?

What would he do if she had? After his own neglect, could he blame her for satisfying herself elsewhere? She had no cause to expect solace at home. *You care nought for me, as I well know....* His fists clenched painfully. How could he have been so stupid? And how could he expect Wroxleigh to bypass such an opportunity? The man specialized in unhappy wives. If she was using him to satisfy the passions that he himself had awakened, he would have to forgive her. But she would never suffer that lack in the future, he swore. It would be harder if she had developed a *tendre* for her lover. Could they eventually reach an accord that would compensate her for giving up her liaison?

As he approached the house, Wroxleigh himself appeared from the other direction, apparently with the same destination in mind. Thomas fought down his instinctive anger. This was a perfect opportunity to warn the libertine away.

"Wroxleigh," he said coolly, inclining his head a fraction.

"Hartford," responded the other. "Is Caroline well?"

"She has returned to Crawley." Thomas had to work to keep his voice level at the intimacy implied by Wroxleigh's form of address.

Drew raised surprised brows. "When I spoke with her yesterday, she had no such plans. I thought you were traveling down together."

"She left early this morning."

"What did you do to her?" Drew's face resembled a thundercloud. "I ought to thrash you for the way you've treated your wife. No one deserves that kind of contempt. Least of all, her."

"My relationship with Caroline is none of your business," he snapped, grinding his teeth in an effort to control his anger.

"I refuse to stand by and watch my dearest friend made miserable because you are too obsessed to believe facts." Drew's fists clenched as his own temper neared the breaking point.

"Friends? I think not. Men like you don't make friends of their women."

"You ought to know," rejoined Drew. "Your reputation is as bad as mine—worse really. I never game to excess. But you are wrong. Caroline is a jewel and it pains me to see her mistreated so badly. You've left her in tears more than once, in case you care."

"How dare you! I ought to call you out for that. And what gives you the right to interfere?"

"Our relationship." He paused at the fury blazing from Thomas's eyes. "You honestly don't know? I can't believe this. No—" One hand lashed out to keep Hartford at arm's length. Fortunately his reach proved longer, for Thomas swung anyway. "It's not what you think. She's my cousin, you fool! I thought everyone in London knew that."

"Cousin?" Thomas sagged in shock, his brain completely blank as he tried to assimilate this new idea. He suddenly burst into laughter at his own ignorance and leaned weakly against the railing. "Why did she never tell me?"

"Did you ever give her a chance? But she probably thought you knew. I'm amazed you did not."

"I might have, if I had ever thought about it. But you can hardly blame me for assuming the worst." He gestured and led the way into the house, ordering Sam to bring brandy to the drawing room.

"I suppose not, given my reputation. Though you were wrong. Not that I didn't try at first. But she drew a very firm line the night we met and I like her too much to try to seduce her past it. You really do not deserve her, you know."

"True, though I hope I can make it up to her now. I have discovered the truth you accused me of ignoring, by the way. Caroline left for Crawley this morning after an assassin hired by Darnley's widow narrowly missed shooting her in the garden."

Drew choked on his brandy. "My God, man, how did you bring her to this pass?"

"It's a long story, and one I might even tell you some day. But I guarantee that it will never happen again. The lady in question has also discovered reality. To her chagrin," he finished grimly.

"I certainly hope so."

"Caroline is safe, and I will join her in a day or two. We are nearly finished with Robert's affairs." His voice wavered at mention of his brother.

"My condolences, Hartford. I should have offered them earlier."

"Thank you. But you might as well call me Thomas. With both kinship and friendship with Caroline, I expect we will be seeing a great deal of each other in the future."

"Thank you, Thomas. And for your trust as well. I am Drew, by the way."

Thomas smiled and settled in for a friendly discussion with the last man on earth he had ever expected to count among his honored guests.

Chapter 18

Thomas arrived at Crawley in a raging downpour.

The discussion with Wroxleigh had cleared most of the remaining obstacles from his mind, leaving nothing but a desire to face Caroline and beg her forgiveness. Earning her friendship became his new goal. Not even Robert's business was more important.

His last interview with his father had reinforced this desire. He sensed a barely controlled fury in his sire as he seated himself by the library fire.

"Thank you for offering Caroline the use of Worth," he began.

"She needed more protection than Larkin could provide, particularly since her dresser will not leave London."

This was something else he had not known. "Is that not a bit sudden?"

"No, Caroline knew of the situation when she hired the woman, but chose to do so anyway."

So Caroline had hired her own dresser. And chosen with great skill. Why was he not surprised? At least Dawson was not scuttling away from trouble. Had Caroline asked her to change her mind? He suspected Cramer entertained more than a little partiality in that quarter. But he dared not pursue the thought yet. His father was still seething. "I am disappointed that you did not tell me Caroline was returning to Crawley."

"She specifically requested that I refrain," he stated in icy tones. "Claimed that you would understand and that she was leaving you a full explanation."

"Both statements are true. There will be no further trouble. I have already seen to that."

"Ah." Marchgate visibly relaxed, his countenance warming to a near smile. Guilty at the realization that his idiotic behavior had been so clear to those around him, Thomas felt a fool. Was all Mayfair discussing his misdeeds?

"I cannot leave her in doubt as to the outcome," he declared firmly. "Can you finish Robert's business without me? I plan to leave at dawn."

"Certainly," agreed the earl readily. "There is not much left to do. And you should be with your wife." *Welcome back, son.*

They spent an hour discussing those items requiring his decision before he excused himself to prepare for his journey.

A sound from Caroline's room drew him through the door. Dawson was busily packing the last of her wardrobe into trunks.

"My lord?" She turned a questioning eye at his sudden appearance.

"Did Lady Hartford make adequate arrangements with you before she left?"

"Yes, my lord."

"I know she would be delighted to retain your services if you have any second thoughts about your original agreement," he offered.

She hesitated, but interest flickered in her dark eyes.

"If you decide to stay with my wife, you would live half the year at Crawley, which is an hour east of Banbury. I will be purchasing a house in London. Once we are out of mourning, we will spend both Seasons in town. Would you like the job?"

Dawson smiled. "Yes, my lord. Your wife is a wonderful lady and a pleasure to work for. Thank you."

"Thank *you*," he replied, hoping Caroline might think better of him for this gesture. "We will leave at first light." His eyes lit on a muddy cloak hanging on the wardrobe door. "What—" he began, a finger tracing the pair of holes. His knees shook.

"She was wearing it this morning."

"Oh, Lord." He struggled between rage and fear.

"She was untouched," added Dawson softly.

He spent his evening at a quiet dinner with George and Jeremy, thanking them for their care of Caroline, making clear without actually saying so that his obsession was terminated and would never rear its ugly head again. He left with messages for her ringing in his ears.

Peters seemed surprised to see him.

"Did Lady Hartford not warn you of my imminent arrival?" he asked, allowing John to remove his sodden cloak. A curricle was not the most comfortable vehicle to drive through the rain.

"She did not expect you for some days," he responded woodenly. "Nor is she here just now, having left this morning for a brief visit to her parents."

Cold terror clutched at his heart. Why would she leave so soon after returning? Had something happened that threatened her life still? Perhaps she was avoiding him. Did she really believe him to be responsible for the attack? And the weather! Larkin was a competent coachman, but what would he have done when this storm broke? It had moved in from the west, so they would have struck it much sooner than he had.

"What time did she leave?"

"She had planned an early start, but the Griggs girl was mauled by a stray dog this morning. She is but four years old. Lady Hartford tended her wounds, so did not leave until nearly eleven. She claimed there was still time enough to arrive before dinner." But Peters cast an uncomfortable eye at the continuing downpour.

Fear overwhelmed Thomas, beyond all logic. Something was wrong. He was sure of it. "Have Greatheart brought around in fifteen minutes." He strode up to his room.

As expected, Caroline had left him a note, but it did not comfort him in the least. In fact, it left the distinct impression that she was considering leaving him.

> *Thomas,*
>   *My apologies for not being here when you arrived, but I did not expect you for some days yet.*
>   *I am visiting my parents. The recent unpleasantness has forced me to take a closer look at the future. Neither of us can tolerate the current situation any longer. I must decide in which direction to move and do not wish to be precipitate. Yet there is no one here I can consult. I need wise counsel, such as my father can provide.*
>
> *Caroline*

Pain lashed him, his dense mind finally absorbing the truth. He loved her. Had probably loved her for some time. His anger at her imagined infidelity was jealousy, not irritation that she ignored the code of honor he thought so important. And he was within a hair's breadth of losing her.

How could he atone for the pain he had caused? *You care nought for me, as I well know. . . .* Or was there pain? *Neither of us can tolerate . . .* Did she refer to the strain of living with his unremitting anger? Or was she acknowledging that marriage had been a mistake and she would be happier living alone?

Shuddering, he considered this possibility. Legally, he could force her to stay. But what about the morals of such an action? If she cared nothing for him, if his own deplorable behavior had instilled a disgust that could not be erased, could he in all conscience compel her to remain at Crawley? Tears welled in his eyes. He could not. Her happiness was more important than his own. He had caused enough harm already and could not inflict more. Why had he never understood this aspect of love? By that one simple criterion, he could never have confused his infatuation for Alicia with love.

He could not wait until morning to follow her. Two forces compelled him into the storm. Something was clearly wrong; he could not shake the certainty that she was in danger. And he was impatient. Questions gnawed at his reason. Whatever the outcome, he had to know what the future held. It was time for honesty. He must admit his guilt and beg forgiveness. Hopefully, she would agree to give their marriage a second chance. Had she retained enough regard to forgive him? Was there any hope his love might someday be returned? But he banished this thought. It would be enough for now to have her at Crawley.

Hours later, his body begged him to reconsider this mad journey. Such a storm had not swept England in years. Even macadamized roads were becoming hopeless mires, and the lanes that offered the shortest route to Sheldridge Corners were virtually impassable. Only the fact that he rode kept him going. No vehicle could have managed.

She had been easy to track during the early stages, relieving one worry. Larkin was following the expected route. But it was becoming more difficult. Darkness was nearly total; storm clouds and curtains of rain blocked all light. Nor was he familiar with the area. Stopping at yet another rustic inn, he prayed fervently that someone had seen the carriage. Greatheart was nearly foundered. He could not push the stallion much farther.

Caroline gazed pensively into the fire, unwilling to remain awake to ponder her problems, yet fearing the dreams of sleep. This whole mad adventure was ill-conceived.

The journey had started late, for Jenny Griggs's harrowing experience could not be ignored. The child suffered numerous cuts and gashes, including several on her face. Caroline had cleaned and bandaged them. A surgeon should have stitched the two deepest, but Mrs. Griggs was reluctant to call him. It seemed the local man was generally too intoxicated to trust, and demanded exorbitant fees besides. When Jenny finally fell into a deep swoon from pain and terror, Caroline took the opportunity to stitch them herself.

She fought down a shudder at the memory. It had taken every bit of her determination not to lose her breakfast. Another hour passed trying to calm Mrs. Griggs. She had sent Talbert after the dog as soon as the attack was reported. It was only when he informed them that the beast had been successfully dispatched that peace was finally restored.

Normally, the delay would not have mattered. But barely two hours into her journey, the heavens opened, creating another dilemma. She had not brought Sarah, expecting to make the trip in a single day and not wanting to admit she had been to Crawley. Thomas would not approve her staying at an inn unaccompanied. Nor could she prove that she was a viscountess. The coach did not yet sport a crest. Larkin wore no livery. Her cards still bore the imprint Mrs. Mannering. She had left town before the new ones had arrived from the printer.

Yet the roads worsened steadily. A growing feeling of *déjà vu* crept over her. Her last journey in the rain had ended in disaster, catapulting her into a sequence of events that culminated in attempted murder. What would happen now?

She was trying to decide whether they should stop at the next inn, regardless of its quality, when fate stepped in. An especially strong gust of wind slammed into the side of the coach. The road surface had turned to slick mud—not deep enough to mire the wheels, but offering no more security than ice. The coach slid sideways, fetching up against a large rock. She screamed as one wheel emitted an ominous crack, shattering as another gust ground the carriage into the boulder.

Thank God the accident was no worse. The coach was immobile until repairs could be affected, of course. But it had not tipped over. Nor was anyone injured, not even the horses. An inn—albeit a poor one—was barely a hundred yards along the road. The ostler and Larkin managed to wrestle the coach into the yard. Both a bedroom and a small parlor were available for hire. Unused to aristocrats, the innkeeper accepted her declared title and raised no brow at her lack of a maid.

Yet she could not shake off a feeling of impending doom.

A knock sounded on the parlor door, surprising her out of her reverie.

"Come in."

A very wet Thomas stepped gingerly into the room.

"What on earth are you doing here?" she gasped, eyes wide with shock.

He gazed warily at her. Her reaction was not encouraging.

"I found your note when I arrived at Crawley this afternoon and feared for your safety in this storm."

She stiffened. "With some justification, it turns out. Did Larkin report the accident?"

"Yes." He nearly added scathing comments on her idiocy in starting a journey when the weather threatened, traveling without a maid, and refusing to stop when road conditions demanded such prudence, but he restrained himself. The last thing he wanted was to hand her another excuse to turn away from him. "You are really uninjured?"

"Completely." Why was he here? She stifled the hope that flared in her breast. Was his abrupt departure from London related to her attack? Had he broken with Alicia? Or was he merely furious at the way she had flouted his authority? His expression was forbidding, at best, but she had resolved to treat him with respect and support in the hopes that they could become friends. Questioning his movements would feed his temper and serve no purpose. And he looked on the verge of explosion. His green eyes snapped fire. Water dripped from every garment. He must be soaked to the skin and freezing. "Your own journey must have been miserable," she commented calmly. "Are you warm enough?"

Ignoring her question, he moved closer to add coal to the fire. "Do you really believe that I engineered the attack on you in London?"

He regretted the words as soon as they were uttered. Would she think the question a denouncement? Yet he was not entirely sorry to have asked. Her suspicions hurt. And it was as good a starting point as any for the discussion they could not avoid if they were to ever begin again.

Surprise widened her eyes. "Of course not. I thought I made that perfectly clear."

"Perhaps I was not thinking sensibly. It seems to be a frequent failing of late. You know who was behind it then?"

She stared at his face a full minute before responding. His shuttered eyes revealed nothing. Could he really be admitting fault? Did she dare press the issue? "Yes. Do you?"

"Yes." He hung his soaked greatcoat over a chair near the fire and held his hands closer to the heat. Eyes on the flames, he licked his dry lips and forced his voice to continue. This was much harder than he had imagined. "I belong in Bedlam. There is much for which I must beg forgiveness. Can you ever consider it?"

Something in Caroline's heart relaxed at the words, but her expression changed not at all. Perhaps she was being offered a second chance. But she would accept it only if they were both completely honest. And it would not hurt him a bit to remain in doubt about her own feelings. "I do not know."

His next words validated her assessment and started a warm glow deep inside, but still she held her pose. Not until everything was in the open would she consider the future.

"We need to be honest with each other, Caroline. I have no wish to inflict more pain than I have already caused you, but understanding requires facts. If I had allowed myself to examine facts sooner, we would not have come to this pass."

"I agree." She composed her face and steeled herself for whatever sins he was about to confess. "Continue."

"You know about the obsession for Lady Darnley I have entertained for the past year." She nodded. "Looking back, I cannot believe how naive I was. She ensnared me with her beauty and a sensual wantonness that raised an answering lust. I named the combination love and proceeded to endow her with every virtue. Nor did I believe any hint that reality was otherwise, letting even the most vicious rumors pass me like the wind."

Caroline gritted her teeth and managed to retain her calm countenance. But her stomach churned at his words.

"Her betrothal tumbled me into that lengthy debauch I described to you once before and ultimately led to our marriage." He paused in thought, pacing the room with restless energy, no longer able to look her in the eye. The easy part was done, for the remainder followed their marriage. He had wronged her more than she knew. But finding the words was nigh unto impossible. How could he confess his guilt without further hurting her?

His voice reflected his uncertainty, no longer exuding his natural charm. "We started rather well until I discovered your artistry on the pianoforte. Clearly you were more accomplished than Alicia, but my befogged mind could not accept that anything about her was less than perfect. I seem to have spent the intervening months in a state of continuous irritation because of that disreputable idea. For you excel in so many ways. Each new realization hurt. Yet I could not admit that I was wasting myself on someone so unworthy."

Caroline's heart broke at his anguish, knowing how difficult this recital was for him. But at the same time, hope surged. Her eyes softened as she gazed at the face she loved so dearly. He did not note the change, still unable to look at her.

"I have also been suffused with guilt. For while at Graystone, I succumbed to her seduction one night and took her to bed." His voice choked at the memory. "I have hated myself ever since for so dishonoring our marriage."

"But you owed me nothing," broke in Caroline in a puzzled voice. "I never expected fidelity."

He smiled grimly. "You hold yourself low then. I gave my word to you and to God, and I do not hold my word lightly. But I swear to you that the lapse in honor occurred only that once. The past weeks have been wrenching. I know I have always had difficulty admitting mistakes. But each day you revealed new truths to my disbelieving eyes that my heart accepted but my brain did not. It became more and more difficult to ignore what everyone else in town already knew—that the object of my insane obsession was the lowest kind of slut. I began to realize the truth that day she asked me to appraise her horses. What she really wanted was to seduce me."

"I know. I saw her intimate greeting at the door. As did Lady Sefton. Fortunately, I convinced Lady Beatrice that you were merely pricing horses."

He slanted a surprised glance in her direction. "Did you indeed? Why?"

She shrugged. "Your family did not need more scandal. Nor did you, for that matter."

"Too true, I fear. I repulsed her advances that day. She was furious. I think that was when I finally began to believe that the rumors were true, though, God help me, I fought the conclusion long enough afterwards. And put you in danger through my own willfulness. I'll not forgive myself soon for that."

"It is over. Don't burden yourself with excessive blame."

"Drew was right. I don't deserve you. He sends you his love, by the way."

It was Caroline's turn to raise a surprised brow. Had Drew been meddling? But Thomas did not appear angry.

"Those accusations I threw at your head were based on nothing more than jealousy," he admitted wryly. "I did not know until yesterday that he was your cousin."

Caroline glared at him. "You *have* been living in another world, haven't you? All Mayfair knows that, Thomas! Your parents, Emily, Uncle William, and Drew jointly presented me to society, making clear their combined sponsorship. They provided me an entree into every fashionable circle. I love Drew dearly, in the same way I love my brother Peter. But Drew has the advantage of being older and part of the *ton* and thus able to advise me. George and Jeremy understand our relationship. Why did they not set you straight?" She knew why, of course. Thomas had never asked. He judged, then accepted his judgment as the truth.

Thomas was unsurprised at his friends' reticence. He was beginning to detect a pattern of omission and praise designed to fan his jealousy and turn his attentions to Caroline. How many others had plotted in the same way? His parents? Sisters? Servants? Caroline herself? But here he shot wide of the mark, he knew. She had done nothing to feed the jealousy and anger.

But it was time to put their future to the test. Nor would he cloud the issue with charm. No longer fighting to hide his pain, he turned his eyes toward his wife.

"I've been a fool, chasing rainbows all this time when I already held the pot of gold. Can you ever forgive me?"

Caroline rose to lay a hand on his arm. "There is nothing to forgive, Thomas. You owed me nothing and made me no promises."

"I would do so now if you will allow it, my dear," he whispered, drawing her into his arms. "I love you, Caroline. I love your calm good sense, your intelligence, and your sunny disposition. The night Robert died would have been far worse without your comfort and understanding. Can we at least be friends, as we so nearly became in the beginning? Perhaps one day I can earn more regard from you, but I so badly want your friendship."

"There is no 'perhaps' about it, for I love you already," she admitted with a smile. "But friendship would make me very happy indeed. Without it, love offers only empty pain."

His arms tightened convulsively as his mouth lowered to hers, parting her lips, his tongue plundering hers with the desperation of a starving man falling on a feast. And she returned his fervor. It had been so long . . . Passion flared, enhanced by a mutual exultation that they had indeed been given a second chance.

"Will you return to Crawley with me, Caro?" he begged raggedly. "Dawson is waiting for you there. She decided to stay in your service."

Her eyes lit up, reflecting her brilliant smile. His heart turned over at the sight. "Of course. I never intended to stay away. I needed time to consider the future in peace, and I thought Father could help. But it would be unfair if your heir was born anywhere but Crawley."

As her last words registered, Thomas's eyes filled with tears. "Oh, God, Caro. Are you sure?"

"Reasonably, my love."

Another penetrating kiss sent fires raging through both. "Where is this room you booked?" he asked huskily some minutes later, pulling her dress loosely over her bared breasts while he trailed fiery kisses up her throat to nibble on an ear. "We have much to celebrate."

Caroline's brown eyes glowed as she led him from the parlor. *Thank you, Lord, for offering a new beginning. . . .*